S̶ ̶ ̶ ̶ ̶E
WITCH

Michael Alexander McCarthy

Rogue Maille
Publishing

This is a work of historical fiction. Any references to real people, events, organizations and places are intended only to give the fiction a sense of reality and authenticity. All names, characters, places and events are either the product of the author's imagination or are used fictitiously.

Copyright © Michael Alexander McCarthy 2021

Michael Alexander McCarthy fully asserts the legal and moral right to be identified as the sole author of this work.

First published in 2021

Rogue Maille Publishing 2021

All rights reserved.

No part of this publication may be reproduced, stored in a retrieval system or transmitted in any form or by any means, whether electronic, mechanical, photocopying, recording or otherwise, without the prior written permission of the publisher, author or their legal representatives.

This book is sold subject to the condition that it shall not, by way of trade or otherwise, be lent, re-sold, hired out or otherwise circulated without the publisher's prior consent in any form of binding or cover other than that in which it is published and without a similar condition including this condition being imposed on the subsequent purchaser.

Also by Michael Alexander McCarthy

The Blood King

Death's Head – Hitler's Wolf Pack

The First War of Scottish Independence Series

KingMaker – Army of God

KingMaker – Traitor

KingMaker – Bannockburn

KingMaker – Death of Kings

Dedication

To Dougal – a source of joy, fun, chaos and wanton destruction.

'Thou shalt not suffer a witch to live.'

Exodus 22:18

Scottish Witch Panics

Witch-hunting plagued Europe during the late 16th and 17th centuries with Germany, Scandinavia, Italy, Burgundy and Switzerland all suffering witch panics during this period. Scotland's witch hunts were particularly severe and boasted an execution rate five times higher than the European average. It is estimated that around 2,500 accused witches, most of them women, were executed in Scotland.

Suffer the Witch

'Has the dirty bitch confessed?' The young man demanded, his handsome and aristocratic features made ugly by his scowl.

The blacksmith gripped his woollen bonnet in his hands and twisted it nervously. He kept his eyes fixed upon the floor in the vain hope of avoiding the Young Laird's fury. Rivulets of sweat ran down his back as he awaited the explosion of rage that would inevitably come.

'No, sir.' He replied, his voice tight with fear. 'She refuses to say a word and will not put her mark upon the paper when we lay it before her.'

'Jesus Christ!' The Young Laird seethed, the words hissed through clenched teeth rather than spoken. 'Did you not do all that I instructed you to?'

'We did, sir. Neither food nor water has passed her lips these past few days. We men have kept a constant watch and have denied her sleep by kicking at her whenever her eyes have fluttered shut. I have heated iron rods in the forge until they glowed bright red and have seared the flesh of her back, stomach and thighs to no avail. She writhes and moans as her skin bubbles and smokes but will not utter a single word. I have jammed slivers of wood under the nails of her fingers and toes but she remains defiant in spite of the agony it causes her. We laid her under the barn door at first light and have spent the morning piling stones upon it. Even with such a great weight bearing down upon her, she remained silent and refused to relent. All five of us then stood upon the door to bring her to submission. We thought that no mortal woman could bear such a great burden but she stayed silent.' The blacksmith paused and raised his head to meet the Young Laird's gaze. 'Twas then the minister came.'

'The minister?' The young man demanded, his face twisted with scorn. 'What business did the feeble old fool have here?'

'He raged at us, sir. He commanded us to release her and told us we would be hanged for murder if the life had been crushed from her.'

'No man has ever been hung for killing a witch when putting her to question.' The Young Laird spat as he shook his head in derision.

'That is what I told him, sir. He insisted that she is no witch until she has confessed to it. Without such an admission, she remains a Christian woman in the eyes of the law.'

'Any fool can see she is a witch! The others broke after much less torture than she has endured. Only a sorceress could withstand such punishment without admitting her guilt.' The Young Laird rapped his knuckles hard against the wooden table in frustration. 'She lives, I take it? I cannot risk having that old bastard run to the authorities in Perth with his complaints.'

'She lives, sir. Her face was purple when we dragged her out from under the door and she crawled on the ground and gasped for air. She then mocked us for our failure though she barely had breath enough to make her voice heard. The wickedness of it caused my skin to crawl.'

'Her wickedness will not go unpunished, I swear it.' The Young Laird rubbed at his beard as he considered his dilemma. 'If the minister means to use the law against us, then I must find a way to outdo him. Go and saddle your horse! You will ride for Edinburgh with a letter for the Privy Council. I will bring the law here and stymie our good minister in his efforts to obstruct us as we go about the Lord's work.'

1

John Seton prodded at the greasy slab of mutton on his plate and sighed as his irate father-in-law continued with his tirade. He was weary after his long journey. The stubble on his cheeks itched from long days of being soaked by the salt spray whipped up from the black surface of the North Sea by the cruel and relentless wind. He was conscious of his unkempt appearance and of the sour stench from his unwashed clothes. His wife and brother-in-law sat opposite him on the other side of the dining table while their father berated him from his place at the head of the table. Elizabeth did not lift her eyes to meet his gaze and had barely been able to bring herself to greet him when the housekeeper announced his arrival. Thomas Carmichael lounged back in his chair and did not trouble himself to hide the glee he took in John's humiliation.

'You are a feckless, wilful, thick-headed oaf!' William Carmichael raged. 'I rue the day you wormed your way into this family's affections. I thought you a rogue and a charlatan the moment I set my eyes upon you but was too soft-hearted and indulgent to refuse my gentle daughter's pleading. Twas a disaster for this family when you won her heart! My own son warned me against you but I was deaf to his words and only now, when it is too late, do I see your defects with absolute clarity.'

John met his father-in-law's gaze and felt his cheeks begin to burn with shame and anger. He imagined himself seizing the ornate glass oil lamp from the centre of the table and breaking it over the old bastard's balding head. The fancy almost brought a smile to his lips as the injury to his skull would be almost matched in satisfaction by the destruction of the expensive and treasured artefact. William Carmichael never tired of boasting about the provenance of the French monstrosity and regaled his guests with stories of its purchase in Bordeaux and of the extortionate price he had paid for it. He might have acted on this fantasy if he had not been in such sore need of the old man's silver to keep his many creditors at bay. He sighed at this unwelcome realisation and bowed his head against the force of the prolonged and spirited reprimand.

'Did I not tell you this enterprise was doomed before it even started? Did you expect the venerable merchants of this city to sit meekly by while some upstart undercut their prices by importing claret from the continent with the intention of supplying it directly to every filthy ale house and tavern without paying what was due? Did you imagine that they would so easily surrender the rights and privileges earned through generations of hard toil and the building of relationships with guilds, councilmen and royal officialdom? I counselled you against such rash action but the lure of easy silver was too strong for such a foolish, naive and work-shy fraudster. You lack both the experience and the instinct to trade successfully. The whole of Edinburgh now laughs behind your back and half of them have your silver in their purses. You were over-charged and extorted at each and every stage. The ship's captain charged you double what he demands of other merchants and the dockers pocketed three times the usual fee. And what do you have to show for it? Two hundred barrels of red vinegar now sit on the quayside in Leith, their contents so bitter that even the poorest dockside tavern will not pay a penny for the foul and undrinkable liquid they contain. The vintners of Bordeaux must have thanked their lucky stars when they saw you coming!'

'What manner of imbecile pays for goods without first testing their quality?' Thomas asked with a dismissive shake of his head. 'You were practically begging them to deceive you and take your coin in exchange for their worthless slop.'

'I tasted the claret from every barrel and found it to be quite satisfactory.' John retorted sourly, though he knew his words sounded weak and succeeded only in bringing a greater smugness to his brother-in-law's insufferable and superior smile.

'I have no doubt that you tasted a great deal of it!' William Carmichael exclaimed as he threw his napkin onto the table. 'And, while you were sleeping off its effects, the French merchants loaded an entirely different product into the hold of your ship! Do you think that fortunes are won so easily? Why would I bother to build up a business over long, hard years of toil if one hasty, ill-conceived venture was enough to make a wealthy man of me?'

Seton groaned inwardly and steeled himself for what was to come. He had heard the tale of Carmichael's journey from poverty to riches so often he fancied he could recite it himself and miss not a single word. He knew the number of sheepskins he had bought and sold in his first year of business and of how he had gone on to trade other skins and hides before branching out into mutton and lamb. He turned his attention to his wife as Carmichael droned on about his ships and his warehouses and as flecks of disgusting, white foam began to collect at the corners of his old and puckered mouth. He realised it had been a mistake to leave her to the mercy of these two pious and poisonous men for so long. It had been nearly three months since he first took ship for France and they had undoubtedly started to work on her from the very moment of his departure. He wondered how long his delicate and pliable Elizabeth had been able to resist them. Her downcast eyes and lack of affection made him fear she was now fully in their thrall.

'You will be relieved to hear, no doubt, that I have made good your debts, much though it pained me to do so!' Carmichael announced as he slapped his hand against the table to punctuate his grand pronouncement. 'Unless there are other creditors I am not aware of.'

'I am very grateful, sir.' Seton replied with all of the humility he could muster. He chose not to mention the large sum borrowed from the Flesher as he knew any admission of dealings with such a low and disreputable money-lender would take him to new depths of condemnation. He would find some other way of settling with the butcher. 'I will repay every penny, sir. You have my word on it.'

'It has gone too far for simple reimbursement to make amends.' Thomas interjected acidly, before exchanging a look with his father that caused Seton's guts to roll in apprehension.

'Indeed.' Carmichael replied, a sudden tension and discomfort evident in his posture. 'The sums involved are perhaps too large for a simple repayment to suffice this time. I have a very different arrangement in mind. One designed to guarantee my debt and clip your wings to deny you the opportunity to trade on this family's name and enter into any further ill-fated ventures.'

'What arrangement?' Seaton demanded, his voice made high-pitched by his trepidation.

'Your debt is now in excess of three hundred pounds. You will work it off by performing the duties of a clerk in my warehouse on the edge of the city. I will pay you eight shillings a week, a generous amount considering you lack the experience to satisfactorily execute the duties required of the position.'

'Eight shillings a week?' Seton exploded. 'It would take me near fifteen years to repay what I owe!'

'Twenty years, Seton.' Thomas corrected him with no small satisfaction. 'When interest is added to the principal.'

'Tis nothing short of slavery!' Seton protested in horror at the prospect of spending long days and endless months counting sheepskins in the stench and gloom of Carmichael's damned warehouse. The thought of subjecting himself to the authority of the two insufferable men before him appealed even less. There was also the matter of the large sum owed to O'Malley the butcher. He would not wait patiently for twenty years while he repaid his debt to the Carmichaels at eight shillings a week. The certainty of a violent death at the hands of the Flesher if he was denied his silver hardened his resolve. 'I cannot agree to this. I will find some other way to compensate you.'

'There is no other way!' William Carmichael snapped in irritation. 'You will sign the papers Erskine has drawn up for us or I will leave you to the mercy of your many creditors. What do you think will happen then? You'll be clapped in irons in the Tolbooth and left to rot for as long as you cannot make good what you owe.'

'Please, good sir, I beg of you.' Seton pleaded in desperation. 'Do not condemn me to this fate. Do I not deserve a chance to redeem myself? I have other ventures in mind and am certain they will come good and allow me to discharge my debt to you before the year is out. Do not tie my hands and make a serf of me. Why endure a trickle of silver in return for your kindness when you know I have the capability to shower you in coin mere months from now?'

'No!' Carmichael replied with a shake of his head. 'The scales have fallen from my eyes and I now see you as you really are. Your honeyed words and easy charm no longer have the power to make a fool of me. There will be no more hair-brained schemes or back street plotting. I will set you to work under my son's supervision and you will learn the value of a hard day's toil. My daughter does not deserve a feckless charlatan for a husband. I will make a man of you for her benefit as well as for your own.'

'Tell him the rest, Father.' Thomas prompted him. 'Tis best that both boils are lanced in a single sitting.'

Seton slumped forward and rested his arms against the tabletop. Every instinct told him that his already wretched position was about to deteriorate. His father-in-law hesitated before he spoke and lowered his gaze as if he could not quite bring himself to look the younger man in the eye.

'The welfare of my daughter is my first concern and I must take steps to ensure she is protected. You know of the provision I made for her when her blessed mother passed from this world and into the next. I cannot risk having those assets fall into your hands so you can squander them on some ill-conceived design. You may be hell-bent on a descent into a life of poverty and squalor but I will not allow you to draw her down with you. While you were away playing at commerce in France, I had your wife sign those assets into her brother's care. Thomas will manage those interests and the income they generate on her behalf. She will want for nothing and need no longer suffer your efforts to prise her birthright from her grasp.'

'Elizabeth?' Seton appealed to his fragile and cowering wife. 'Why would you treat me so?'

A single tear ran down her pale, white cheek and caused his heart to melt. He loved this gentle and beautiful woman and found he could not be angry with her when it was he who had abandoned her to the attentions of her sanctimonious father and greedy brother. He turned his rage towards his tormentors.

'Are you happy now, Thomas? Happy that not a single shilling of your father's fortune will slip through your fingers?' He pushed himself to his feet and met his brother-in-law's self-satisfied gaze steadily. 'Shame on you both! You have insulted me and treated my wife most shabbily! I will not stand for it. Toss your damned agreement onto the fire. I will neither sign it nor abide by its terms!'

He then turned for the door with a flourish and strode out into the hall satisfied that the sudden manner of his departure would leave them reeling and dumbfounded. The drama of the gesture was somewhat lessened by Thomas calling out to him in amusement as he reached out to open the door into the street.

'Go and drown your sorrows as you always do when you are unable to face the consequences of your foolish actions! Just be sure to be waiting at the door of the warehouse by first light on the morrow. I'll dock a penny from your wages if you are not punctual!'

The bastard's laughter followed him out into the road and was still audible after he slammed the door shut at his back.

2

Seton clenched his fists and muttered to himself in anger as he stepped out into the muddy street. Thomas had succeeded in blunting the effect of his exit and his impotent rage smouldered as he tramped along at a furious pace in a bid to put the fine houses of Edinburgh's Cowgate behind him. He had left in such haste he had neglected to take his cloak with him and the light but persistent rain soon plastered his brown, shoulder-length hair to his scalp and began to seep through his clothes. Light and laughter spilled out from the inns and taverns he passed but he resisted the shelter and warmth they offered as he was keen to avoid the merchants and burghers who frequented them. He had no desire to endure the mockery they would undoubtedly subject him to on account of the failure of his latest venture. His face reddened at the thought of being the butt of their jokes and the object of their derision.

He fixed his gaze on the distant, dark silhouette of Castlehill and set course for the Grassmarket.

He was so engrossed in his own misery he paid little heed to the few people who had braved the weather and now scurried along with their heads bent against the drizzle intent on finding the shelter of home or some drinking den. He pushed on resolutely until the fragrances of sawdust and new leather heralded his arrival in the Grassmarket with its many timber yards and shoemakers. Few merchants would lower themselves to drink in the taverns in this part of town and he was confident that the tradesmen who patronised these humble establishments would know nothing of his recent disgrace. He made for the door of the Black Swan, a small, rough tavern reputedly named in honour of an exotic bird brought to Edinburgh by a French lady-in-waiting back in the days of Queen Mary. Local legend had it that the poor creature had lasted less than a month before finding its way into a Grassmarket cooking pot. Whatever the truth of it, the bird had lived long enough to inspire some tavern keeper to immortalise its image on a sign that was now so worn and faded it was impossible to make out the image or decipher the name.

'My God!' The innkeeper declared in surprise when Seton pushed the rough wooden door closed at his back. 'I barely recognised you, John Seton! I thought you to be a drowned rat when I set my eyes upon you.'

'I came away without my cloak.' John replied with a wry smile. The warmth of the greeting had cheered him. It had been months since he had last set foot in the place and he was surprised he had been remembered so fondly. He recalled the innkeeper quite well on account of his badly disfigured face. A childhood accident involving a cart had left his skull misshapen and had gouged an ugly scar from forehead to chin leaving his left eye milky-white and sightless. He judged his mangled smile to be genuine and returned it in kind.

'I'll take a tankard of ale by the fire, Peter. The first will warm my innards while the other dries my clothes.'

'Not claret then, John?' The innkeeper enquired, a twinkle of amusement in his good eye. 'I heard you were uncommonly fond of the stuff. They also said you had five hundred barrels of it on the dock at Leith.'

'Kiss my arse!' Seton retorted wearily in response to his laughter. 'Bring my ale to the table and put it on my slate.'

'I'll need your pennies first, I'm afraid.' Peter replied, his tone suddenly quite serious. 'I hear whispers of monies owed to all and sundry, including some quite unsavoury characters. I'll take your coin before I serve you. I have no desire to become another of your creditors.'

Seton sighed, paid for his ale and made his way to the table on the far side of the roaring fire. He nodded to acknowledge the small, rough-looking man on the bench opposite as he took his seat. He returned the gesture with a weak smile, his lips parting enough to reveal a set of blackened, uneven teeth. They sat in silence as they drank and Seton took the opportunity to study him out of the corner of his eye. His clothes were of good quality but were worn and dirty. He might have thought him to be a lowly clerk but for the dirt beneath his fingernails and the lack of ink stains on his fingers. His face was thin and pinched, his eyes small and the skin around them dark and somehow unhealthy. His features lent him an untrustworthy, rat-like countenance and made Seton conclude there would be no advantage in engaging him.

He dismissed the fellow from his thoughts and set himself to drinking and wallowing in the injustice of his present misfortune. He wracked his brain in search of some solution to his predicament but his thoughts seemed to swirl around in an endless circle of hopelessness. Old Carmichael would throw him to the wolves if he refused to buckle down and sign his life away to him and his damned son. However, if he agreed to submit himself to servitude, he would lack the means to repay the Flesher and he would end his days hanging from a hook in the butcher's yard while his skin was peeled from his bones. He had used his wits to extricate himself from many a difficult situation in the past but he feared he had over-reached himself this time. He gave in to despondency and wondered how long Elizabeth would grieve for him before taking a husband less likely to be a disappointment to her. He drained his third tankard of ale and sighed in despair. His preoccupation was such he did not realise he was being addressed until his black-toothed neighbour repeated himself.

'I thought to drink my sorrows away but it seems your misery is even greater than my own. What ails you, my friend? You sigh so much I am certain you have suffered a calamity even greater than the one I have endured.' The stranger's voice was low and hoarse and the sound of it grated on Seton's ears.

'I have brought myself to ruin through rash and foolish actions. Pride and arrogance blinded me to my own stupidity and now I find myself in a desperate and precarious position with no way out in sight.' Seton paused and met his companion's gaze. His small, close-set eyes put Seton in mind of a pig and he decided he had no desire to confide in him. He attempted to bring the conversation to a close. 'Tis a sad and pathetic tale and I will not burden you with the telling of it.'

'I will happily listen to it.' The man replied. 'I would rather hear tell of your misfortune than continue to dwell on my own suffering. Perhaps we can divert each other from what troubles us for a short while. I would welcome a distraction from the dark thoughts weighing down upon me.'

Seton groaned and tried to think of some polite excuse to avoid having to give voice to his shame and humiliation. He glanced around the crowded tavern to see if anyone lurked close enough to hear them, but all of the gathered tradesmen and assorted labourers were too absorbed in their own chatter and arguments to pay any attention to the two miserable souls sitting hunched at the fireside. He could not say if his lips were loosened by the strength of the thick, black ale or by the darkness of his mood, but he fell to unburdening his woes on the unappealing stranger. He did not spare himself or conceal any of his failings but spoke freely as if he was in the confessional. He castigated those who had sinned against him but saved the bitterest and sharpest of his criticisms for himself. He bared his soul with a candour he had never bestowed on any other person and did not withhold even the most embarrassing and shameful details. The stranger listened with rapt attention, speaking only to order the innkeeper to bring more ale to wet his companion's throat and so lubricate his vocal cords.

Seton slumped back in his chair when he had finally divulged all of his secrets, sins and fears. He was surprised to find so many empty tankards littering the table and was pleasantly shocked to realise that the weight of his concerns no longer lay so heavily on his shoulders.

'Tis a sorry tale, right enough.' The stranger intoned with solemnity as he wiped foam from the stubble on his chin. 'It will do nothing to console you, but my own problems now seem puny in comparison.'

'I thank you for giving me your ear. I find my spirits less downcast than before, though my condition remains as wretched as it ever was.'

'Will this butcher really resort to torture and murder if your debt is not repaid? These backstreet moneylenders often spread such dark tales about themselves so their reputation will dissuade borrowers from reneging on their arrangements.'

'Tis sadly true. I have heard of finger bones and teeth being found in the meat pies sold in the Grassmarket taverns he supplies. I would counsel you against exchanging your pennies for one should I disappear in the days to come. The pastry is buttery and tempting but the filling might sit heavily in your stomach.' Seton shivered and then tried to put the unsavoury thought to the back of his mind. 'What of you, my friend? Would you have me return the favour? I will hear your sad story if you are of a mind to tell it.'

'I will do it gladly, though my losses and perils are much less than your own. I am William Kincaid and, like my father, I am a farm labourer out of Stirlingshire.'

'You surprise me, William.' Seton interrupted with a raised eyebrow. 'You do not dress like a labourer. Your doublet and trews are of a fine cloth far beyond the means of such men.'

'You have a keen eye, John. The clothes upon my back were not bought with pennies earned from breaking hard earth or from long hours of wielding a scythe. It was my good fortune to happen upon a much more lucrative trade a few short months ago. A river of silver has flowed into my purse since then and I have lived a life beyond the wildest imaginings of my poor father, God rest his soul. The river has now run dry and I am left to rue the riches I have squandered on ale, whores and at dice. I was a fool to think it could last!'

'What trade?' Seton demanded, the prospect of easy silver causing his ears to prick and his hopes to rise.

'I will come to that in good time, John, but you must call me Will. It would not do to stand on formality when we have already shared so much. My story began when the ground was still hard with frost and the baillies and good burghers of Fife called on the Provost of Edinburgh to prosecute Margaret Aitken, a widow of the hamlet of Balwearie, on charges of witchcraft, sorcery and of consorting with the Devil himself!' Will announced this last part with a flourish, his gleeful expression showing he fully expected his pronouncement to incite astonishment in his audience.

'The Great Witch of Balwearie?' Seton gasped with sufficient wonder to gratify his companion. 'I have heard dark tales of her. Tell all! I would hear of this, good sir!' He insisted, his curiosity so piqued he fell to silence to allow the fellow to speak unhindered.

'If you know the story, then I will move quickly to my part in it. The witch confessed her sins under threat of grievous torture and was duly and rightfully condemned to be strangled and burnt at the stake. The old bitch then bartered with her prosecutors to save her scrawny neck. She offered to use her ability to recognise other witches from a special mark in their eyes left there from gazing into the face of Satan himself. She was granted clemency and was taken from town to town to detect whatever witches were lurking there. She found the mark in the eyes of near fifty women and filled the air with the black smoke of their pyres before she came to Glasgow and fell into the custody of the minister at the Cathedral there. John Cowper set her to work immediately and was set on scouring the town of all vile sorcery but was baulked by other lesser clerics who were envious of his success and the renown it earned him in high places. King James himself sent word of his approval and this incensed these small and petty men. Twenty witches were exposed by Margaret Aitken and then condemned to death by Cowper but the Presbytery refused to approve the executions solely on the word of a woman who had confessed to such grievous sins herself. Cowper then sent out a plea for good men and good women to step forward to provide other evidence of their guilt.'

'And that is where you came into the story.' Seton guessed with no small excitement.

'Like you, I am not a man to miss an opportunity when it presents itself. I was in Glasgow to sell mutton on my master's instructions and was sore fed up when I could not command a decent price for the meat. I took to a tavern to drown my sorrows as I knew I would be sorely reprimanded when I returned with less coin than was expected. It was there I heard of Cowper's call for men skilled in the pricking and swimming of witches.' He shrugged his shoulders and held his palms out to demonstrate his honesty. 'I freely confess my ignorance of both practices and admit I would have given the matter no further thought if not for an ancient and shrivelled hag who babbled and gossiped at the table next to mine. She captured my whole attention when she said that Cowper would pay ten shillings for a single test and would double the amount if it was successful and proved a witch's guilt. My mind reeled at the thought of it. With twenty women already accused, a bold and clever fellow could easily walk away with ten if not twenty pounds in his purse.'

Seton let out a low whistle and drained the gritty dregs from his tankard. It did not escape him that such a sum would be sufficient to save him from a meat hook in the Flesher's yard.

'I used my last pennies to buy a shot of whisky for the wrinkled old whore in the hope of inducing her to spill her guts. I listened with rapt attention as though she spoke the Gospel. She was ignorant and foul-breathed but knew enough of pricking and witches' marks to embolden me to try my luck.'

'You answered Cowper's call though you knew nothing of the craft.' Seton announced in amazement. 'I cannot help but admire your nerve.'

'I believe we are of a similar bent and have courage enough to refuse to accept our lot in life when opportunity beckons us on. I went directly to the market, sold my master's mutton for a scandalously low price, bought an old bodkin from a shoemaker and had my knife ground until it had a wicked edge. Then, before my courage faded, I went to the Cathedral and presented myself before John Cowper. He questioned me severely and I feared he saw through my lies when I boasted of learning my craft at the witch trials in

Berwick. He knew immediately that I would have been only a boy at the time but I thought on my feet and claimed to have been assisting my father in the work. I thought myself a clever fellow at the time but now realise he was less concerned with the truth of my account than he was with securing convictions. He engaged me on the spot and even gave me advice on how to conduct the tests and told me what words I should use to better convince the gathered elders of my competence.' Kincaid paused to drink from his tankard and, on finding it empty, tapped his index finger against it to signal his need for more ale.

'I conducted my first test the very next morning.' Will continued as Seton gestured to the innkeeper. 'The elders and ministers glared at me so fiercely I could scarcely keep my hands from shaking. Tis a wonder the first wretch did not bleed to death when I tried to shave her. My knife was so sharp her skin parted whenever the blade touched her.'

'You have to shave them?' Seton blurted out in surprise.

'Aye!' Kincaid informed him. 'The Devil leaves his mark on any witch who swears herself to him but it is never left in plain sight. You have to strip them and shave their hairy parts to reveal them.' Kincaid gave a sickly smile as he spoke and Seton felt a prickle of revulsion at the sight of his wet tongue sliding over his rotten teeth. 'You would not believe the number of teats and cunnies I have set my eyes upon these last few weeks. More than most men see in a lifetime, I would wager. Old, young, fat, thin, fair and foul, it makes no difference to me. There is a great thrill to it and it is not lessened by repetition. A pricker does more than look, John. I must touch and spread them with my fingers to reveal what Satan would hide from good Christian eyes. The truth is I would gladly do it for no reward at all. The silver Cowper showers upon me merely sweetens the deal still further.'

'How much did you make?' Seton asked, his curiosity driving him to risk being impertinent. 'Surely not twenty pounds? It seems such a fantastical sum.'

'Twas much, much more than that, my friend.' The pricker replied with a smile of smug arrogance. 'A hundred more witches have been convicted since the first twenty burned. You have a head for numbers. Count it for yourself!' Kincaid's face then fell as he was hit by an unwelcome realisation. 'Tis such a pity I wasted it all. The well has now dried up and left me with nothing to show for it.'

'Are there no more witches to find? I suppose there must be a limit to their number.'

'Tis not that.' Kincaid croaked in his misery. 'In fact, I am here in Edinburgh on Cowper's instructions to collect a commission from the Privy Council to prosecute three witches up near Perth. The documents were barely in my satchel when I received word of the disaster that has befallen us.'

'What disaster?' Seton asked, though his enthusiasm for the subject had waned just as the prospect of easy silver had diminished.

'Those bastard dogs have undone us! Cowper's petty and spiteful rivals have brought proceedings to a halt with their trickery. Margaret Aitken looked into the eyes of twenty accused women a month ago and found the Devil's mark in the eyes of ten of them. Those snivelling and jealous shits washed the accused, dressed them in new clothes and presented them to her again a week later. The decrepit, thick-headed bitch gazed into their eyes and declared every last one of them to be innocent, even those she had condemned only seven days earlier. When confronted, the witless beggar confessed to deceit and to falsifying her powers. The scheming ministers now denounce her as a fraud and demand an end to both trials and executions. Cowper had strength enough to resist them at first but some bitter Glasgow widow has laid her hands upon Aitken's confession and is having it read aloud in every inn and tavern in the town. The people are in uproar and the trials have been halted by the Presbytery. I am ruined and cannot help but blame myself for parting with so much hard-won silver so foolishly.'

Seton could think of no words to console the pricker and so feigned some fascination with the contents of his tankard. A heavy and prolonged silence fell between them as both men fell back to wallowing in their own sorrows. Seton was about to offer some excuse to allow him to withdraw when Kincaid suddenly sat bolt upright with a thoughtful look on his face.

'I may have the answer to both of our prayers, my friend!' He announced, his expression both solemn and hopeful. 'Would you hear my proposal? I cannot tell if my notion is the result of madness born of desperation or if it is the product of some sweet inspiration. Hear me out so I might have your opinion of its wisdom and practicality.'

Seton gestured towards the tavern keeper and held up two fingers to indicate that two more tankards were required.

3

Seton had never known such pain. The clatter of hooves and cartwheels in the street outside seemed to cause a thousand pins to pierce his brain. The fine needles Elizabeth used in her embroidery would not have inflicted such agony. Only the long, blunt implements wielded by rough-handed sailors when repairing torn sails could be responsible for boring into his skull with such savagery. He squeezed his eyelids shut against the oppressive morning light in a bid to steady himself against the waves of nausea washing over him. A sickening dizziness threatened to overwhelm him and cause him to lose the sour contents of his churning guts. Vague fragments of the night's events flashed through his mind but full recollection of what had occurred remained frustratingly beyond the grasp of his fevered and faltering memory.

A hazy picture of a bucket of oysters on the tavern table caused him to groan and tentatively shake his head in an attempt to take refuge in denial. No sane man would purchase shellfish so late in the day when so many hours away from the sea would have turned them bad. An image of Will Kincaid grinning as he sucked an oyster between his rotten teeth caused his stomach to roll and he sucked in great breaths of air to steady himself. Just when he thought he had won this battle, his tongue found a remnant of the rotten feast stuck between his teeth. The briny tang was enough to send him crashing to his knees in a panicked scramble for the chamber pot he shared with his wife. He could not tell if Elizabeth had used it during the night, but the sickly turd floating in two pints of thick, dark and frothy pish was undoubtedly his. The stench of it caused him to vomit until the pot near overflowed with pish and watery puke. He continued to retch painfully once his stomach was empty, the force of it so great he half feared his innards would be torn asunder and fleshy chunks ejected into the bowl.

He groaned and sat with his back against the bed when the spewing fit had passed. His head still throbbed but he no longer felt as if he was dying. The momentary relief brought on by the improvement in his physical condition did not last for long. The familiar shadow of drunkard's shame descended upon him with a vengeance. The unshakeable feelings of guilt and regret served to keep his spirits low. His mind reeled with thoughts of his personal and financial predicament and he struggled to recall what had passed between him and the pricker during the course of the previous evening. He remembered talk of witches, warlocks, trials and silver but could not order the long discussion in his mind. He closed his eyes and forced himself to concentrate and recollect what had caused him to carouse and celebrate with the odious and repugnant stranger.

He groaned when the remembrance came to him. The pricker had proposed some wild scheme in which he would impersonate the witch prosecutor John Cowper and they would travel to Perthshire and execute the Privy Council's commission under false pretences. He shook his head and cursed himself for his stupidity and gullibility. The prospect of dividing the sum of sixty pounds between the two of them had been enough to sweep all of his doubts aside. Ale and oysters had fuelled them as they plotted long into the night. Now, in the hard, cold light of day, the proposal was clearly preposterous and more likely to see him jailed or dead than freed from his current plight. He silently berated himself for his impetuosity and idiocy. What did he know of witches or the law? Even the lowest half-wit would see through his thin deceit in a heartbeat and he would be denounced and put to trial for fraud. His cheeks turned red at the thought of the Carmichaels hearing of this foolhardy plan. They would rightly decry him as nothing more than an irredeemable cretin.

The fragrance emanating from the chamber pot was not improving as its foul contents festered and fermented. The stench caused bile to rise in Seton's throat and the threat of further painful retching forced him to his feet. He gripped the overflowing receptacle in his shaking grasp and edged slowly towards the open window. He could not prevent some of the foul liquid from spilling onto the wooden floor and had to concentrate hard to keep the turd from floating over the edge and splattering onto the bare boards below. He was on the verge of pouring the rancid brew over the sill when he caught sight of his father-in-law out in the street. Carmichael's face twisted in contempt and he glared up at Seton in fury. He shook his head dismissively as he jabbed his right index finger in the direction of the warehouse Seton was supposed to have graced with his presence some two hours earlier. The old man then stomped off without looking back.

Seton was gripping the chamber pot so tightly it left his knuckles white. He tossed the putrid night soil out into the street in temper and paid no heed to the scurrying citizens who called out in anger at having so much excrement cast in their direction. He was still directing silent threats and curses at the insufferable and pompous merchant's back when his eyes fell on a figure loitering on the far side of the narrow, winding lane.

The tavern lamps had been kind to William Kincaid. The light of day revealed him to be seedier, dirtier and rougher than Seton had thought him to be. He would have hesitated to give the peasant the time of day if he had encountered him in the street. The pricker tapped his cap's worn brim with his index finger in mock salute and bared his blackened, misshapen teeth in what was probably intended to be a smile, though the gesture was more reminiscent of a snarl. Seton raised his own hand in reluctant greeting and gritted his teeth in frustration and annoyance. He could not risk Elizabeth or Thomas encountering his fellow conspirator if his lunacy was to be concealed. He dressed as quickly as his throbbing head would allow and hurried downstairs intent on sending the ruffian away and bringing their unfortunate association to an end.

'By Christ, I have seen corpses with more colour in their cheeks, my friend!' Kincaid announced happily as Seton crossed the street towards him. 'Was it the ale or the oysters, do you think? My guts bubble and churn so ferociously methinks the shellfish were to blame. Tis a wonder I did not shit myself in the night!'

'A bit of both perhaps.' Seton replied, hesitating before grasping the nettle of extricating himself from their foolhardy arrangement.

'Was that your father-in-law who glowered up at you so fiercely?' The pricker demanded as he scratched at a patch of dry skin on his neck. 'I can see why you are unwilling to submit yourself to the authority of such a mean and hateful old bastard. I would rather have the dreaded Flesher peel my skin away than bow and scrape to such a tyrant. Twould be more than I could stand.' Kincaid shook his head in disapproval and sent a stream of saliva shooting towards the ground from between his teeth. 'Are you set, just as we agreed? We can be at the Forth by dusk if we have the horses as you promised.'

'I am less certain now my belly is not so full of ale.' Seton countered as he struggled to meet the pricker's eye. 'I doubt my ability to hold up my side of the pretence. I have little knowledge of either law or kirk and even less of trying witches. I also doubt I would have the stomach to condemn a woman to burn, even if she was deserving of such a fate.'

'Do not let your courage fail you, John Seton. Do not let this rare opportunity fall from your grasp. Think of the silver we could wring from the purses of those simple country folk. They will gaze at the Article of Commission from the Privy Council in awe and submit to whatever we demand of them. Would I risk the noose myself if I did not have faith in you? Think of all those men you persuaded to invest in your recent venture. Hardened merchants do not so easily hand their silver to someone who is lacking in credibility. Have courage! Have faith! What knowledge you lack I will impart to you as we go. By the time we ride into the hamlet at Marlee, you will know all I have learned from a hundred trials and more. Those peasants will revere your wisdom and bow down to your authority.'

'Tis too great a risk, Will. A single slip will lay our deception bare and we will be undone. We would surely be hung if we were caught!'

'Would you rather stay here and crawl to your father-in-law while you live in dread of the Flesher's hook and the edge of his blade? Why suffer such a short and miserable life when another path beckons? I did not hesitate when opportunity favoured me but rode my luck with no little success. We can repeat the feat if only we have courage enough to do so. There is risk, I do not deny it, but I will have your back. You have a gift for speech and can be most persuasive. Think of the prize you landed when you married. A faint heart did not win you a wife from such a wealthy family when you yourself came from such humble beginnings. Even your strict and stern father-in-law fell for your charms, your fine frame and your handsome countenance. If such a worldly and successful man could be so taken in, these country mice will not stand a chance.'

Seton found himself torn between facing the consequences of his actions and taking a gamble more likely to end in failure than success. The thought of trudging to the warehouse to be scolded by his brother-in-law tipped the balance in favour of abandoning all caution.

'Damn it!' He exclaimed to Kincaid's delight. 'What difference does it make how I die? The butcher's knife and the shame of servitude will separate me from my soul just as surely as the noose. It is God who will decide our fate whether we will it or not.'

Kincaid waited in the street while Seton rushed back inside to see to his packing. The smothering and casting aside of all doubts had left him elated and almost giddy at the prospect of leaving the Flesher, the Carmichaels and all of his debts behind. With both William and Thomas already away to the warehouse, there was only the housekeeper, the errand boy and Elizabeth left in the house. He sent the boy to the stables to order the groom to bring both of the Carmichael's horses around without delay. He was keen to avoid both of the women and the unwelcome questions they would undoubtedly ask him. The clatter of dishes in the pantry signalled that the housekeeper was busy clearing the breakfast table and would likely be so occupied long enough to allow him to finish his task. He pressed his ear against the drawing room door and could just make out the sound of Elizabeth gentling humming to herself as she did when she was engrossed in her embroidery. She would stay hard at it until the housekeeper brought her a tray of refreshments in the middle of the morning. When he was confident he would not be disturbed, he made his way upstairs, taking care to go slowly and to tread lightly so the boards would not creak and give his presence away.

It took only moments to pack his own belongings. Most of his clothes were still dirty and unlaundered following his return from France and he cast these aside in favour of the few unsoiled items he had left behind when he set off for the continent. He added his comb, wash-cloth and a small knife to the meagre pile. He then tiptoed across the landing and made for his father-in-law's chamber. The old man did not stint when it came to his wardrobe and Seton found his drawers stuffed so full it took all of his strength to wrench them open. He helped himself to two pairs of trews, two doublets and six sets of stockings, though he wrinkled his nose and declined to take anything from the drawer filled with his undergarments. The thought of nestling his private parts in cloth that had previously enwrapped Carmichael's shrivelled and wrinkled genitalia caused him to shudder in disgust.

He turned his attention to the wardrobe in the far corner. He knew this would contain the old man's most treasured finery for it had been placed close to the fire to keep its contents free of damp and mildew. The need for such care was evident the moment he pulled the door open. Carmichael must have parted with a great weight of silver to purchase such an array of exceptional and exquisite attire. Cloaks, coats and doublets hung from a row of pegs, caps and hats sat in a neat line on a high shelf and the wardrobe bottom was filled with polished and spotless boots and shoes. Seton doubted that any of it had been worn for there were no creases or specks of dust to be seen on any of it. The quality, cost and pristine condition of these items were such Seton hesitated to so much as touch them. He did not dither and ponder for long.

'Hell mend me!' He told himself in a whisper as he made his selections. 'If I live long enough to come back here, I'll have silver enough to replace it all.'

Kincaid let out a long, low whistle when Seton emerged from the Carmichael house and made a show of examining him from head to foot.

'My God, John.' He exclaimed in admiration. 'You cut a more imposing figure than Cowper himself. Even King James would take you for a witchfinder if you presented yourself to him at court as such. If I had any small misgivings, they have been blown to the four winds by the sight of you.'

Seton could not help but smile at the pricker's compliments. He felt powerful in William Carmichael's Sunday best. The knee-length boots were tight at the toes but the discomfort was worth enduring as the black leather was polished to a shine so deep it exuded both fine craftsmanship and great expense. The cloak and trews were of equal quality and lent him an air of wealth and authority. The hat was of black felt and, though a little old-fashioned in style, the wide brim was reminiscent of clerical garb. Old Carmichael had undoubtedly chosen it for this very reason as he set great store in his position as an elder of the kirk. Seton tossed a cloth bag to Kincaid and waited while he pulled the drawstring open and examined its contents

'My brother-in-law's church clothes will suit you well, though you may need to fold the trews at the bottom. He is a little taller than you.'

Kincaid raised an eyebrow in an unspoken question.

'Tis better to be hung for a sheep than for a lamb, is it not?' Seton retorted with a wide grin. 'The theft of their clothes will be little felt in comparison to the loss of their horses. Come! Their groom brings their horses! Let's away without delay. It would not do to encounter any of them now!'

4

Seton's spirits lightened as they put the stink and smoke of Edinburgh behind them. A weight seemed to lift from his shoulders as the distance between him and his troubles increased. He smiled at the thought of how much consternation his sudden disappearance would cause. The Carmichaels and the dread Flesher would be driven to impotent fury when they came to realise he was far beyond their grasp. He allowed himself to bask in daydreams of their reaction when he returned in triumph with pockets heavy with silver. The clearing skies and weak summer sun caused his mood to brighten as they went. The only cloud to blot his horizon was the regret he felt at having abandoned Elizabeth to her family once again. He put the unwelcome thought to the back of his mind by telling himself he would be better placed to make amends when he had money in his purse.

Kincaid proved to be a surprisingly good teacher for a man so rough and poorly educated.

He regaled Seton with tales of his experiences of the witch trials in Glasgow and was able to recite Cowper's prosecutorial speeches as if he had learned them by heart. He showed himself to be adept at mimicry by imitating the good minister's tone and gestures as he delivered the great man's arguments. Seton drank in every detail and, to Kincaid's delight, was soon able to incorporate this rhetoric into his developing repertoire and imbue it with sufficient bluster and eloquence to be convincing. The pricker applied himself to these preparations with admirable thoroughness and missed no opportunity to put Seton through his paces.

'I used to practice in my chamber at night.' Kincaid confided in him whilst attempting to convince him of the value of repetition in improving his performance. 'The poor innkeeper must have thought me to be in the grip of insanity after hearing me talk to myself for hour after hour. His eyes would grow wide with fear whenever I encountered him and he would flinch away from me if I ever came too close to him.'

Once Seton had mastered the vocabulary of prosecution, the pricker sought to test him by subjecting him to the challenges Cowper had faced at the hands of the jealous and petty clerics who were intent on doing him down. John's ability to rebut these spirited assaults improved steadily as they wound their way through Fife and on towards the Tay.

'My God, John!' He exclaimed after a particularly robust and bombastic performance in a cramped and smoke-filled tavern as they awaited a ferry to take them across to Dundee. 'These peasants will quail before you! Even my own cheeks grew flushed as you lambasted me! Cowper himself would struggle to have the better of you!'

Seton basked in the face of the pricker's praise and felt his confidence soar. His pleasure in his achievements was such he found he was able to overlook the aspects of Kincaid's character and conduct he found to be repugnant and objectionable. His eating habits were not the least of these. John had learned to keep his gaze fixed firmly on the plate before him when they ate to spare himself the sight of Kincaid's gaping maw as he gnawed and chewed noisily at his food. The disgusting spectacle of the pricker's teeth and chin smeared with the yolks from a plate of eggs had given him the boak. The vulgar fellow slurped at broth and gruel with such relish the mere sound of it was enough to make him gag. Then there was the matter of his lack of care when it came to his cleanliness and personal hygiene. Even the finest of gentlemen cannot spend a day in the saddle without falling prey to perspiration and the grime of the road. Seton would call for a jug of water and a washbowl on arriving at each and every tavern and inn and would not sit down to eat or drink until he had made himself clean and presentable. The pricker showed no such scruple and would take to his bed with the day's dust still in his hair and smeared across his cheeks. He reeked so badly it caused Seton's eyes to nip if he was trapped with him in close proximity for too long.

His lack of manners at table and his foul odour were less odious than the greatest of his unsavoury appetites. When the day's lessons and tests were done, he would invariably indulge himself in recounting the more obscene duties demanded of him as Minister Cowper's pricker. He needed no encouragement to enthusiastically launch into detailed descriptions of the indignities he was required to inflict on the women accused of witchcraft and was both blind and deaf to Seton's silent disapproval.

'You would not believe the great size of the old bitch's cunny!' He exclaimed as he nursed a pot of ale whilst lost in reminiscence in the tavern at Meigle. 'I doubt she had to push when birthing her brats. The poor bastards must surely have fallen out and thumped straight onto the floor.'

Seton would mask his distaste and make discrete attempts to steer the conversation onto topics other than the debasement of these unfortunate women, but Kincaid's pleasure was such he could seldom be diverted. When his revulsion at the pricker's drooling lasciviousness threaten to overwhelm him, he would feign fatigue and take himself off to bed. Once safe behind his chamber door, he would go immediately to the washbowl and scrub at himself to cleanse his skin and stop it from itching in disgust.

He was also somewhat troubled by Kincaid's failure to reassure him about the possible dire consequences of the deceit they were about to enact. When he gave voice to his reluctance to condemn anyone to death by burning or any other means, the pricker would berate him for his squeamishness.

'I was just the same when I first started out.' He declared in a manner Seton found less than convincing. 'You'll feel differently when faced by one of these vile and despicable creatures. You will see it as your duty to God and nation to scour their filth and malice from this earth.'

When Seton displayed a reluctance to be persuaded, Kincaid would invariably turn to the amount of silver they could win if only they had courage enough to see their pretence through to the end. The fee for an execution was not a trifling amount and the thought of it was sufficient to somewhat subdue Seton's misgivings without extinguishing them entirely.

The minister squinted against the sun and let his gaze travel along the track as it wound its way through the glen's green fields and pastures. He let out a sigh when he caught sight of the two horsemen in the distance. A weariness fell over him and his thin and heavily wrinkled face seemed to crumple in defeat as he observed their progress. He did not turn when the door to the big house creaked open behind him with a squeal piercing enough to set his teeth on edge. The housekeeper wheezed as she padded to his side, the great weight of her bosom, full cheeks and large, round belly causing her to become breathless from the exertion of only a few steps.

'The witchfinders come.' He announced in a dull and disheartened monotone.

'Then all of our prayers have fallen on deaf ears.' The housekeeper replied.

'The Lord is not deaf to us.' The minister corrected her. 'But it seems he is cruel. I was certain the authorities in Edinburgh would have the wisdom to refuse the Young Laird's request. My faith in them was clearly misplaced. City walls obviously offer no more defence against lunacy than open fields.'

'Will you wait to greet them, Minister?' The housekeeper asked, the forced lightness of her tone failing to disguise her anxiety.

'No.' He replied with finality. 'I have not the stomach for it. I will take to the fields and spare myself their company. I will likely have to suffer enough of it in the days to come.'

If he saw the sour expression on the woman's face, he gave no sign of it, but hobbled off as quickly as his stiff knees and thick cane would allow him to.

Seton took several deep breaths to steady himself as Marlee House came into view. His nerves settled a little as they approached for the place seemed less imposing the closer they came to it. Distance had lent it an impression of grandeur but proximity lifted that veil and exposed a long history of neglect and decay. A thick carpet of moss lay heavily on the thatch of the sagging roof, the stonework was worn and cracked and the doors and shutters were rotten and hung askew in their frames. The grounds were similarly unkempt and the air was heavy with the smell of mildew and rot.

'Look at the size of that bitch!' Kincaid exclaimed as he caught sight of the figure of the rotund housekeeper awaiting their arrival. 'Her teats hang down below her waist. If she gets much fatter they'll drag along the ground as she walks.'

'Wheesht!' Seton growled at him. 'You'll give us away if you speak out of turn!'

He then urged his horse ahead of the pricker's as the master would be expected to go ahead of his servant. He tipped his hat to the housekeeper as he reined in before her.

'Good morrow, good woman.' He greeted her, perfectly capturing the tone of disdain his father-in-law reserved for servants, beggars and the many others he considered to be beneath him. 'Allow me to introduce myself. I am John Cowper, Minister of the Cathedral of Glasgow, and this is my man, William Kincaid. We are expected by your master, I presume?'

'We thought you might come.' The housekeeper replied, unable to stop her voice from faltering and her hands from kneading each other in nervousness. 'Though Laird Marlee had no word of your arrival. Come! I will take you to him. He is ill in bed but is eager to renew your acquaintance and make you welcome here.'

Her words chilled Seton the bone and he saw panic in Kincaid's eyes when they exchanged a glance as the housekeeper led them up the worn and rickety staircase. The pricker was glancing about himself so wildly Seton feared he was on the verge of bolting for the door.

'Hold your nerve!' He hissed at him as the housekeeper puffed and gasped ahead of them. 'We will flee only if we must. I doubt she would have breath enough to pursue us or if the Laird would leap from his sickbed to capture us. Let us ride our luck till it has run out!'

Kincaid nodded his agreement though his eyes still danced with fright. Seton tilted the brim of his hat downwards in a bid to conceal more of his face as the housekeeper led them to the bedside. The air was thick with the stench of disease and stale piss. The withered and desiccated figure in the bed before them seemed to drown in the blankets heaped over him. The Laird's eyes flickered open at the sound of the housekeeper's voice. The features of his skull were clearly visible through a thin covering of wrinkled, mottled skin and only a few pathetic wisps of grey-white hair remained upon his head. Seton clenched his fists tight to steady himself and then breathed a sigh of relief when he saw that the old man's eyes were as cloudy as milk and likely sightless.

'I did not think we would meet again, John Cowper.' The old man croaked before reducing his eyes to slits to peer up at him. 'You do not seem to have aged a single day.'

'If only it was true, Laird.' Seton replied, taking care to deepen his voice to give the impression of greater maturity. 'I think your eyes deceive you into so complimenting me.'

A strange grating noise came from the Laird's old throat and his body began to shake, causing Seton to fear he was suffering a fit. He only realised the old man was laughing when he broke into a wide grin and revealed the gummy interior of his mouth.

'Tis true, Cowper. My sight is almost lost to me now. It was already bad when last we met. Can you recall the location of our meeting?'

Seton's mind raced in panic as he struggled to remember what Kincaid had told him of Cowper's history. A slip here would surely bring their enterprise to an abrupt, premature and unprofitable end.

'It must have been before I was appointed to the ministry in Glasgow, though I have been there for near ten years now.' He began, watching the old man's face closely to detect any reaction in his expression. 'It would likely have been in Edinburgh, though so much time has passed I could not swear to it. My powers of recollection seem to lose sharpness with each passing year.'

'Your memory is not at all impaired, Cowper. I spoke to you after you had delivered a sermon at the cathedral there. You will remember I complimented you on its brevity and for sparing me from the discomfort of long hours on the cathedral's hard pews. I had the misfortune of suffering there in the days of John Knox. That man never tired of the sound of his own voice and would talk on until the poor congregants' arses were so numb they would pray for the good Lord to strike them down just to bring an end to their pain.'

Laird Marlee wheezed horribly as he spoke and the effort brought on a fit of coughing. He gestured at the housekeeper with his fingers and she quickly snatched up a cup of water and held it to his thin and puckered lips. He did little more than sip weakly at the liquid but it was sufficient to lubricate his throat and allow him to continue.

'Twas a rare thing in those days to encounter a pastor not drunk on piety and set on haranguing his flock and terrifying them with visions of the burning hell and eternal torment awaiting them the moment their last breath rattled in their sinful and unworthy throats. I sought you out to praise you for your moderation and restraint in the hope of encouraging you to continue to resist the increasing harshness and inhumanity of the kirk's rhetoric. It is why you came to mind when my errant son made it his business to persecute these poor women. I am certain you possess both the moral strength and the authority to steer him from his misguided course. I will rest easy now you are here.'

Seton glanced at Kincaid as the old man reached out and grasped his hand in fingers made thin and twisted by age. Some colour had returned to the pricker's face and he no longer appeared to be on the brink of fleeing.

'I tire so easily these days and must regretfully leave this matter entirely in your hands.' He croaked, his eyelids already fluttering and his voice now faint and distant. Margaret will show you to your chambers before serving you with refreshments after your long journey. God bless you for coming. I will sleep easier now.'

'Jesus, John!' Kincaid exclaimed in relief when Margaret had left them to huff and puff her way downstairs to see to their food and drink. 'I thought we were undone. My heart lurched in my chest when the old biddy revealed that Cowper and Marlee were already acquainted! I do not know how you held your nerve! I saw a great strength in you when we first met but I now know I sorely underestimated you. I was close to shitting myself and you just stood there all calm and full of confidence. Thank Christ the old bastard is blind as blind can be!'

Seton grinned in response to the praise though his knees still trembled and sweat ran in rivers down the small of his back.

'I would rather have avoided the encounter, Will, but it has won us great advantage. No one will doubt us when the Laird, in his dotage, has confirmed my identity. Let us press on as quickly as we are able. My nerves are jangling so hard I am eager to have this business over and done with.'

'Let us not be so hasty.' Kincaid cautioned him. 'The longer we can drag this out, the more silver young Marlee will be forced to part with. The father is eager to have the prosecution dismissed while the son is set on seeing it through. Such division cries out to be exploited. Let us take our time in examining both the case for and the case against. We must be compensated for each day we are here. The longer the arguments rage, the fatter our purses will grow!'

5

Seton gazed around the cavernous dining room as the clatter of his footsteps on the worn, wooden floorboards echoed back at him off the panelled walls. The dark interior spoke of past grandeur rendered scuffed and shabby by neglect and the passing of the years. Whatever source of wealth had funded the expensive furnishings and exquisite craftsmanship of Marlee House had clearly dried up long ago. The space was dominated by a dining table large enough to comfortably seat thirty guests. A thousand scratches on its surface hinted at the hundreds of lavish entertainments it had witnessed in better times and the mismatched chairs set around it told of the Laird's inability to pay for repairs to the original seating or to replace it with items of similar quality. Six ornate, brass candelabra hung from the smoke-blackened ceiling but they were dark and held only ugly clumps of ancient, melted candle wax turned grey by age and decades of accumulated dust. A single taper provided a faint light at the far end of the table and illuminated Margaret as she bustled and fussed around with plates, cups and jugs.

Seton called out a greeting as he approached, his stomach rumbling at the sight of bread, cheese, boiled mutton, trout fried with onions and a whole roast pigeon. He let the housekeeper serve him a little of each dish until his plate was piled high with food. He set about it with great relish, pausing only to offer his compliments to the cook. Margaret blushed with delight and encouraged him to eat as much as he liked. Kincaid, for his part, ignored the food and poured himself a cup of wine.

'The Laird was pleased to see you here.' She stammered, her hands clasped together in nervous agitation. 'It did my heart good to see him in such good spirits when he has had so much to trouble him of late.'

'The good Lord will ever seek to try us, Margaret.' Seton replied, eager to engage her in conversation in order to glean whatever morsels of intelligence might prove useful to their deceit. 'Pray tell us how he has tested the good Laird in recent days?'

'There has been no end to the torments visited upon him.' The housekeeper exclaimed with a rueful shake of her head. 'The last three harvests have been as poor as any I can remember in my thirty years on this estate. There's barely enough to feed us let alone any surplus to sell to pay for maintenance and repairs. Hunger is our constant companion and you would not believe how much weight I have lost these past few years.'

'What?' Kincaid demanded, almost choking on his wine. 'Just how fat were you before?'

Seton glared at the pricker to silence him before bidding the red-faced Margaret to continue.

'Then there is the Young Laird.' She continued hesitantly, her glance flicking constantly towards Kincaid in fear of further insult. 'He vexes his father more than any good son should. Even as a boy he was ungrateful and full of avarice. If his father offered him a spoon of jam, he would reach out and demand the whole pot for himself. The Laird is a kind and gentle man and the boy takes advantage of his generous nature. He demands silver when there is none to be had and will settle for nothing less than the best of everything. He rides the finest stallion this side of Perth and dresses in clothes from the finest and most expensive tailors in Edinburgh. The Laird thinks only the best of him and makes his excuses for his behaviour. When he sent the boy off to study in St Andrews at no little expense he was certain it would be the making of him. He was sore disappointed when he abandoned his studies after less than a year and returned home with only rich friends and heightened expectations to show for it. He will ruin his poor father before he is done.'

'What of this current business?' Seton enquired gently, noting that Margaret kept glancing in the direction of the front door with no little trepidation. 'The Laird is clearly at odds with his son as far as this matter is concerned.'

'I have never known him to be so angry with the boy!' The housekeeper replied, her head bobbing in disapproval so furiously the action set her chins to quivering. 'There is no witchcraft at the root of this! Tis the Young Laird's greed that drives it and the spite and lust of others that spurs him on. If there is evil in this parish, it does not come from any of those poor women now chained in horse stalls in the barn behind this house. Each one of them is blameless and they are undeserving of the false accusations made against them. Agnes Nevie was the kindest and most Christian of women and was known to give her last crust to another if they would only ask for it. Half the women of this parish cried out for her when giving birth to their bairns and she was ever willing to rush to their sides no matter the weather or whether it was night or day. Farmers would beg her to tend to their animals when they sickened or when their milk dried in their teats.'

'She was a healer then?' Kincaid demanded, his face set hard in suspicion. 'Such acts are considered to be witchcraft no matter whether the intent is good or ill.'

'She was good with beasts and bairns, that is all.' She protested. 'She had nothing but good in her heart and would refuse any reward for her work. Those she once helped turn upon her in ingratitude now she is no longer able to serve them in her decrepitude. Neither is Elspet Leyis a witch, though I will not deny she is a vile, spiteful and ill-tempered creature who would test the patience of Christ himself. I doubt there is a single man or woman in this parish who has not suffered her foul-mouthed rage but that does not make her a witch. She is no more in league with the Devil than you or I.'

'What of the third accused, Violet Frazer?' Seton asked, recalling the final name listed on the Privy Council's commission.

'It is the worst of them all.' Margaret spat, her eyes flashing with anger and her cheeks turning a darker shade of red. 'Her crime, if she is guilty of any, is to have been born a woman and to have grown up fair. If she was plain and had not inherited her father's land, she would not have been so badly mistreated. If she had given in to the demands made of her, our shameless menfolk would have had no good reason to call you here.'

Seton did not know how the man had managed to enter the house so silently when the outer door screeched on its hinges at the slightest touch and the floorboards groaned under the weight of the lightest of footsteps. He was only alerted to his presence when a surprisingly girlish squeal came suddenly from Margaret's throat and she scurried away in fright.

'I must offer you my apologies if Margaret has been afflicting you with her ignorant and inane chatter, gentlemen.' The dark figure declared in a deep and authoritative voice as he advanced into the single candle's flickering light. 'I have often had cause to chide her for her gossiping but she is not happy unless her tongue is wagging and her gums are flapping. I have often urged my father to dismiss her from his service but some sense of ill-placed and undeserved loyalty makes him deaf to my counsel.'

Seton disliked the Young Laird on his first sight of him. Tall, handsome, broad-shouldered and impeccably dressed, there was a smug confidence in his swagger that put him in mind of his brother-in-law, Thomas Carmichael. The set of his jaw projected a level of arrogance, self-satisfaction and expectation possessed only by those who had been born to wealth and privilege and who had been brought up to be certain of their God-given right to their advantages. Seton was intimidated by his greater height, grace and rank and had to steel himself to present himself as his equal, if not his superior.

'James Moncur, Young Laird of Marlee, at your service, gentlemen.' He announced with a bow. 'I cannot tell you how pleased I was to hear of your arrival. I rode here will all speed so we can set proceedings in motion without delay. I hope Margaret caused you no offence. She is inclined to blethering and enjoys precious few opportunities to so indulge herself when she is shut away with only my ailing father for company. Pray forgive her foolishness and do not let her nonsense influence you. I will join you at table so we may drink to a successful and speedy prosecution.'

The Young Laird called for Margaret to bring more claret and set about ingratiating himself with his guests without dwelling overlong on introductions or ceremony.

'I am glad we were able to entice you away from Glasgow when all reports of that poor, bedevilled place talk of a plague of witches the like of which has never been seen before. It makes me shiver to think of the evil that is abroad and I pray nightly for the good citizens who have been so afflicted.' Moncur raised his cup and drank a toast to the health of the witchfinder and his pricker. 'I would not have asked you here if our need was not so great. The godly people of this good parish are under siege from evil-doers and are sore afeart. Three witches might seem insignificant when compared to the hundreds you have exposed in Glasgow, but our terror for our very souls is no less urgent and we are desperate to purge this vile contamination from our midst.'

'The whole kingdom is consumed by darkness and despair.' Seton replied, rising to the performance required of him. 'The Devil is at work across our nation with few places spared his malevolent attentions. I will not lie to spare you from the horror of what now faces us. We are at war with Satan and the legions he has sent against us. He has cursed us with famine and disease and sends his wanton servants into our midst to weaken us with dark magic and naked malevolence. Each new day brings fresh reports of demonic possession, of great congregations of witches gathering to worship at Satan's feet and to fornicate with the Beast in renunciation of the laws of God and of sinners communicating with spirits, familiars and the fairy folk! Battles are being fought in Aberdeen, Edinburgh, Fife and Glasgow and only God knows what abominations are lurking in the lands of the heathen Highlanders. We are in a fight for our very souls and have only ourselves to blame! None of us can boast of unwavering vigilance when we have allowed the practice of white magic, healing and midwifery to proliferate unchallenged in our own parishes. We have left our doors ajar and let Satan enter while we were distracted by more earthly matters. The tide can be turned but the struggle will be long and hard and must be fought wherever the contamination of evil is to be found. We will, with God's help, fight it here and bring relief and salvation to the good people of Marlee!'

Seton paused and wiped at the flecks of spittle that had gathered at the corners of his mouth as he waited to see the effect of his words on James Moncur. He kept his gaze fixed on the Young Laird but saw Kincaid nodding in approval from the corner of his eye. Moncur's reaction was all he had hoped for.

'My father was right to recommend you for this undertaking.' He announced with a burst of enthusiasm. 'He was certain you possessed the strength, determination and moral rectitude required to bring these matters to a righteous conclusion. Let us drink to our success!' He refilled their cups before continuing in a tone of earnestness. 'We must bring this vile business to a close without delay. I will move heaven and earth to clear your path towards an early and just resolution.'

He pulled a heavy leather purse from the folds of his cloak and let it thump down onto the table. Kincaid sucked in a breath from the shock of seeing their prize so early in their endeavour. Seton felt his heart flutter in his chest but held the young aristocrat's gaze as if the weight of silver was of little concern to him.

'With your services in such great and urgent demand, I thought it better to resolve the issue of your fee before the proceedings begin.' He paused and licked his lips, a look of triumph shining in his eyes. 'I would not want such petty and administrative matters to distract you from the efficient execution of your duties. I will settle the more minor matter of your daily expenses as we go.'

With the Young Laird's desire for haste clearly established, the conversation turned to the arrangements for the trials. Seton was in such a daze he struggled to concentrate on the details and found himself agreeing to whatever Moncur proposed.

'It is settled then!' The Young Laird declared with finality as he pushed himself to his feet. 'We will conduct the trials here in Marlee House. I will have this room set out so the proceedings can begin at dawn. It would make no sense to waste time transporting the three accused from my barn to the kirk each day when expediency is the order of the day. I will bid you goodnight, gentlemen. We shall meet again to break our fast at first light.'

Seton and Kincaid made straight for their chambers where they would be better able to converse without being overheard. The pricker had the foresight to take the half-filled jug of claret with him so they might drink to celebrate their early windfall.

'My God!' Seton hissed in delight as he poured the contents of the purse onto the blanket on his bed. 'Tis the full amount! My portion will be sufficient to repay the Flesher in full with a bit besides to salve his temper for my unannounced departure.'

Joy and relief pulsed through him and left him dizzy after the strain of having to perform his part under the scrutiny of both the Old Laird and his son. He thrust his hands into the pile of coins and luxuriated in the cold heaviness of the silver against his fingers. Kincaid slapped him firmly on the back before whispering in his excitement.

'I will confess to feeling my courage melt away when the Young Laird crept out of the darkness and caught us listening to the fat housekeeper's gossip. I wilted under the fierceness of his gaze and was certain he would see through our subterfuge. I feared the worst when you hesitated and seemed about to falter in giving him a response.' He shook his head in admiration and bared his blackened teeth in a grin. 'I will never doubt you again, John Seton. The moment you cleared your throat and parted your lips I knew we would succeed. You spoke with so much confidence and authority even I was taken in and half-believed you to be a formidable pastor set on scouring the land clean of evil-doers and their foul works. Did you see James Moncur's expression as he listened to your words? He thought to bring a stern witchfinder to his parish and is now convinced he has accomplished it. I doubt if even the court of King James boasts a play-actor more accomplished than yourself.'

Seton accepted the praise gratefully though the effort of the pretence had left him drained and exhausted.

'Let us take ourselves away under the cover of darkness rather than stay here and risk discovery and the loss of this silver.' He gripped the pricker's wrist as he made the suggestion to emphasise its gravity. 'Why take the gamble when the money is already in our possession?'

'Why would we skulk away now when we could extract the same amount again from Marlee's purse if only we have courage and keep our wits about us? With expenses for each day spent in prosecuting the cases and fees for pricking, ducking and burning, we can prise more coin from the Young Laird's tight fists.' Kincaid kept his eyes locked on Seton's as he urged him to stay the course. 'I am certain young Marlee will urge us to haste but we must use the authority of the commission to resist him and stretch the process to its extremity. We have wit enough to achieve it!'

'Tis too much of a risk, Will. The longer we tarry here the more likely we are to be exposed. What then? We will lose what we have already won and be left with only the shadow of the gallows in its place.'

'I thought you to be a man of ability and ambition, John. Do not be faint-hearted! If you can steel yourself to last just one full week, we will near double our purse! If we can induce even one of these foul hags to turn against their neighbours and accuse them of witchcraft, we could still be here a month from now and will have drained Laird Marlee of all of his wealth.' Kincaid now dug his fingers into John's wrist with enough force to cause him to wince. 'Think of what my master achieved in Glasgow! One witch led to near two hundred others being accused and tried, a hundred burnt and two dozen branded and exiled.'

'Aye!' John retorted as he pulled his hand away. 'Look where that has led your master! We should learn from his mistake and take care to avoid stretching our luck too far!'

'If you play your part well enough, my friend, we will have no need of luck. Let us judge when we have squeezed the last drops of blood from these fools and we'll be away as fast as our full and heavy pockets will allow us!'

Seton sighed in frustration and let his gaze fall to the scattered mound of coins on the bed. He remained silent as a brutal battle between caution and greed was fought in his mind. This struggle between two mismatched forces was short-lived.

'Very well!' He declared in solemn and reluctant resignation. 'Let us see how events unfold and we will judge when the moment has come for us to flee.'

6

John Seton was torn from his fitful sleep by a great screeching and a thumping powerful enough to cause the floorboards to shudder and rattle beneath his bed. He leapt up and snatched at his breeches in panic intent on dressing before tearing the shutters open and making away in the weak morning light. His mind reeled as he tried to imagine how they had come to be unmasked as impostors while the house slept. He froze at the sound of hushed voices from the floor below and strained his ears in an attempt to catch their words above the thunder of his racing heart. He could discern nothing of the content of the conversation but could detect no hint of anger or alarm in the tone of the exchange. One voice was louder than the others and seemed to bark out terse instructions. This was followed by more banging and scraping, though the din was more muted than before.

He dropped to his knees and pressed his ear against a crack in the rough wooden boards. The

Young Laird's voice was muffled by the thick timbers but Seton was able to make out the words 'chairs' and 'back wall'. The tension melted away from his shoulders when he realised the man was concerned with the arrangement of furniture in the hall rather than with the presence of fraudsters in his house. He exhaled sharply in relief and sent a silent prayer of thanks to God for sparing him from the shame and ignominy of exposure and from being pursued and captured for his deceit. The reprieve was only momentary and his heart seemed to shoot up into his throat when boots clattered across the landing floor and his chamber door was swept open hard enough to send it crashing against the wall.

'Ha!' Will Kincaid crowed in amusement. 'You look set to shit yourself in fright! Your face is as white as a baby's arse! Did you imagine you were about to be dragged from your bed and strung up from the nearest tree?'

Seton cursed at the pricker and bid him to close the chamber door so he might gather himself and prepare for the performance to come.

'We will do it just as we rehearsed as we travelled here.' The pricker declared when his hilarity had subsided sufficiently to allow him to turn to the serious matter in hand. 'The Young Laird has been true to his word and the dining room is now arranged just as we agreed. The feasting table has been pushed back against the wall and the serving table is now positioned in the centre of the room with chairs behind it for the two of us. A low stool has been placed before it so the accused can be seated and subjected to questioning. A bench has been carried in for the other women to sit upon while they await their turns. There are chairs for the Young Laird, the minister and the other worthies and there is standing room for a dozen witnesses and for twenty villagers to come and gawp and attest to the justice of the proceedings.'

'I did not expect the gathering to be so large.' Seton moaned, his stomach churning at the thought of such a large audience. 'My mouth is dry and my knees tremble so fiercely I fear they will knock against each other loud enough to be heard.'

'You must pull yourself together, John.' Kincaid reassured him as he placed his hands on his shoulders. 'Remember what I told you. Dominate the room, just as Minister Cowper does. Neither the minister nor the Young Laird has any authority here. Order them to silence if they speak! Let them see the Privy Council's warrant. The sight of the seals and the ribbons will cow them into submission. Project your voice to every corner of the room. Make judicious use of silence and let it hang in the air until it grows oppressive. They believe you to be here with all the authority of the king himself. Do not refrain from reminding them of that fact. If you do these things, we will run rings around these slack-jawed, in-bred simpletons.'

Seton nodded and tried to steel himself for the ordeal ahead.

'Be merciless in challenging every accusation, statement and assertion. Harsh words and cold-heartedness will harden your authority and will draw out the proceedings as they scramble to find new evidence and make new arguments to bolster their case against your questioning and objections. Think of the silver we will gain with each passing day!'

The pricker's words succeeded in settling Seton's nerves and his confidence grew as he dressed himself in his father-in-law's fine Sunday clothes. The effect of the long boots, black cloak and wide-brimmed hat was evident in Kincaid's admiring gaze.

'Let us go and do God's work!' He announced, jutting his chin out in determination.

The hum of conversation rising from the floor below had increased in both volume and ebullience while Seton was dressing and repressing his nervousness. The sound of his boot heels on the stairs caused it to fall away to a murmur and then to come to complete silence when he strode into their sight. The gathered villagers gawped at the imposing figure of the witchfinder and seemed to hold their breath as he took his place at the table and laid his documents out before him with exaggerated care. He let the stillness hang until the weight of it bore down heavily on all present and made them fearful of making the slightest sound or movement. He then surveyed the room with deliberate slowness, letting his eyes bore into those of every man and woman there as though he judged them and found them wanting. He was heartened to see that his control was absolute. Even the Young Laird fidgeted uncomfortably when subjected to his glare. The other peasants, tradesmen and farmers quailed under his harsh scrutiny and most dropped their eyes to the floor rather than meet his gaze. Seton then lifted the Privy Council commission from the table and held it out so its seal and ribbons were clearly displayed to all sides of the room. Several people jumped and jerked in fright when he finally spoke, the sudden thunder of his voice shattering the silence as it reverberated around the worn, wooden walls. He continued to hold the parchment aloft as he recited its contents from memory.

'By the royal authority of His Majesty King James, Prince of Scotland, it pleases the honourable Lords of the Privy Council, in response to the humble supplication of the Presbytery of Marlee, to grant warrants and commissions for the trying and administering of justice upon Agnes Nevie, widow of the Parish of Marlee, Elspet Leyis, widow of the Parish of Marlee and Violet Frazer, maid of the Parish of Marlee and upon any other such persons similarly accused of the crimes of witchcraft, sorcery and necromancy in defiance of the Laws of God. These warrants and commissions hereby invest John Cowper of the Presbytery of Glasgow with the authority of King James and the Lords of the Privy Council in the advancement of the gospel and the punishment of vice.'

John surveyed the room as he spoke and observed the effect of his performance with no little satisfaction. Men winced as he detailed the punishments he was empowered to inflict should the accused be found guilty of the crimes they were charged with.

'Without exception for age, sex or rank, those found to be magicians, sorcerers or witches are to suffer just punishment according to the Laws of God, the civil and imperial law and the municipal law of all Christian nations. Such punishment includes, as is deemed appropriate, execution by hanging and burning, branding, banishment, indefinite imprisonment, public humiliation, flogging, the seizure of all goods and property and, by way of excommunication, exclusion from the sacraments and services of the Christian Church.'

He took great care to enunciate each one clearly and paused to let the enormity of his powers sink in. The faces gaping back at him were grave and filled with anxiety and tension. It seemed that Kincaid was right to believe these peasants would be no match for them. He was surprised to realise he was actually enjoying himself when the time came for him to call for the first accused to be brought forward to stand before him.

Two burly men dragged Agnes Nevie through the crowd and forced her down onto the stool set there for that purpose. Seton scowled at his first sight of her and shook his head in honest disapproval. He could not recall having ever set his eyes upon a woman in such a wretched and pitiable condition. Her clothes were torn and filthy, her skin was mottled and wrinkled with age, her calves were covered with open, festering wounds and her feet were broken and blackened with only bloody scabs and weeping, suppurating sores where her toenails had once been. Her face was gaunt and hollow from lack of sustenance, her eyes were wide and unfocused and she was clearly unaware of anyone or anything around her. Seton felt a sudden surge of anger well up in his chest so strongly he could not stop himself from giving vent to it.

'This woman may stand accused but she is to be considered innocent until the moment she is condemned.' He growled through teeth so tightly clenched they ground against each other. 'Whoever has so mistreated her must hang his head in shame! Is it not plain she is too feeble to be put to question? Did no one think to feed her?'

'We put porridge and gruel before her but she would not touch it.' James Moncur protested, his cheeks reddening in spite of the defiance in his tone. 'I thought it a pity to waste good food on her when it is likely she will burn before too long.'

'That is not for you to determine!' Seton roared with enough ferocity to leave the Young Laird blinking in surprise. 'Call your housekeeper here and command her to take this woman away so she can be washed, dressed in clean clothes and fed some broth. I will hear no word of evidence against her until this outrage has been remedied.'

Moncur opened his mouth to object but quickly closed it again rather than risk further censure. He rose from his seat in a sulk and went in search of Margaret, calling her name in irritation as he went.

'Jesus, John!' Kincaid whispered, his mouth hidden behind his hand. 'Even I near pissed myself when you barked at him. There is no doubting who is the authority in this room. We will drive events just as we discussed. The Young Laird thinks to have this hag found guilty and condemned before this day is done. Challenge each and every piece of sworn testimony and see how far we can drag it out!'

Seton gave only a curt nod in response and kept a serious expression on his face though he was exhilarated by the way the morning had unfolded. His trembling and nausea were long forgotten and he could not help but dream of what his silver might buy him.

Agnes Nevie looked only a little better when she was returned to her place on the stool. Her expression was as blank and unseeing as it had been before and the act of washing her face and feet had succeeded in removing the dirt only to reveal dark bruising and swollen flesh. Seton shook his head and gestured for the first witness to step forward. The woman was of middle age, was plainly dressed and the roundness of her cheeks suggested she had means enough to keep herself far from hunger. Her feet shuffled in nervous agitation but there was a bitter hardness in her eyes and a sense of determination in her stance. Seton had her swear an oath to speak the truth and instructed her to give voice to her accusation.

'I am Anna Kerr, wife to William Kerr, blacksmith of this parish, and I do denounce Agnes Nevie as a witch, may God strike me down if I do not speak truly, sir. I did dream of the old wife one night last winter and, when I awoke, I found my youngest boy insensible with fever. I applied poultices and cold compresses and had my good husband buy beef to make broth to revive him. I knew it was witchcraft when no cure could be found to remedy his condition. Any natural fever would break when treated so but this one endured for almost a month and left the boy slow and dull-witted. Only a spell or curse can explain such a thing, all people agree that this is true.'

'Children are often sick.' Seton replied with a weary sigh. 'And dreams are no proof of anything. I once dreamed of falling from a great height. The vision was so vivid I cried out in my sleep and awakened in my bed in a fit of terror. It was merely a nightmare just the same and I suffered no injury from it. Do you have any evidence, apart from this dream, of Agnes Nevie playing any part in causing harm to your son?'

'I just know it, sir.' She snapped back, her face twisted in annoyance. 'I know her to be a witch and know she should burn for it!'

'Knowing her to be a witch and thinking her to be a witch are two very different things, good wife.' Seton scolded her. 'Step back if you have no proof and give way to any other witness more likely to convince me of her guilt.'

Anna Kerr opened her mouth to protest and turned towards the Young Laird in search of his support. James Moncur glared at her before giving a curt nod to indicate that she should withdraw.

The second witness was a younger woman of no more than twenty years of age. She blushed beetroot red when she introduced herself as Marie Shaw, wife to Robert Shaw, a tenant farmer on the Marlee estate. Seton examined her in silence for several moments, not with the intention of discomfiting her, but because there was something in her face he found troubling. He could not quite put his finger on the cause of his disquiet and so took her oath before instructing her to testify.

'All here know Agnes Nevie to be a witch.' She began, her voice low and hesitant and her cheeks burning a darker shade of red. 'She is never without a black dog at her side. Tis her familiar spirit and she was given it by the cunning folk. I know this to be true because she talks to it, calls it Bunnykins and lets it suckle at her teats.'

The gathered men and women let out a collective gasp at this shocking revelation but fell to silence immediately when Seton scowled in annoyance.

'Tis also true that she sits by her fire at night fashioning charms and likenesses from clay and wax to use in spells intended to do harm to good, God-fearing folk.'

'Tis no sin to talk to a dog.' Seton interrupted her. 'The good minister did exactly that when he arrived here and settled his old hound down by the fire. No reasonable man would condemn him for so comforting an old and faithful friend. Allowing such a beast to suckle at her breast would be unnatural and quite another matter altogether. Tell me how you came to witness this and her other nocturnal activities. I assume she does not bare herself in the street or make her charms within the sight of the good people of this parish.'

'No, sir.' The girl replied. 'I saw her from her step when I crept up to her hovel. She did not know I was watching her. The beast lapped at her as she busied herself with her enchantments.'

'Tell me more about these charms. If she spends her nights in their concoction, she must have used a great deal of clay and wax and will have produced a whole host of them.'

'Aye, sir. There were dozens of them scattered about her hearth.' She announced, her confidence and enthusiasm growing in response to Seton's encouragement. 'Some for luck or fertility and others to bring misfortune upon her neighbours. The sight of them filled me with such terror I have seldom slept since then. I doubt I will rest easy until she is condemned and burnt.'

'You have done your duty to God and parish by having the courage to testify before us this day, good wife. I will pray for you and beseech the good Lord to grant you peaceful slumber now you have shared your burden with us. Please step back and allow the next witness to come forward.'

The third witness was even more nervous than the last. He shuffled uncomfortably from one foot to the other and kept his eyes cast downwards, lifting them only to exchange glances with the Young Laird and the swarthy, unsmiling fellow at his side. His red and bulbous nose stood out in a pale face not weathered by long days in the fields exposed to the cruelties of wind, rain and sun. His hands were calloused and scarred from hard labour, his fingernails ragged and black. He spoke in a dull monotone and his delivery reminded Seton of his own performances when his schoolmaster had made him recite biblical passages by rote.

'I am Samuel Cartwright, apprentice to William Kerr, blacksmith of this parish. I know Agnes Nevie to be a witch and so accuse her.' His hand shook as he raised it and pointed towards the insensible old woman on the stool. 'She did scold me for taking a crab apple from her tree. When I cursed her as a witch she grew angry and shrieked at me as if she was demented. 'If witch I be.' She screamed. 'Then great misfortune will befall ye, you rude and impudent oaf!' I was so afeart I ran from her and did not stop until I reached the forge. A great misfortune did befall me that very afternoon, just as she had foretold. My hammer slipped as I worked at repairing a plough and took my forefinger off at the first knuckle.' He held his hand out to display the mangled digit. 'All men know me to be sure of hand so the injury could only be the result of that vile witch's sorcery! God knows she should burn to spare us all from her devilry!'

'Show me your hands.' Seton instructed him. 'Hold them out for all to see!'

Cartwright complied with evident reluctance, glancing over his shoulder in the hope of some support from the Young Laird and his companion.

'I see injuries to several other fingers and burn marks on both the backs and palms of your hands. Were they all caused by the malevolence of this or other witches? What of your master, William Kerr?' He demanded, gesturing towards the man at the Young Laird's side. 'Let us see his hands to determine if they be free of blemish and disfigurement.'

Kerr looked to James Moncur for permission before slowly extending his hands towards Seton for his inspection.

'A lifetime at the forge has left you with a myriad of bruises, lacerations and contusions, Mister Kerr. Will you seek to persuade me that each one of them was caused by witchcraft rather than by the rigours and perils of a blacksmith's lot?'

The blacksmith grimaced and attempted to hold Seton's gaze but his defiance was short-lived and he bowed his head in submission.

'Let us now move to consider the witch's confession.' The Young Laird barked in anger at seeing the testimony of the last of the witnesses dismissed. 'It will confirm all claims against her and provide irrefutable evidence of her malfeance.'

'I have not yet completed my examination of the witness testimony, good sir.' Seton retorted. 'You will accord me the courtesy of allowing me to conduct the proceedings as I see fit and resist the temptation to provide direction when I have requested no such counsel. We will adjourn for a while and the good pastor will accompany me to the auld wife's hovel to assist me in my enquiries. We will seek evidence there to corroborate or disprove the accusations made during the course of the morning.'

'You will find nothing there that these gathered elders cannot vouch for here and now.' Moncur protested, his cheeks flushed in annoyance. 'You should not waste our time or your own, not to mention the silver I will be required to pay out for your expenses.'

'I waste nothing, sir, and will spare no effort in my search for the truth. You should remain here and await our return.'

7

Kincaid had good reason to be pleased as the afternoon dragged on. Seton's excursion had all but ensured that the first trial would not be completed for another day. His companion was playing his part with great confidence and skill and would doubtlessly earn them much more in the way of coin. The pricker had also benefited from remaining at his place while his co-conspirator ventured out. He stayed at the table and hunched over the Privy Council documents in a pretence of studying their contents though he could not read a single one of the words scratched onto the parchments. This left him largely undisturbed and unobserved and so enabled him to watch and listen to everything done or said in Seton's absence. He was able to deduce that those gathered in Marlee House fell into three distinct and separate groups. Those around the Young Laird were his supporters and were strongly and openly in favour of seeing the accused women condemned and executed. Another smaller and less vocal party congregated around the minister's wife and satisfied themselves with shooting disapproving looks at James Moncur and his acolytes. The remaining folk were in the majority and could be categorised as gawpers drawn there in search of excitement to distract them from the banality and suffering of their daily lives. Kincaid drank this all in thirstily and committed it to memory to be used when it might bring him some advantage.

The Young Laird took no pleasure in the passing hours. His scowl tightened and his countenance grew increasingly sour as time wore on. He was pacing and muttering to himself in irritation when a stable boy came with word of Seton and the minister's approach. Moncur met them at the door and, gripping Seton's wrist with no little force, pulled him aside.

'The day is almost done without a conclusion to this business.' He hissed in the witchfinder's ear. 'I trust you have not been unduly influenced by our good pastor. He is, as I am sure you have already realised, a weak and feeble-minded man. He is too easily swayed by tears and protestations of innocence and lacks the backbone required to stand up to his soft-hearted and interfering wife. I would urge you to discount his opinions and place your faith only in the evidence before you, though I doubt your little outing has revealed anything of note.'

'On the contrary, good sir.' Seton replied as he pulled his wrist from the Young Laird's grasp. 'The pastor was most informative and our efforts proved to be more worthwhile than I had hoped. If you would be good enough to resume your place, I will disclose all we discovered.'

Seton favoured Kincaid with a wink as he crossed towards him. The pricker remained impassive in spite of his rising excitement. He was certain he was about to enjoy the next part of the proceedings. Seton took a moment to compose himself before revealing his findings.

'I am dismissing the testimony of all three accusers.' He announced, the bluntness of his pronouncement causing a murmur of surprise to spread around the chamber. 'I am discounting Marie Shaw's testimony on the grounds of falsehood. The minister and I stood upon the auld wife's step and could not see her hearth from that vantage point, no matter how far we leaned inside her door. There is no clear line of sight from doorway to hearth. Therefore, it is clear she could not have seen what she claimed to have seen. We also took the opportunity to conduct a thorough search of the hovel. We found neither charms nor any sign of the wax and clay required in the making of them. If she spent her nights in their manufacture, as Anna Kerr asserted, then surely some evidence of this nefarious activity would remain. Mrs Shaw also spoke of a familiar spirit in the form of a black dog. We found just such a dog skulking around her hovel. He is grey of chops and foul of breath but does not seem in any way demonic or elemental. If he was reliant on his mistress for sustenance, he must surely be ravenous after so many days away from her and would be unable to resist throwing himself upon her to suckle at her teats.' Seton paused for effect and slowly surveyed the room. 'Let us see for ourselves, shall we?'

The minister called out and a boy led a dirty and mangy dog in through the doorway. His old ears pricked up at the sight of Agnes Nevie and he went to her, his tail wagging furiously as he licked at her unresponsive fingers. All present held their breath in anticipation of witnessing proof of witchcraft with their own eyes. Some sighed in disappointment and some in relief when the hound showed no interest in Agnes Nevie's breasts but instead chose to curl up at her feet and close his watery eyes.

'I also dismiss the testimony of Anna Kerr and Samuel Cartwright out of hand.' Seton declared with a wave of his hand. 'Children grow sick and blacksmiths mash their thumbs without the aid of sorcery or spells. When the good Lord sees fit to test us with misfortunes, we must suffer those torments with courage and forbearance, not seek to attribute them to witches and spirits. We must also resist the temptation to covet our neighbours' goods, to bear false witness against them and to take the Lord's name in vain. Anna Kerr, Samuel Cartwright and Marie Shaw have all broken these three sacred commandments this day!'

Seton jabbed his finger at each of them in turn as he accused them.

'What did I find when I visited Agnes Nevie's hovel?' He demanded, his face red with rage. 'I found a blacksmith's forge on the land adjacent to it. I had detected some familial similarity in the faces of the witnesses but thought little of it until I called into the forge and found it abandoned apart from an old woman sunning herself there on the step. She was most forthcoming in answering my questions and unwittingly damned all three of you. I now know you to be the wife, daughter and son-in-law of William Kerr, good blacksmith of this parish. I now know that all three of you live under his roof and that you expect to be granted Agnes Nevie's land should she be condemned and executed. You lied under oath and bore false witness against this poor woman. Your unfounded accusations were driven by greed and not by any sense of Christian duty! Go! Take yourself from my sight! I will summon you when I am ready to pronounce sentence for your crimes!'

Their shame-faced departure was accompanied by a heavy and oppressive hush. The blacksmith and his wife remained in their places, though neither of them could meet the eyes of their neighbours and both were flushed crimson with embarrassment. Even the Young Laird seemed stunned into silence, doubtlessly cowed by the unspoken implication that it was he who had promised Agnes Nevie's land to the blacksmith's family once she was dead.

'Let us adjourn for the day.' Seton announced with genuine weariness. 'We will reconvene in the morning to consider the matter of the widow's confession.'

'Tis an outrage!' Seton raged when he and Kincaid were left alone to take their meal at the prosecution table. 'I have seen some low tricks in my time but never a scheme as vicious and as contemptible as this. Half the parish have conspired to condemn this poor woman to burn in full knowledge of the falsity of the charges. I can scarcely believe the Young Laird's part in it!'

'Tis often the case.' Kincaid replied, gravy running down his chin as he spoke. 'Folk will use the trials to settle petty grievances and old rivalries or to gain possession of long-coveted goods or chattels. I have seen it all before. You should not fret nor be roused to anger. Few prosecutions are ever decided on testimony alone. The weightiest evidence is usually the witch's confession or the results of the tests and we will get to those tomorrow. Satisfy yourself with a job well done, my friend!' Kincaid reassured him, raising his cup to give toast to him. 'I bow my head to the quality of your performance! Even the Young Laird now quails in your presence and hesitates before urging you to greater haste. I do not doubt he will thank you as we relieve him of his silver.'

'I am certain Agnes Nevie is guilty of only age and infirmity.' Seton persisted. 'I will not condemn her when I know the accusations to be false. I could not live with myself!'

'Do not let your conscience trouble you, John. Attack the testimony and the confession as fiercely as you like, then leave the rest to me. The tests will determine guilt or innocence and absolve you of all responsibility. What do we care if the old bitch burns? Her mind is so far gone it would be a mercy to put an end to the misery of her existence. If we were to earn six pounds for her execution, so much the better.'

Seton nodded at the thought of so great a sum of money but could not shake off the sense of unease brought on by seeing the auld wife so badly mistreated. He could find no way to soothe his troubled mind and what little sleep he enjoyed was fitful and plagued by a restlessness of spirit.

There was no artifice to his demeanour when he took his place at the prosecution table the next morning. His grim and fierce expression perfectly reflected the sourness of his mood. He eschewed all niceties of courtesy and procedure and moved directly to his examination of the confession.

'Whose hand is this?' He demanded, the bluntness of his question matching that of his tone. He held the square of rough parchment aloft and jabbed at it with his finger. 'The widow Nevie made her mark upon it. If she could not sign her name, I must assume she did not write her own confession.'

'It is in my hand.' The minister declared as he hobbled forward, his walking stick clacking against the floorboards as he advanced. Seton doubted he had ever seen a man less comfortable in any setting. 'The Young Laird and William Kerr took her confession and repeated it to me so I might record it.'

'The Young Laird and the blacksmith?' Seton replied, fixing the pair with a look heavy with disdain. 'Tis fortunate, is it not, that two such fine, upstanding gentlemen were present to hear her damn herself? Come then, Minister Logie, pray read her confession to us so we might judge its veracity.'

The old man shuffled forwards and took the parchment from Seton's hand. His eyes reduced to slits as he peered at the document and began to read it aloud, his voice faltering and hesitant.

'I, Agnes Nevie, do freely confess to the practice of witchcraft, to consorting with the Devil and to giving him use of my body. I have used charms and spells to enchant my neighbours, to do harm to them and their beasts and to cause their crops to fail. I am guilty of sorcery, necromancy and of all manner of malevolent acts. I willingly renounced my baptism when induced to do so by Satan. I did kiss his private parts in return for a promise to free me from want and suffering. I swore myself to him and his diabolical works and did take a familiar spirit from the cunning folk. I did deny the Gospel and took dark communion in defiance of the Laws of God. I did consort with witches and demons and fairy folk.' Minister Logie lowered the parchment and met Seton's gaze, all colour drained from his face.

'Would you describe the widow Nevie as an educated woman?' Seton asked, his tone light.

'No, Minister Cowper.' He replied. 'I would not describe her as such. She is a simple woman of lowly birth and can boast of little education.

She can neither read nor write and so made her mark on this confession. She was unable to sign her name.'

'Did you not find it peculiar that her confession was so articulate? I have met my share of simple and lowly folk and not one of them possessed either the vocabulary or the turn of phrase present in this document.'

'I wrote only what the Young Laird bade me to, sir.' The minister responded.

'Her words were slurred and jumbled.' James Moncur interjected. 'I may have paraphrased in places for the purposes of greater clarity.'

'So, it is not the verbatim confession it was purported to be but your interpretation of what the widow might or might not have said.' Moncur began to protest but Seton cut him off. 'Was the confession extracted under torture? The injuries on her person would seem to stand as testament to that fact.'

'Only legitimate and proportionate measures were employed, sir!' Moncur retorted, his jaws clamped together in suppressed fury at being so challenged in his own house. 'We denied her food, water and sleep and then teased the truth from her with hot irons, pliers and the laying of weights upon her feet. There was nothing improper in our conduct!'

'Who would not confess when subjected to such torture?' Seton seethed back at him. ''Tis likely that every man here would confess to anything asked of him in order to bring such suffering to an end. This confession is as false as the testimony of the witnesses you set before me yesterday!'

'You would accuse me of such falsehood?' The Young Laird raged, his anger propelling him across the floor until he and Seton were so close together their noses were almost touching. 'I will not stand for it!'

'I will not go before the Privy Council to defend an execution on such flimsy, fabricated evidence! They would surely hang me for it and you would swing and jerk on the gibbet next to mine!'

Kincaid inserted himself between them and gently pushed them a few inches apart.

'Control yourselves, gentlemen!' He ordered them, keeping his voice low so he would not be easily overheard. 'Tis not seemly for you to bicker so when all the small folk are here to witness it. Why fight over witness testimony and the confession when neither were ever likely to be conclusive? Let us now adjourn to allow tempers to subside and cooler heads to prevail. When we reconvene, we will turn to science to prove guilt or innocence. Witnesses can be unreliable and confessions subject to doubt, but the integrity of the swimming test and of pricking are beyond question or reproach. Let us set our differences aside and put our faith in the scientific approach.'

The intervention brought Seton back to his senses and he turned away from the confrontation to announce the adjournment. The Young Laird held his ground for a moment longer before turning to join the village elders and the small folk as they left the chamber.

'What the hell was that?' Kincaid demanded when they had the room to themselves. 'Your task was to prolong proceedings, not to bring them to a violent and early close! Do not seek to provoke the Young Laird! Do you forget he is our paymaster? He is so enraged it is likely we will be murdered in our beds! Even the blacksmith now glares at you with naked malice. It would be better if I was to take the lead in conducting the proceedings this afternoon. Tis my area of expertise and the less they hear from you, the faster resentments are likely to abate.'

8

Seton would have nursed his fury throughout the afternoon if Kincaid's performance had not so distracted him. He played his part with as much flair and polish as any of the players he had seen plying their craft in the squares and streets around Holyrood Palace when the king was in residence. What he lacked in manners and refinement, he more than made up for in enthusiasm and his ability to enthral his audience. They nodded and gasped at his command and stood wide-eyed when he chose to linger on the more salacious aspects of his craft. The elders and the small folk alike sat in rapt attention as he explained the scientific infallibility of pricking and of the swimming test. His deft delivery, honed to perfection during the course of a hundred witch trials, even succeeded in coaxing the Young Laird out of his sour temper.

'King James himself.' The pricker declared with a courtly bow to indicate his deference to the monarch. 'Has provided us with the methods to be employed in determining the innocence or guilt of those accused of witchcraft. Witness testimony and confession, though they are not so easily set aside, cannot always be relied upon. It is not unheard of for neighbours to make accusations out of greed or spite or for confessions to be falsely made. Most of those so accused are women and, as we all know well, a woman's word cannot be depended upon for they are weak and petty creatures who will spout falsehoods and shed tears at every light occasion. This is why the king has commanded us to turn to science to provide irrefutable proof of a witch's guilt. This is why we must subject Agnes Nevie to the swimming test and then to pricking.'

Seton found himself shaking his head in admiration of Kincaid's skill. When he demanded answers of the crowd, they roared their responses back at him. It put him in mind of peddlers drumming up business at summer fairs before charging inflated prices for inferior goods.

'Do witches deny the Gospel and renounce their baptism?' The pricker cried.

'Aye!' They called back at him, some stamping their feet to demonstrate the strength of their agreement.

'Aye!' Kincaid confirmed with great enthusiasm. 'That is why the good Lord has provided us with a supernatural sign of the monstrous impiety of witches by decreeing that the water will refuse to receive in her bosom those who have shaken off the sacred waters of baptism and wilfully refused the benefit thereof! Any witch cast onto the water will therefore float, while any good Christian will sink immediately into the depths. This is the first of the scientific tests and the first that Agnes Nevie will be subjected to.'

The sight of Kincaid's tongue snaking out between his rotten teeth told Seton the performance was about to take a more salacious, less wholesome turn.

'Whenever a witch has renounced God and her baptism to swear herself to Satan's service, the Devil will seal their unspeakable, unholy pact by leaving his mark upon her. He does this by tooth, tongue or claw while the two are locked together in the throes of bestial congress. But the beast will not leave his mark where it might be seen and so expose the witch as his disciple. He takes care to mark them in their most secret, private places.' The pricker waved his finger around his chest and his genital area to suggest where these places might be. 'This is why the accused must be stripped bare, shaved and searched in her most intimate places.'

Seton cast his eyes around the hall as Kincaid spoke. Most of those gathered there seemed shocked by the obscenity of the pricker's speech but others were clearly excited and enthralled by it. Both the minister and the Young Laird were stony-faced while the blacksmith and several other elders seemed to be relishing the prospect of the stripping and the shaving as much as Kincaid himself.

'Once found, the blemish must be put to the test by pricking.' Kincaid pulled a bodkin from his pocket and held it out for inspection. The thin spike was set in a worn, wooden handle and was of a similar length to a man's middle finger. 'If the witch feels no pain and sheds no blood when the mark is penetrated by this spike, then it is no natural blemish. It can only be the work of Beelzebub and her guilt will be proven beyond all doubt or argument!'

The swimming test was as grim a procedure as any Seton had suffered the misfortune to attend. Agnes Nevie was dragged from Marlee House to the banks of the River Ericht. She shivered as her hands and feet were tied with separate lengths of rope, though Seton could not tell if this was from fear or from the chill of the rain that soaked her clothes and plastered her wispy grey hair against her skull. Kincaid ordered two men to take hold of each rope and instructed three others to lift the widow's frail and emaciated body and toss her out into the dark, slow-flowing waters. No sign of shock registered on her slack, unmoving face as she hit the freezing water and sank beneath its surface. All present seemed to hold their breath as the old woman disappeared from sight. They then exhaled in collective shock when they caught sight of the widow's pale form rising up from the murky depths. She broke the surface and floated there, the folds of her dress filled with air and billowing around her.

'The bitch floats!' The blacksmith cried out in triumph, his face twisted in the joy of vindication. 'She is a witch! A dirty witch! We will see her burn, praise God!'

Even as he spoke these last words, a great bubble of air burst between the widow's legs and the swollen material of her dress sagged and deflated like a burst pig's bladder. The waters swallowed her immediately, her pale face sinking away into the green depths until it could no longer be seen.

'Haul her in!' Kincaid ordered when long moments had passed with only a thin stream of air bubbling to the surface.

'Wait a little longer, sir.' The Young Laird implored him. 'The waters will reject her. I am certain of it. Give them enough time to do their work, I beg of you.'

'Pull her in!' Seton barked at the men holding the ropes. 'Or I will hold you responsible should she drown.'

They shot nervous glances at James Moncur before obeying the command. Agnes Nevie vomited a great flood of water as she was dragged into the shallows and was seized with a coughing fit as she gasped horribly in an effort to draw air into her lungs. Laird Marlee's housekeeper dashed forward and slapped at the old woman's back to force more water from her throat. Seton could not help but pity the poor and wretched creature as she lay wheezing on the stones and mud. Her vacant eyes suggested she remained insensible to the ordeal she had just suffered, but

Seton found he could take little comfort from that small mercy.

Kincaid then surprised him by ordering two farmhands to carry the widow back to the big house so the housekeeper could dry her clothes, warm her by the fire and spoon hot broth into her mouth.

'Such kindness is to your credit, Will.' He told him as they followed the rough path back towards Marlee House. 'I, too, could not help but pity her.'

'My only concern is for our pockets, my friend.' Kincaid replied, tapping his forefinger against the side of his nose to emphasise his cunning. 'I mean to draw out the swimming test and earn us another full day of expenses. We will duck the rancid bitch twice more before darkness falls. The time it takes to warm and dry her between the tests will eat up the entire afternoon.'

Agnes Nevie was cast into the waters of the Ericht twice more before the day was done. Each test produced the same result as the first. The frigid water sucked her down and stubbornly refused to expel her from its bosom as it would surely have done if she had renounced her baptism. The light was fading when she was dragged ashore for the final time. Seton gazed at her blue lips and limp and lifeless body and thought her dead. Each thump of Margaret's meaty fist upon her back produced only a hollow, watery sound and sent a shower of drool and spit flying into the air. The effort of her ministrations caused the housekeeper to pant and her face soon grew slick with sweat. The violence of her blows intensified as her desperation increased and seemed hard enough to break the old woman's thin and fragile spine. Minister Logie stepped forward to still her arm but stopped himself when Agnes suddenly arched her back and suffered a convulsion so powerful it caused her eyes to roll back in her head until only the whites were visible. The minister jumped back in fright at this ghastly sight but was not quick enough to avoid having his shoes and hoes soaked by the torrent of foul water Agnes spewed out onto the river bank.

'It seems a pity to have caused so much suffering to this poor and feeble creature.' Seton moaned when Kincaid came to his side to observe the old woman's struggle. 'It is a wonder she did not drown and it will be a miracle if she survives the night after such prolonged and repeated immersion in those frigid waters. Look! She shivers uncontrollably! Poor woman!'

'You are too soft-hearted for this work.' The pricker retorted, his tone cold and devoid of sympathy. 'Leave this part to me if you find it unpalatable and lack the stomach for what is necessary. You should save your pity for she may yet be proved a witch. She might have cheated the waters, but she will likely find the pricking a test beyond her powers. You will think differently when I have spiked her, you have my word on it.'

Seton was not persuaded by Kincaid's reassurances and could find no way to ease his conscience when they returned to Marlee House as the light began to fade. He had so little appetite he did not join in with the pricker's complaints about the plain and tasteless fare when only ale, bread and cheese were provided for their dinner. He took a cup of ale in the hope of dulling his senses but the bitter brew did nothing but sour his guts and cause hot bile to rise to the back of his throat. The pricker seemed entirely untroubled by his conscience and was so ravenously hungry he cleared both of their plates and set about draining the jug of its contents. Seton made his excuses and retired to his bed as early as he was able but sleep eluded him until the small hours of the morning. Each time he closed his eyes, he was confronted with an image of the widow gasping for air as she struggled to clear her water-filled lungs.

Word of what Kincaid intended had clearly spread far and wide. Seton had to push through a great throng of people packed into the hall of Marlee House when he descended from his chamber a little after dawn. Barely a yard of the floor was left unoccupied. The air was heavy with the stench of bad breath and unwashed bodies. Distant flocks and farmsteads had been abandoned so filthy and ragged shepherds, labourers and hermits could tramp across the hills to revel in the coming spectacle. Seton did not think he had set his eyes upon so many unkempt beards and threadbare coats since he witnessed King James and Queen Anne distributing alms to hordes of unwashed beggars at the gates of Holyrood. Minister Logie accosted him as he pushed his way through to the prosecution table.

'Tis not seemly.' The old man complained, his face wrinkled in consternation. 'These sinful and lascivious reprobates are not drawn here by any sense of Christian propriety or from a desire to see justice served. They come only to satisfy their indecent curiosity and to indulge their carnal and filthy appetites by delighting in the old widow's humiliation and shame! Look! The slack-jawed imbeciles have brought bread and cheese to gnaw upon just as they would when entertained by jugglers or dancing gypsies at the summer fair. Send them away, good minister, in the name of Jesus! Spare poor Agnes the indignity of their gawping and jeering!'

'Mister Kincaid is master of these tests.' Seton replied. 'But I will apprise him of your concerns and inform him of my own misgivings. There is an air of pageantry here I do not much like. Be sure that I will urge him to clear the chamber before he begins the test to ensure propriety is maintained.'

Will Kincaid was honing the edge of a razor with a leather strop when Seton came to his side. His tongue lolled between his uneven teeth as he worked and his eyes shone with excitement at what lay ahead. The grin on his face did not falter when Seton made his reservations known but his eyes seemed to lose their sparkle and harden as he listened to his fellow conspirator urge him to clear the room of all but elders and minister.

'There are enough of them to testify to the outcome of the test.' Seton argued. 'The presence of these leering half-wits brings us no benefit and will only add to the poor widow's shame and suffering. Let us remove them before we begin! The air in here is already so bad I can scarcely draw breath.'

'That would not be wise.' Kincaid growled, his glare cold and his tone icy. 'The Young Laird has charged them two pennies apiece for the privilege of witnessing these proceedings. If we send them away, he will have no money with which to pay us. You must choose what is dearer to you. Is it the old bitch's dignity or the weight of your purse? Will you come to regret your sentiment when she is exposed as a witch? Do as you see fit, my friend, I have my own work to attend to.'

Seton wrestled with his conscience for several moments before surrendering his morals in the face of the strength of his own self-interest and greed. He took his place and kept his eyes resolutely forward in order to avoid Minister Logie's disapproving gaze. His sense of self-reproach was not eased by the showmanship of Kincaid's performance. He winced and felt his cheeks burn when the pricker sliced at the widow's stained undergarments with his razor and let them fall to the floor with a flourish. The peasants gasped at the sight of her nakedness, their eyes dancing with delight at the shame and obscenity of it all. Seton lowered his eyes rather than gaze upon the wretched creature's shrunken and wizened breasts and her exposed privates. Kincaid subjected himself to no such restraint or sense of pity but drank in the sight greedily, his eyes wide and his tongue pink and moist as he licked at his lips.

'Christ!' A grizzled, dirt-smeared villain cried out with a bawdy laugh. 'She has a haystack betwixt her thighs!'

'Out!' Seton roared at him as he leapt to his feet and brought the rising hubbub to silence. 'This is no dockside tavern or house of ill-repute. Take yourself away before I have you whipped for your impertinence! Go now! Before I do something you will regret!' Seton glared at the oaf as he skulked off towards the door. 'The rest of you will remain silent or you will suffer for it. Treat this commission with dignity and due respect or take yourselves away from here!'

There were no further interruptions as Kincaid had the insensible Agnes Nevie laid out upon a table and set about examining every part of her naked body. He drew his inspection out for more than an hour, though most of his attention was focused on her breasts, crotch and nether regions. He took great care in shaving her hairy parts but was lacking in the skills required to avoid breaking her skin as he went. Her flesh was soon streaked with blood and the loss of so much of it caused her face to become ever paler as he progressed. Seton's stomach turned in revulsion when the repugnant pricker peered up at him from between the widow's bare thighs and favoured him with a filthy wink.

'See!' He declared, pointing his finger at the woman's private parts. 'The Devil left his diabolical mark upon her cunny when he had use of her. Elders! Ministers! Come hither to bear witness!' He gestured at them to come forward to see it for themselves. 'Look! It is as clear as the nose on my face.'

'Tis a flea-bite!' Minister Logie protested after examining the small, red blemish indicated by the pricker's outstretched finger. His lips were pursed in distaste at being in such close proximity to her sex and he leaned backwards in a vain effort to distance himself from it. 'I have suffered worse myself and so has every other person gathered here. This proves nothing to my satisfaction.'

'Tis the Devil's mark, good pastor, I have no doubt of that.' Kincaid insisted. 'I have seen it a hundred times before and know this to be the same. I will test it now before your very gaze and will drive all doubt from your mind.'

He pulled the bodkin from the pocket of his coat and stabbed it into the tabletop to demonstrate its strength.

'When penetrated by this spike, all natural flesh will bleed and all natural women will feel the pain of it. Watch now!'

Kincaid stabbed the spike into Agnes Nevie's calf and elicited a soft moan of pain from the mouth of a woman insensible to all other provocation. He then withdrew the spike and nodded in satisfaction when blood flowed freely from the wound. He repeated the procedure on her belly, arm and cheek with the same result. He then parted her lifeless legs and moved around her body to position himself between her thighs. He checked to ensure the elders were paying close attention before touching the tip of the spike against the mark he had attributed to the hand of Satan himself. He kept it pressed there for several moments before ramming it home with no little force.

'Did she whimper or recoil from the injury, good pastor.?' He demanded of Minister Logie to draw the reluctant cleric into his performance. 'Was her response different to that when I pricked her belly, arm and cheek? Did she give any sign of suffering pain?'

'She gave no sign of feeling it.' Logie replied, his voice flat and his face pale with shock. 'I would not have believed it if I had not seen it with my own eyes.'

'Then let us see if she bleeds as good Christians do when their flesh is pierced so deeply.'

Kincaid slowly and deliberately withdrew the spike from the widow's genitals. All eyes followed the implement and gasped to see not a single drop or smear of blood upon it.

'She does not bleed!' The Young Laird announced, half in disbelief and half in triumph. 'See! The spike has left no wound in the disfigured flesh! Tis the Devil's mark right enough! She is a witch, just as I said she was!'

Seton was struck dumb by the shock of it. His mind could not accept the evidence of his eyes. He had seen the spike pierce the widow's flesh but the deep incision had produced no blood and left no wound. His proximity to the Devil's work caused his skin to crawl and he staggered back away from it.

'She is a witch!' He stammered, his heart hammering in his chest.

'Minister Cowper has condemned the bitch!' Kincaid cried out in an effort to draw attention away from Seton's clear distress. 'We will burn her for her vile heresy along with any other so condemned!'

He then called for the witch to be tightly bound and returned to the barn with two men to guard her there. The proof and declaration of Agnes Nevie's guilt caused sufficient agitation to transform the assembly into a rabble. Men called out to curse the widow and pressed around her as she was led away. She would likely have gone down under a hail of fists and feet if Minister Logie had not put himself between her and the vengeful throng. Kincaid made good use of the distraction and guided Seton out of the chamber and upstairs to the safety of his chamber. The younger man's legs seemed to give way beneath him the moment the door closed at their backs and he sat down heavily upon the bed.

'I can scarce believe my eyes!' He gasped, still aghast at what had occurred. 'You stabbed her to the bone and she neither gave sign of any sensation nor spilled a single drop of blood! Tis not possible!'

'Did I not tell you to save your pity?' Kincaid snapped back at him. 'She is a witch and is not deserving of your mercy.'

'But she is so old and decrepit and is no longer in possession of her wits.'

'What do we care of that? Think of it as a mercy if it pleases you. It will surely be a blessed relief for her to end her life when she is in such a wretched condition. We must think only of ourselves. The Young Laird practically danced with delight when the verdict was made and his happiness will serve to loosen his purse strings in our favour. I will fetch wine to soothe your nerves and carry you to sleep. I will need you rested and in full possession of your wits when dawn breaks and the second trial begins.'

9

'Let us be done with this and make away without undue delay.' Seton implored Kincaid as he and the pricker watched the locals file into the hall full of anticipation for the trial ahead. 'My nerves are stretched so tight I fear they will break.'

'You must gather your courage and hold tight to it!' The pricker urged him. 'If you can draw this out for two full days, you will have the respite of the Sabbath and the Young Laird will be forced to pay our expenses even though we rest. Another shilling in your purse means one less day of servitude in your damned father-in-law's putrid warehouse. Keep that in mind to still your knees as they knock together and your fingers as they tremble! You have shown your power to control events, find it now and do not falter!'

The dark rings around Seton's eyes spoke of a night of sleeplessness. He rubbed at his face in a bid to revive himself and restore his mettle. A few days of tension and discomfort were worth suffering if they were to spare him months of purgatory counting rotten sheepskins under Thomas Carmichael's constant scrutiny. He cursed under his breath when he caught sight of James Moncur striding towards them with a look of determination upon his face.

'Let us move quickly to the tests!' The Young Laird demanded without doing them the courtesy of offering a greeting or inquiring after their health. The air of arrogance about him suggested that the previous day's verdict had restored his confidence. 'I see no point in dwelling on testimony and confession when you are clearly unwillingly to reach a judgment based solely on either one of them. We should let Mister Kincaid be about his work without any further procrastination. I am certain he will have proven all outstanding accusations before the day is out.'

What Kincaid had failed to achieve through encouragement and persuasion, James Moncur accomplished with his imperious and irksome manner. Seton's sudden irritation served to banish all anxiety and drove him to reply with equal haughtiness and disdain.

'Your suggestion is both improper and illegitimate, sir. The Privy Council has set out the procedure to be followed in prosecutions such as these. No lawful judgement can be reached if corners are cut and protocols cast out for convenience sake.' Seton felt his courage soar as he spoke and he pulled himself to his full height to better impose himself on the unsmiling Moncur. 'If the Privy Council were to conclude that we failed to adhere to due process of law, any sentence laid down against these women would be deemed illegitimate and you and I would be held accountable for it. The guilt of the accused would be set aside and we would be judged guilty of the murder and torture of innocent subjects. Would you risk such an ignominious fate for the sake of a few shillings?'

'Very well!' Moncur snapped, his cheeks reddening from anger and embarrassment. 'If we must do it, then let us do it quickly. Bring the accused forward to the stool and call on Minister Logie as the first to testify. I trust you will not accuse him of falsehoods as you did the other witnesses!'

Elspet Leyis was dragged forward from the back of the hall but was proving to be less docile and biddable than the inanimate Agnes Nevie. She struggled furiously and cursed horribly as she came, her swollen, bruised and dirt-smeared face red and twisted in fury.

'Bastards one and bastards all!' She screeched through teeth so tightly clenched it was a wonder they did not break. 'Get your filthy hands off me you scabbit rogues! Away you stinking, fatherless knaves!'

The mere sight of Minister Logie sent her into greater paroxysms of rage. She kicked out wildly with her bound feet with enough force to send the heavy stool flying across the floor to crash into the shins of the village elders. A stream of foul invective poured from her mouth and was only stemmed when Seton had her gagged with one of the housekeeper's dirty cloths. This served to muffle her continued profanity and she glared at him, her eyes bulging in fury and the veins at her temple pulsing with such intensity it seemed likely they would burst. When order was finally restored, Seton commanded Minister Logie to speak his part.

'I have known Elspet Leyis for many a year.' The old man began, casting disapproving glances at the still struggling accused as he spoke. 'And can honestly attest that she is as vile, ill-tempered and sharp-tongued as any woman I have ever had the misfortune to encounter. She has plagued her neighbours with her malicious gossiping and you will find no man, woman or child in this vicinity who has not borne the brunt of her objectionable, argumentative and unpleasant nature. It is well known that her relentless haranguing and chiding of her husband sent him into a fit of apoplexy and condemned him to an early and unjust grave. He was a simple man and well-liked but she granted him not a moment's peace from one dawn to the next. All here would swear they could seldom pass her door without having their ears assailed by her shouting and screeching as she scolded and berated him for not applying himself with sufficient vigour to whatever chore she demanded of him.'

'I have suffered her screeching for myself, good pastor.' Seton interjected. 'And unpleasant though it was, it does not constitute a sin worthy of condemnation. If every wife who badgered and tormented her husband was guilty of witchcraft, we would not have wood or peat enough to burn them all.' He paused to let the laughter of the assembly die away. 'Do you have anything of any substance beyond your unfavourable judgment of her reprehensible character?'

'She has turned from the path of righteousness.' Logie persisted, the harsh nature of the question causing him no small degree of vexation. 'She has forsaken the church of her baptism and, as all here would attest, has been absent from the kirk on every Sabbath Day these two long years past. The whole village speaks of it and knows it can only be because she has cast off a life of Christian duty and now devotes herself to the works of Satan!'

These words caused Elspet Leyis to struggle against her bonds with such ferocity she toppled to the floor and struck the boards with a sickening thud. The impact of skull on solid oak did nothing to curb her foul temper and she continued to squirm and jerk against her ropes and the thick, saliva-soaked rag jammed into her mouth was not enough to completely silence her muffled and unintelligible protestations.

'I would hear you Mistress Leyis.' Seton informed her, bringing her struggles to an end. 'But will only have the gag removed if you affirm your willingness to address this commission with civility and all due respect. I will not hesitate to silence you by having the cloth forcibly replaced should you once again resort to profanity or abuse.'

Elspet breathed heavily and met Seton's gaze with cold defiance before giving a curt nod to indicate her acceptance of his terms. She leaned down to wipe the drool from her chin onto the arm of her ragged dress the moment the cloth was pulled from her mouth. She set her eyes on old Logie as she spoke, the burning malice in her eyes causing him to blink in fear and lean away from her.

'Tis not the Devil who keeps me away from the kirk.' She hissed. 'Tis the unbearable length and monotonous delivery of your dull and tedious sermons. I would rather pluck out my own eyes than cause myself to suffer through the slow torture of your bleak and dismal monologues. Your poor congregation is only kept from falling into despairing unconsciousness by the hardness and discomfort of your pews.'

'I must protest!' Logie spluttered in dismay at being so maligned. 'Tis well known that she consorts with sprites and fairy folk and has herself admitted to calling upon the Sithean to assist her in the making of charms and the casting of spells. There are good Christian folk here who will swear to it. Call on Douglas Crichton, Laird Marlee's tenant, to testify if you will have the truth of it.'

Seton duly called him forward and made him swear his oath. The tenant farmer gripped his cap so tightly in his fists it seemed likely he would tear the cloth and be left with one half in either hand. A lifetime of heavy drinking had left him with a nose redder than his burning cheeks and so riddled with broken veins it appeared to have suffered some injury or disease. What little hair he had left reached only a little above his ears and encircled a crown of pale and mottled skin.

'I lost my good hunting knife when returning from Perth after selling my two best cows.' He began, his voice low and hesitant. 'It was given to me by my father and to him by his father. Its loss left me sorely vexed and I spent long hours tramping the Perth road in search of it. I was so desperate to recover it, I was driven to approach the widow for her help. She told me she could invoke the fairy folk and have them search for it in return for two silver shillings.' This revelation caused a brief murmur of conversation but it faded quickly under Seton's disapproving glare. 'It was more than the knife was worth but I was so downcast I agreed to her price. Not two days later, the widow came banging at my door with my father's knife in her hand. She demanded payment for its return and I gave her three pennies for her trouble. Twas a fair reward for I doubt the blade is worth a penny more. She raged and riled at me and called me a dirty cheat and a lying whoreson. She then cursed me and swore that I would not prosper. The very next day, my wife caught her skulking behind my house and chased her away. She encountered my neighbour as she made off and told him she had buried a dead cat beneath my hearth to bring me all the ill fortune I was deserving of.' Crichton paused to wipe the sweat from his brow before continuing.

'From that day to this, I have endured all manner of misfortune and know myself to be accursed.' He then listed the calamities he had suffered as a result of the widow's sorcery. 'My bull was rendered impotent. He has not sired a calf nor shown any interest in mounting a cow for more than two years. How can this be when he could barely be restrained from mounting the whole herd in the past? That vile bitch has all but ruined me with her damned spells. Then there is my cart. Two wheels have broken in less than a year after five years with no such troubles. Even the blacksmith was left scratching his head and could offer no good explanation for the damage. Then there is the matter of my crops. My bottom field has been ever fertile but now produces less barley with each passing year. Tis unnatural and can only be caused by witchcraft!'

'What colour was the cat buried under your hearth?' Seton demanded, the bluntness of the question causing the farmer to blink in confusion.

'I could not say, sir, for I never laid my eyes upon it.'

'But you must have seen it when it was dug up from your hearth.' Seton insisted. 'How else could the spell be broken?'

'The minister told me to leave it there so as to avoid fouling my hands with her dark magic. He said a blessing before my fire and sprinkled the earth with water from the kirk's font.'

'Good!' Seton exclaimed, pushing himself to his feet 'He was right to do so and, as a consequence, has left us with solid evidence to prove the truth of your accusations. Minister Logie will accompany me to your home and we will unearth the unfortunate creature. We will bring what remains of its carcass here and confront the accused with it as proof of her crimes. I will examine this bull of yours while I am there.'

The Young Laird did not wait for Seton to formally call the adjournment but stormed off into the back of the house in a sulk.

'We will return directly.' Seton informed the pricker as he and the minister turned for the door. 'The farm is only a short walk away.'

'Take your time,' The pricker replied with a grin. 'I have patience enough for both Moncur and myself.'

'You do not believe him.' The minister huffed as he led Seton along a well-trodden track in the direction of Crichton's land.

'It matters not what I believe, good pastor.' Seton replied, cheerful now they had left the oppressive and stuffy confines of Marlee House behind them. 'It matters only what I can prove and your farmer has provided me with the means to test the veracity of his accusation one way or the other. We will have the truth with only a little digging.'

Kincaid gave an almost imperceptible nod of his head to signal his approval of the length of Seton's absence. The late afternoon sun was already fading and any further witnesses would not now be questioned until the following day. Seton took his place and made a pretence of studying his papers in order to allow a sense of anticipation to build amongst the gathered elders, farmers, tradesmen and peasants. When he finally spoke, his tone was curt and unapologetic.

'Mister Crichton, I have no choice but to dismiss your testimony in its entirety.' The ruddy-faced farmer began to object but was brought to silence when Seton held up his index finger in admonishment. 'There never was a cat beneath your hearth, not for witchcraft nor for any other purpose. Minister Logie and I excavated the floor around your fireplace until our exertions left us breathless and soaked in our own sweat. We were both so caked in dirt and wet with perspiration we were forced to call into the tavern to avail ourselves of washbowls to clean ourselves and to order a good draught of ale with which to moisten our throats and revive our strength. Our diligent efforts to locate and disinter the unfortunate feline unearthed nothing other than earth, stones and pebbles. Whether you lied or were mistaken is of little consequence, I find your accusation of sorcery to be disproven.'

'I turn now to the matter of the series of misfortunes you have suffered in recent times. I lay no claim to any degree of expertise in animal husbandry, but even I and the good pastor were able to deduce the reason for the lack of vigour displayed by your bull. All creatures, even us men, lose potency as we age, much though we may regret it. Your own beast is cursed by nothing more sinister than the passage of time and the ravages of the years. Age has caused the hair around his muzzle to turn from black to white and he is so decrepit he scarcely has the strength to support his own weight. I would counsel you to purchase a younger replacement if your fortunes are to be restored. You would also be well advised to invest in two new wheels for your cart as those not already replaced are rotten and brittle. We found them to be in a lamentable condition. Minister Logie was able to dig his fingers into the wood in several places and scratch away great lumps of rot. A lack of care is the source of your ill-luck, not curses or spells.'

'What of the missing knife?' The Young Laird demanded, his face turned sour by the spectacle of yet more testimony being discredited and discounted. 'You cannot dismiss that accusation with such casual abandon. How could a mere woman search such a large area in so short a time? She could not have found it without some unnatural and diabolical assistance.'

'Tis a fair question.' Seton retorted. 'What say you, Mistress Leyis? How could you locate the item so quickly when Mister Crichton could not do so after long hours spent scouring the verges and hedgerows betwixt here and Perth? Do you deny offering to harness fairies and sprites in the finding of it?'

'I do not deny saying it!' Elspet Leyis spat, her expression bitter and full of spite. 'Though I required no dark or diabolical powers to aid me in the finding of bald Crichton's knife. I spoke of fairies only to encourage him to part with more silver in return for my aid.'

'Then how did you find it with so little delay. It would seem an impossible task when there are so many miles of narrow, twisting track between here and Perth.'

'Twas not hard!' Elspet explained, a smile of disdain on her thin lips. 'The lazy drunkard is overly fond of his ale and fills his guts with gallons of the stuff every market day. He then staggers home in the darkness and will always stop at the minister's gate. It was there that I found it. It must have fallen from his belt when he dropped his breeches to pish on the vegetables the minister's wife grows there. He does it every time he passes and will sometimes squeeze out a fat turd for good measure.'

Seton knew the truth of her claim from the look of abject horror on Crichton's face. He turned so pale it seemed likely he was about to faint. Minister Logie and his good wife were so appalled at the thought of what might have garnished their greens, they both looked set to vomit. Seton had to avert his gaze to keep himself from laughing out loud.

'Why on earth would he even contemplate such a repulsive act?' He demanded of the accused.

'He took an ill-will towards the minister when he scolded him from the pulpit for being a drunkard and a wastrel. I have heard him mutter to himself as he sprays the minister's cabbages. 'You might have made a fool of me but it is not I who is idiot enough to gobble vegetables soaked in piss.' I have also heard him chortle at the thought of Mistress Logie collecting the turds he left for her.'

It took every ounce of Seton's self-control to keep himself from sniggering at the thought of the pious minister's wife dutifully harvesting the foul fruit deposited from the vengeful farmer's arse. His condition was not much helped by Kincaid and the shaking of his shoulders as he fought to repress his mirth. It took several minutes of pretended absorption in the Privy Council papers before he was once again in full control of his faculties.

'I move to dismiss this testimony in its entirety.' He announced whilst fighting to keep his expression suitably grave. 'There is evidence of nothing more than petty spite, the majority of it being on the part of the witness rather than on that of the accused. We will adjourn until dawn, at which point we will hear the testimony of the remaining witnesses before moving on to consider the alleged confession.'

Kincaid and Seton took their leave as quickly as they were able and gave vent to their hilarity the moment the chamber door was closed behind them.

'Jesus, Will!' Seton howled as tears ran down his cheeks. 'I thought I would surely burst when she spoke of Crichton emptying his bowels on Mistress Logie's onions. I doubt they will ever eat cabbage again!'

'You did well to keep your face straight, John. I know not how you did it. You grow more accomplished with each passing day. When you dismissed that miserable farmer, you did so with such authority I almost forgot you are neither minister nor prosecutor. I am confident you will eke the witnesses and confession out sufficiently to fill the day. Then we will have the respite of the Sabbath to regain our strength.'

10

It proved impossible to take up the entire morning with the examination of the witnesses. The milkmaid, the servant and the saddler's wife were uniformly unimpressive and all three looked constantly to the Young Laird for approval and encouragement. Their testimony had clearly been rehearsed and all three of them were vague and evasive when pressed on the details of their accusations. The servant girl sought sanctuary in her tears when Seton questioned her honesty.

'I know her to be a witch!' She wailed before descending into a fit of sobbing severe enough to render her insensible and unfit for further interrogation.

Her antics drove Seton to distraction. He had seen the same trick performed more than a thousand times in the past. It was the ruse his younger brother would employ whenever he was caught stealing apples from the minister's tree, throwing stones at the hens or engaging in whatever mischief took his fancy on a particular day. When his father went to scold him for his misdeeds, he would fall into convulsions of crying so fierce his cheeks would be soaked with his tears and he would blow great streams of snot from his nose. His father would invariably throw his hands up in disgust and abandon his scolding only for young Andrew to recover in an instant and grin in triumph at his back. Seton still rankled at the memory of such devious cunning even though he had been heartbroken when his brother was carried off by the pox before the first hairs had appeared on his chin.

'Then offer some credible evidence in support of your claim!' Seton snapped in frustration. 'The widow Leyis cannot be condemned on the basis of something you might or might not have seen!'

He could only shake his head in disgust when his question set the empty-headed girl to weeping and snivelling with renewed vigour. Kincaid could offer no good suggestion as to how they might proceed and simply shrugged his shoulders when Seton asked him if he had any questions he wanted to put to her. This left them with no choice but to dismiss the wretched girl after only a few minutes of cross-examination.

The morning did not improve much when the second witness was called forward. The saddler's wife was so ignorant and stupid she drove Seton to new heights of exasperation. After delivering her faltering monologue in the most unconvincing fashion, she proceeded to respond to all questions with nothing more than a blank expression and a weary shrug of her shoulders. Seton ordered her removal when she had roused him to such a rage he lost his temper and denounced her as a 'brainless wench!'

The milkmaid was the worst of them all. She told her story well enough, but smiled with relief when she reached its end, much like a boy who has successfully recited the biblical passage his pastor instructed him to commit to memory. That sweet smile of satisfaction did not last long under Seton's harsh questioning. She grew flustered and was soon contradicting her own testimony and seemed incapable of remembering facts she herself had presented only moments earlier.

'If your father believed Elspet Leyis was responsible for poisoning three of his sheep with her spells, why would he then call upon her to tend to his ram with her potions when it sickened?' He demanded in exasperation. 'You damn her as a killer in one breath and then as a healer in the next. It makes no sense to me and any reasonable and rational man would dismiss it as the height of absurdity!'

'Hold your temper!' Kincaid cautioned him from the corner of his mouth. 'This horse is quite dead! No good will come from flogging its carcass.'

The truth of the pricker's words prompted him to pause for a few moments while he regained his composure. He dismissed the milkmaid with forced courtesy and prepared to give his judgment.

'Tis a disgrace that such flimsy and baseless testimony was deemed sufficient to justify the seeking of a commission from the honourable Lords of the Privy Council. These three witnesses were no more credible than the imbecile Crichton who stood before us yesterday. We were offered little more than contradictions, evasions and barefaced falsehoods. All three told the self-same tale. They sought the assistance of the accused when either children or livestock fell sick and then reneged on the agreed payment when full health was restored. Their accusations of sorcery and necromancy came only when Elspet Leyis cursed and berated them for failing to pay what they had agreed to pay. They were motivated by spite and not by any sense of Christian duty. All here should be repulsed by their dishonesty and their willingness to condemn to death one whose only crime was to aid them in their time of need and then denounce them for their greed and tight-fistedness. I must hereby dismiss all testimony in this case and move to consider the evidence gained by means of confession.'

'I took the confession of Mistress Leyis.' Minister Logie announced as he stepped forward. 'Would you have me read it?'

'Aye, sir.' Seton replied with no small amusement at the sight of Logie lifting the parchment so close to his eyes his nose almost brushed against its surface.

'I, Elspet Leyis, widow of this parish, do freely confess to wilfully and knowingly engaging in foul acts of maleficium in flagrant opposition to the laws of God and Kirk.' The minister's eyes were reduced to slits as he peered at the neat script. 'I did practice acts of witchcraft and did cast spells and enchantments to cause dire misfortune to befall my good and blameless Christian neighbours. I did renounce my baptism and invoked the Devil and other foul spirits to so aid me in the execution of my malicious plots. When the Devil appeared to me in the form of a rough, dark and uncouth man, he promised me I would lack for nothing and would be free of want and harm if only I agreed to serve him. I gave my oath to him and raised my skirts to expose my private parts so he might have use of them. I let him lick me there and moaned like a wanton whore when he penetrated me with a tongue that was as cold as ice and unnaturally long. I let him take me then and cried out in unnatural ecstasy when his cold semen squirted into my belly though it chilled me to the bone. I then fell to my knees to kiss and suckle upon his bestial, huge and misshapen manhood and willingly let him have the pleasure of my lips and tongue.'

Kincaid's own tongue licked furiously at his bottom lip as the minister spoke but his eyes were fixed firmly on Elspet Leyis. Seton fidgeted in disgust as the pricker's breathing grew shallower and more rapid as his excitement grew.

'I did, with malice aforethought, take a black toad and string it up by its heels to gather its venom as it dripped from its back. I then crept into the big house while the housekeeper was in the washhouse and stole a napkin the old Laird had used to wipe his mouth when at his supper. It was thick with the gravy and grease wiped from his old chops. I then made a spell by soaking the napkin in the toad's poison and did cause the old man to sicken and suffer such agonies he was driven close to madness.'

'I know this to be true!' The Young Laird cried out, stepping forward to the minister's side. 'I heard her curse my father when he chased her away from his door when she came crawling in false obsequity to beg him to put silver into a poor widow's palm. When he refused her pleading and ordered her away, she did abuse him horribly without a shred of respect for either his rank or his good standing in this parish. She cursed and called him a wizened and feeble old bastard and vowed to send him to an early grave. She was not abashed when he denounced her as a vile and vicious witch but retorted furiously with words I shall never forget. In a tone of icy certainty, she screeched, 'If witch I be, then your heart will not beat long in your breast! Those few days remaining to you will be filled with pain and misery and your nights will seem an eternity of sleeplessness, torment and agony!' She then made the sign of the evil eye and strode off in her temper. My father began to sicken within the week and took to his bed not long after. What further proof is required? She is a witch and must be burned to break this spell and release my father from his suffering!'

'A more damning confession I have not heard.' Kincaid announced when the chamber fell to hushed silence. 'Let us adjourn to take sustenance and allow Minister Cowper sufficient time to prepare the questions required to further test its veracity.'

Seton had Margaret bring bread, cheese and ale to his chamber for them to eat while they prepared to subject the accused to cross-examination. They dawdled over their meagre repast but had soon reduced it to dregs and crumbs.

'I doubt I will be able to stretch this out sufficiently to take up the entire afternoon.' Seton admitted with a shrug. 'The witness testimony was so weak and full of holes I can justify no further scrutiny of any part of it. The Young Laird already glares at me and will lose all patience if I indulge in any such transparent time-wasting. Perhaps we should concentrate solely on the confession and then move onto the swimming test. We will then have the respite of the Sabbath before you prick her on Monday morning.'

Kincaid grimaced as if the suggestion had caused him pain and shook his head while trying to dig some stubborn morsel out from between his rotten teeth with a dirty and ragged fingernail. He did not speak until the troublesome piece of crust had been extracted, examined and then consumed for a second time.

'I have full confidence in you, my friend.' He drawled, smacking his lips. 'The Young Laird has no choice but tolerate a slow and deliberate examination if he is to secure the verdicts he so desires. Do you not remember how frustrated and irate he became when Agnes Nevie was before us? All fury and animosity evaporated entirely the moment I pricked the bitch and proved her guilt. It will be the same with this vile and foul-mouthed whore. Let him glower and fume to his heart's content. He might snarl and growl but has no choice but bend to your authority. If you can withstand the enmity of this spoilt and entitled boy, you will fill our purses while you empty his.'

The pricker's words were sufficient to strengthen Seton's resolve and steel him for the task ahead. He strode back into the hall intent on employing whatever tricks and stratagems were necessary to frustrate Moncur's desire to move quickly to the tests. He first subjected the accused to a long and pious sermon on how she was expected to conduct herself and threatened to have her gagged if she was foolish or disrespectful enough to give vent to hysteria, profanity or blasphemy. He was encouraged to continue in this vein by the assembly's evident approval of the widow's scolding. Several of the men and many of the women clearly revelled in the spectacle and even James Moncur nodded in agreement when he berated her for her previous bad behaviour.

Seton then provided her with the opportunity to answer each and every accusation made against her, even those already proven to have little substance or merit. The widow managed to keep a civil tongue in her head and gave clear and courteous answers to every question she was asked. Her expression was sour and furious throughout, but she succeeded in restraining her temper and in limiting herself to treating her accusers to nothing worse than black and murderous looks. The Young Laird was the main recipient of these, though he returned them with equal hostility and increasing frustration as the credibility of each witness was destroyed. He rolled his eyes and muttered under his breath when Seton finally turned to the examination of the confession.

'Did you curse and abuse Laird Marlee?' Seton asked her. 'You confessed to it and his son has testified to the truth of it.'

'Aye.' The widow Leyis admitted without hesitation. 'I was weak from hunger and was made furious by his lack of Christian charity and his tightfistedness. Tis hard for a widow to make ends meet without a man to provide for her. I cursed the old bastard just as much as he deserved.'

This admission was met by a collective gasp and Seton had to bang at the table to bring the proceedings back to order.

'Then you admit to using witchcraft to cause the old Laird to become ill?'

'I admit to no such thing!' She retorted, her chin thrust out in a show of defiance. 'Tis true that I cursed him, but there was no sorcery to it. I did call him a feeble and wizened old bastard but there was no spell, toad or napkin. If he sickened, he sickened because he is an old man and not because of anything I have done.'

Seton nodded and held her gaze, his eyes searching hers for any sign of a lie. Her words had the ring of truth about them and he had always prided himself on his ability to tell when he was being deceived. Even his recent experiences with the devious and duplicitous wine merchants of Bordeaux had done little to dent his confidence in this regard. He then took her through her confession line by line, giving her the opportunity to respond to each part of it. She denied it all. The enchantments intended to cause dire misfortune to befall her neighbours, the practice of witchcraft, the consorting with spirits and the renouncement of her baptism were all dismissed as falsehoods. The appearance of Satan, the raising of her skirts, the giving of her private parts for his twisted pleasure and the suckling of his bestial and misshapen manhood were all fiercely refuted as the lies and perverted fantasies of her accusers.

'Then why, Mistress Leyis, did you confess to it all?' Seton demanded, suddenly conscious of every man and woman in the hall holding their breath in anticipation of the widow's response. 'Why did you make your mark upon the confession when you must have known it would damn you?'

'I refused to confess when they denied me food or water for days on end. Even when I was dizzy from hunger and so thirsty I was tempted to drink my own piss, I would not comply. When they kicked and punched me to keep me from sleeping, I cursed them for their cruelty and swore I would never be compelled to give truth to their lies. When they burned my flesh with hot irons and crushed my feet under great weights, I prayed for death and for God's strength to keep me from relenting.' A single tear ran down Elspet's cheek and all defiance seemed to leave her as her face crumpled in despair. 'But when they hammered splinters under the nails of my fingers and toes and began to tear them away with their pincers, I could not endure the agony of it. I begged them to stop and vowed to do anything they asked of me. I made my mark on their damned parchment so the pain would stop and I would make it again if they were to subject me to such torment anew.'

Seton waited patiently for her sobbing to ease, his heart sore at the sight of a woman reduced to such a wretched condition in both body and spirit. A cold fury began to build within him at the injustice and cruelty of her treatment on the basis of such flimsy and spiteful testimony. He clenched his fists and fought to control his temper and to resist the urge to denounce and castigate her accusers. He sucked great breaths of air into his lungs and reminded himself of the purpose of his presence in Marlee House. He had calmed himself by the time the widow's weeping subsided and was able to ask his final question without betraying his anger.

'What does 'maleficium' mean, Mistress Leyis?' He asked with forced lightness, though he spoke the words through gritted teeth. 'You used the word in your confession. I would like to know where you learned the term.'

'I learned it from the minister, Mister Cowper.' Elspet replied, her eyes widening in surprise on realising the question was intended to discredit rather than support the legitimacy of her confession. 'I learned it when he wrote it in my confession.'

Minister Logie grew ashen when Seton set his gaze upon him and was only able to lift his eyes from the floor to cast sullen and furtive glances of accusation in the Young Laird's direction. James Moncur, for his part, met Seton's eyes with steady and steely determination and seemed undaunted by the disintegration of the case against Elspet Leyis. This brazen arrogance prompted Seton to give vent to his fury, though his delivery was controlled and cloaked in moderation and restraint.

'All here should hang their heads in shame and pray to God for forgiveness for their part in these proceedings. A woman has been subjected to torture and pillory on the basis of falsehoods and testimony so driven by spite and petty malice it has been sickening to behold. I would have each accuser and witness horse-whipped through the streets if only my commission gave me the authority to inflict such just and deserved punishment upon them. Those involved in the extraction of her confession are deserving of more severe chastisement.'

'The minister is right to so rebuke the witnesses.' Kincaid interrupted, stemming the flow of Seton's tirade. 'And we will seek the authority of the Privy Council to bring them to justice, if that course of action should prove to be appropriate. The veracity of the confession is also in doubt but it cannot be dismissed in its entirety solely on the word of a mere woman when a man has attested to the truth of it. We will have to turn to the tests to determine innocence or guilt. We will now adjourn until first light after the Sabbath day.'

'Why wait until then?' The Young Laird objected. 'We could duck her in the river before nightfall.'

'I will not be rushed in my work.' Kincaid snapped back at him. 'Would you have her found innocent when the fading light conceals her guilt?'

The Young Laird shrugged his reluctant agreement and the trial was adjourned.

Seton felt as if a great weight had been lifted from his shoulders when he and Kincaid stepped out into the cool night air and made for the village tavern. The short walk was enough to clear his head after so many hours of tension and of being forced to breathe the hall's cloying stench of bad breath and unwashed bodies. The relief of escaping the oppressive atmosphere of Marlee House proved to be short-lived. The babble of conversations and arguments faded to near silence the moment they passed through the tavern door. A few isolated discussions carried on amongst the more inebriated of the tavern's patrons, but even they died away when the change in atmosphere penetrated the fog of their intoxication. Seton hesitated when confronted by the sea of faces turned in their direction. Kincaid was undeterred by their sullen scrutiny and advanced towards a table by the fire. He jerked his head to one side and the abrupt gesture was sufficient to send the table's occupants scurrying away with their ale pots in their hands. He waved Seton into one of the newly vacated chairs and called for the tavern keeper to bring a jug of ale.

'Jesus!' Seton muttered. 'They stare as if they would murder us. I cannot tell if they wish us ill because we try the witches or because we do not condemn them readily enough.'

'Tis neither!' Kincaid chortled, his face creased in amusement. 'Their eyes are filled with fear and not with hatred. They gaze upon the witchfinder and tremble at his power. They may be simple and ignorant peasants but they know that you need only point your finger in their direction to condemn them to burn. Enjoy it, my friend. When this week is done and we have left this place behind, you will never again experience the thrill of striking terror into the hearts of all who encounter you! Word of the scolding you inflicted on the Young Laird and the minister will have reached their ears. To them, the man who has the authority to humble those who rule their daily lives is a man who fills them with naught but dread.'

The truth of the pricker's words was confirmed when a plain tavern maid brought a jug of ale to their table. She could scarcely bring herself to look at them and her hands shook so badly the dark brew spilled as she lowered the vessel and left a puddle of the dark and foamy liquid on the wooden boards.

'They deserved to be scolded.' Seton declared before taking a long draft of the bitter ale. 'The witnesses they put before us were worse than simpletons. Elspet Leyis is undoubtedly a vile and ill-tempered woman but there was not a single shred of evidence of any involvement in witchcraft. Their lies lacked both substance and conviction and only served to expose their own pettiness and spite. Neither was I persuaded by the confession. Her protestations seemed genuine to me. I know I would admit to anything if you threatened to sear my flesh or tear my fingernails out. I would make my mark before you even approached me with pincers or hot iron rods. You may think I went too far, but I do not regret it, even if it angered James Moncur.'

'Do not fret, John.' Kincaid replied as he wiped the froth from his lips. 'You have done no harm to our cause. The Young Laird was aggrieved but still parted with his silver to cover our expenses for the week.' He patted his pocket as he spoke to indicate the location of the coins. 'He thinks you are too soft-hearted for this work but I was able to persuade him to trust in the tests to find the truth of it. I reminded him of your misplaced sympathy for the widow Nevie and of how you were inclined to deny her guilt until I stuck her with my pin. He laughed heartily at my recollection of the shocked expression on your face when I pierced her and she neither bled like a good Christian woman nor felt the injury.'

'I would not have believed it if I had not seen it with my own eyes.' Seton replied with a shiver of revulsion. 'It was the most unnatural thing I have ever witnessed. Only witchcraft could explain such a thing.'

'That is the beauty of these scientific tests.' Kincaid replied. 'The findings cannot be disputed as testimony and confessions can. Do not concern yourself with Elspet Leyis. The waters and the bodkin will give you the proof you need. Let us drink and speak only of the silver we have won and what we will do with it. None of this will trouble you when the Flesher and your father-in-law have been repaid and you have taken your sweet Elizabeth back into your embrace.'

11

In the end, the Sabbath did not provide the restorative respite Seton had longed for. He and Kincaid had filled their bellies with ale in the tavern before staggering back to Marlee House to count their silver and talk of how they would spend it. Kincaid had stalked off into the house's dark interior without a candle to light his way and quickly and gleefully returned with a jug of claret from the Laird's kitchen. Neither of them could say when they had fallen into unconsciousness, but Seton would swear he had slept for only a few moments before being awakened by the light of dawn streaming through the cracks in the shutters. He winced when he rose to empty his aching bladder for the movement this entailed caused his head to throb painfully. He groaned when Margaret knocked at his door with a bowl of porridge and told him they must leave for the kirk within the half-hour.

Kincaid's face was as pale as his companion's as they trudged miserably towards the church.

Minister Logie's sermon was as bad as Elspet Leyis had claimed it would be. The length of it was unbearable, the delivery was monotonous and its content was dull and insufferably tedious. Seton was certain there was an underlying message in Logie's preaching but he was in no condition to discern it. While the old man recited long passages from Corinthians and emphasised that the foolishness of God is wiser than men, Seton concentrated on breathing deeply enough to keep himself from vomiting the sour contents of his stomach onto the floor. Waves of dizziness threatened to overwhelm him every time the minister instructed his congregation to take to their knees for the purpose of prayer.

The eyes of his fellow worshippers followed his every step when he rose to take his leave at the end of the service. He felt so wretched he was not troubled by their scrutiny as he had been the night before. Their nervousness and reluctance to engage with him were a blessed relief and the prospect of escape caused his languid spirits to soar. When the minister was kind enough to invite them both to take refreshment with him and his wife, they politely declined, citing the need to prepare for the next day's proceedings as their excuse. They employed the same justification back at Marlee House to spare themselves the housekeeper's company and so allow them to retire to their chambers and crawl back into bed.

It was twilight when they finally resurfaced and made their way downstairs. The housekeeper greeted them with a look of sour disapproval but was good enough to bring them cold beef, bread, ale and water. Seton could stomach only the bread and the water while Kincaid was fully restored and set about the beef and the ale with gusto.

'By God!' He declared happily. 'It is good to have something solid in my stomach! I felt so weak in the kirk, it was all I could do to stop myself from staggering.'

'It was a mistake to so disgrace ourselves.' Seton moaned in disgust at his own pitiful condition. 'I am certain we have damaged our credibility with these people. Let us bring this business to a close as quickly as we are able. It would be foolish to prolong the process and risk having our deception exposed.'

'Nonsense!' Kincaid retorted as he tore at a crust of bread. 'If anything, our reputations are enhanced. Apart from sailors and Irishmen, clerics are drunk more often than any other group of men. I have seen Cowper preside over trials with lips still stained red with claret and with dried vomit crusted on his cloak. Do not fret! We'll see this week out and ride off with our purses full to bursting. I will eat up a full day ducking and pricking Elspet Leyis and then you must stretch out your examination of the case against the third accused. If fortune favours us and you can keep your wits, we'll draw this out to the next Sabbath day.'

Elspet Leyis unwittingly aided them in their scheme. The early morning light did not fall upon the sobbing and broken creature who had slumped before them on the stool not two days past. The moment the barn doors creaked open, it was clear the widow was fully revived. No longer forlorn and defeated, her eyes burned with hatred and defiance.

'Bastard dogs!' She snarled, twisting and struggling as men bent down to pull her to her feet. 'Worthless sons of bitches and whores!'

'Filthy bitch!' The blacksmith cried out in disgust as he wiped the widow's phlegm from his face. 'You would spit on me? See how you like it!'

He stamped down on her head with the heel of his boot with vicious force and, as she lay stunned, leaned down to spit directly into her face.

'Away!' Seton roared at him, clenching his fists at his sides. 'Away from her, you contemptible rogue! You are too fond of lifting your hand to defenceless women for my liking. She is bound hand and foot yet still you feel the need to kick at her. Away before I raise my own fists against you! Bring another man forward who is capable of subduing her without doing her harm.'

The glowering blacksmith stood his ground until the Young Laird ordered him to withdraw and gestured for Peter Myles to take his place. The young carpenter was twice the size of Elspet Leyis and had strength enough to haul her upright with one jerk of his thick right arm. He dropped her again just as quickly when she sunk her teeth into the flesh just above his wrist. He squealed like a girl as he tried to stem the blood flowing from the gaping wound and cursed when the widow spat a gobbet of flesh onto the earth of the barn floor.

'You're a miserable turd, Peter Myles.' She taunted him, her lips red with his blood. 'Do you forget who pulled you into this world from between your mother's fat, hairy thighs? Would you drown the woman who thumped at your back to force your first breath into you? Ungrateful and treacherous pup! I'll tear holes in your flesh every time you attempt to lay your hands on me!'

'Fetch a pole so we might string her up!' Kincaid ordered, his expression one of fascination and amusement. 'She can gnaw at the wood as much as she likes while we carry her with arms and hands safely beyond the reach of her fangs.'

'Mistress Leyis!' Seton admonished her. 'I will have you suspended from a pole if you refuse to conduct yourself in a civilised and Christian manner. The test will be administered whether you will it or not. Your violent and unseemly struggling will not prevent us from executing our duties as required by the law. If you comply, you will walk to the river on your own two feet and spare yourself the discomfort of being carried there like a carcass. If you continue to defy me and threaten these good men with physical harm, I will be forced to have you borne there in a manner likely to cause you great pain and risk tearing your shoulders from their sockets.'

The widow held his gaze for several moments as if she was giving careful consideration to his words. Seton began to hope he had succeeded in bringing her to reason. He sighed in frustration when a sly and insolent grin spread across her face.

'Kiss my arse!' She spat at him, taking great care to emphasise each individual word in order to imbue the insult with as much potency as she was able. 'Drown me if you will. I will give you no help in the doing of it.'

'Have it your own way.' He conceded with some reluctance. 'Bring a pole so we might hoist her up!'

A hitching rail was brought from Laird Marlee's stable and was thrust roughly between the ropes binding the widow's hands and feet. Two men lifted her up but progressed no more than a dozen paces before the wood splintered under her weight and sent her crashing down onto the damp earth. A close and prolonged examination of the rail led to a heated debate about what had caused it to break. Some said it was the work of common woodworm while others pointed to the dry flakes of wood and attributed age and rot as the cause of the breakage. The discussion eventually moved on to consider what might serve as the best replacement. A shaft from Minister Logie's cart was suggested by the hesitant and soft-spoken cartwright who had built it for him several months earlier. The minister was reluctant to see his cart dismantled but was forced to agree due to his inability to propose a suitable alternative and because of the weight of opinion against him.

Kincaid and Seton exchanged knowing glances as the minutes passed without any progress being made. Elspet Leyis had lain still and quiet while all this unfolded but threw off all passivity the moment an attempt was made to insert the shaft between her bonds. She bucked and convulsed like a woman possessed, making it impossible for the men to complete their task. Seton could not help but admire her vigour and stamina. Her face grew red and streaked with sweat from the effort of twisting and throwing her body violently from one side to the other. She gasped for breath from her exertions but curses and obscenities continued to flow from her lips without interruption. It was Peter Myles who finally succeeded in threading the needle. Still smarting from his humiliation at the widow's hand, he had the patience, skill and strength to force the shaft home the moment she weakened and her thrashing slowed.

The indignity of being hoisted aloft served to reinvigorate her and she flailed against her bonds like a fish writhing on a hook. Blood began to flow from her wrists and ankles from the chafing of the ropes and she screeched and shrieked as if she had been driven to madness.

'Jesus!' Kincaid cursed when they came in sight of the riverbank. 'You should have let the blacksmith crack her skull. My ears are sore from her yelping and my head throbs as if my brain has been pierced. Let us waste no time in ducking her. The sooner the water chokes her throat the sooner we will have peace.'

The ducking of Elspet Leyis did not go as easily as Kincaid had hoped. She yanked at her ropes so fiercely the four men chosen to hold them had to brace themselves in order to contain her. The unfortunate Peter Myles was strong enough to keep his grip but could do nothing to save himself when the stones shifted beneath his feet and pitched him headlong into the water. He blushed red when he surfaced and redder still when the tavern keeper caused great mirth by declaring that he had sunk so fast he was proven to be no witch.

The waters no more rejected Elspet Leyis than they had the hapless carpenter. She sank the moment the tension on the ropes was eased, leaving only ripples and water bubbles to disturb the surface.

'Let us leave her a few moments longer.' Kincaid declared happily. 'So we might enjoy a little quiet.'

The widow coughed and spluttered when she finally broke the surface but took only a single breath before giving vent to her spleen.

'Cockless bastards!' She croaked, her face twisted in rage. 'Sodomites! Dirty whoresons! Stinking, pox-ridden whores!'

Kincaid groaned, held his head in his hands and jabbed his finger at the water to signal that she should be ducked again. She sank into the dark, green depths the moment the ropes were slackened. The sudden tranquillity was welcomed by all there. The silence was broken by nothing other than the sounds of birdsong, the light breeze in the branches of the trees and the gentle lapping of the water against the riverbank. Long minutes passed before Seton spoke.

'You had better bring her up, Will.' He insisted when he began to fear she might drown.

'A moment longer.' The pricker replied without any hint of urgency. 'Let the water take the strength from her lungs so we might be spared any more of her nasty squawking.'

Only water spewed from the widow's mouth when they hauled her in. Her face was a dark purple and her lips were blue from lack of air. She retched horribly and seemed to vomit a greater volume of water than her body had the capacity to hold. Her fingers clawed weakly at the mud on the bank as she hacked and wheezed in her struggle to draw breath.

'Isn't that better?' Kincaid enquired with no small satisfaction. 'I doubt she will have the strength to scorn or assault us.'

'She has had enough, Will. The waters did not refuse her. We can consider the test to be complete.'

'The third time's the charm, John.' Kincaid replied with a wink. 'There can be no deviation from the process, as well you know. I'll give her a few minutes to recover herself out of concern for your sensitivity, but then she must be ducked again.'

Elspet Leyis uttered no curse or insult while she lay upon the bank and offered no protest when the ropes were tightened to pull her back into the river. She made no sound before the waters closed over her head and confined herself to coughing and spluttering when she was pulled from the waters for the last time. She cast no aspersions on the parentage, morality or sexual proclivities of those who watched as she struggled for breath. No pole was required to carry her back to her prison and she did not fight when rough hands seized her shoulders and dragged her back towards Marlee House.

'We have broken her spirit.' Seton observed when the listless and submissive form of Elspet Leyis was lowered onto the stool before them.

'Good!' Kincaid declared with a snort. 'It is a bastard job to prick these bitches when they make a fight of it. I thought I might have to knock the teeth from her head if she tried to take a bite out of me as she did with that great hulk of a half-wit this morning. It will go easier for her now she is subdued.'

'What if she is innocent, Will? We will be shamed if we have broken her for no good reason. I fear she is innocent. I am certain of it.'

'Do not waste your pity on her as you did with the wizened old hag. My spike will find the truth of it and leave you to rest easy in your bed.'

The widow offered no resistance when Kincaid stripped her clothes from her. She leaned forwards and crossed her arms across her chest in a feeble attempt to cover her nakedness but meekly let them fall back to her sides when the pricker pushed them away. The evidence of her torture was laid bare for all to see, the bruises and burns dark and angry against the paleness of her skin. Her left foot was blackened and misshapen and three of its toes were topped with thick scabs in the place of the nails torn out to bring her to confession. She lay still while he shaved her, though she winced when he nicked her with his razor and screwed her eyes tight shut when he inspected her intimate areas.

Seton found he had no stomach for the spectacle the second time around. He lowered his gaze to the floor rather than let it linger on the widow's shame and humiliation. A sideways glance was sufficient to confirm that only a few of her neighbours were willing to deny themselves the opportunity to gape at her bare paps and private parts. The minister alone had closed his eyes and his lips seemed to move in a silent prayer to God to bring the distasteful ordeal to a close. The damned blacksmith stared without shame, his eyes wide and unblinking in his determination to miss not a single detail.

Will Kincaid practically drooled as he went about his examination with exaggerated care and thoroughness. Not an inch of flesh was neglected, with her breasts, cunny and rectum receiving the closest scrutiny and a great deal of poking, prodding and squeezing. He might have been mistaken for a surgeon if it had not been for the obscenity of his tongue protruding between his teeth like a disgusting, glistening slug. Seton might have been able to dismiss this evidence of his companion's lecherous depravity if it had not been for the bulge at Kincaid's groin betraying his arousal. He tried to think of the silver and of how it would bring his Elizabeth back to him but he could not so easily dismiss the feeling he was somehow stained by his involvement in this sordid business.

'It is here!' Kincaid announced, his voice loud and heavy with import and his finger pointing at the widow's raw and naked groin. 'See! The Devil has left his unholy mark upon her!'

Seton strained his eyes but could see nothing more than a small patch of discoloured skin in the crease between her privates and her thigh. He thought it to be the kind of blemish likely to be caused by the chafing of sodden undergarments. Bitter bile rose to his throat as he watched Kincaid begin the pricking ritual. He held the bodkin aloft as if it were a holy relic before thumping its point down into the wooden tabletop in a theatrical demonstration of the strength of the spike.

'By God's grace, this humble implement will shine the holy light of truth and so expose the corruption of this wretched creature!' He bellowed. 'Let us put her to the test to determine guilt or innocence and so set all doubt aside.'

Seton held his breath and prayed silently for the test to exonerate the widow. It would be a mercy to bring an end to her suffering, though he feared she was already ruined and would likely never fully recover from her ordeal.

Kincaid brandished the bodkin in his fist and let his gaze pass slowly over all those present in the hall. They were entranced by his performance and leaned forward in eager anticipation. He pointed the spike at Elspet's waist and drew it back before pausing as though he had been frozen just as he was poised to strike. Long moments passed before he stabbed the spike into the widow's side with vicious force. Her scream pierced the heavy silence, its sudden violence causing all to jump in fright. Mistress Leyis writhed in agony and clutched desperately at the bodkin in an effort to pluck it from her flesh. Kincaid knocked her hand aside before slowly withdrawing the spike. Blood poured from the wound and began to pool on the wooden boards.

The pricker took great care to clean his instrument before repeating the procedure with the same result. Elspet Leyis cried out when he pierced her shoulder and fell into a fit of sobbing as her blood dripped onto the floor.

'See!' Kincaid boomed. 'Behold the effect of steel on uncorrupted flesh! Even the strongest of men will bleed and cry out when their skin is punctured. Only flesh tainted by Satan's touch is impervious to pain and injury. Let us test the mark on this woman's most private place. The steel will reveal its impurity!'

The pricker crossed to the far side of the table to put the widow's prone figure between him and his audience. He parted her thighs and leaned down so his eyes were only an inch away from her blemish and his nose only an inch from her sex. He did not stab at her but pressed the point of the bodkin against her skin with unexpected gentleness. Seton held his breath and watched with astonishment as the spike slid slowly and smoothly into her flesh until it was embedded there to its very hilt. Elspet Leyis still sobbed softly but gave no sign of suffering any pain or distress despite being pierced so deeply. The shock of it caused him to gasp and he gazed transfixed as Kincaid withdrew the spike from the wound. The steel was not so much as smeared with gore, no blood flowed and there was only unbroken skin where there should have been a deep and gaping hole.

'Witch!' Kincaid bellowed, his finger pointed at the widow in accusation. 'Witch!'

The cry was taken up by Elspet's neighbours, its intensity increasing with each repetition. Seton was rendered dizzy by what he had just witnessed. The phenomenon was so unnatural he could scarcely believe the evidence of his own eyes.

'Burn the witch!' Kincaid roared, rousing the villagers to a frenzy. 'Burn the witch!'

12

'Do not look so grave.' Kincaid commanded Seton when he joined him for breakfast in the small drawing room adjacent to the dining hall in Marlee House. 'All is well with the world. With two witches condemned and one still to be tried, our enterprise is almost complete.'

'Let us away with the silver already in our possession.' Seton pleaded. 'I do not have the stomach for more of this. I could hardly sleep for thinking of the widow Leyis and that damned mark between her legs. I scrubbed myself raw at my washing bowl but my skin still crawls from my proximity to such corruption. I am not hardened to it as you are.'

'Nonsense, my friend.' The pricker dismissed him as he heaped bread and eggs onto his plate. 'The worst is already behind us. Even the Young Laird is satisfied and no longer chides us for emptying his purse. Look at the fine spread he has laid on for us in gratitude for two trials brought to a successful conclusion. He will let us proceed with no further interference. If you have the courage and the wit, we will see out the week and leave this place weighed down with more silver than we dared to dream of.'

The sight of Kincaid's teeth coated in yolk as he talked with his mouth gaping open caused Seton's stomach to churn and robbed him of what little appetite he had left.

'It will take a day to prick and swim this last bitch.' Kincaid continued, blissfully unaware of his companion's revulsion. 'And with a day to erect the stakes and gather sufficient wood and peat to reduce them to ash, we can burn them on Saturday and so relieve the Young Laird of every last shilling we could hope for. All you need do is draw out the examination of the evidence for two full days.'

'I doubt it is possible.' Seton moaned, not bothering to disguise his reluctance to tarry for a moment longer than was necessary. 'There is no confession to be considered and the witnesses to come will likely be as feeble and witless as those who have preceded them. I will probably be done before the morning is over.'

'Pish!' The pricker retorted as he helped himself to more of the eggs. ''Tis only your soft-heart that holds you back. You have both the intelligence and, when it pleases you, the cheek to bend these peasants to your will. Find your courage and hold hard to it! Then you will return to Edinburgh in triumph and free yourself from the bonds of penury.' Kincaid leaned in close and gave Seton a lecherous wink. 'Think of your wife if it hardens your resolve. What would you give to have her back in your bed to bring other parts to stiffness? A few days longer in this damned place is surely a very small price to pay for such a rich prize.'

It revolted Seton to hear the pricker refer to Elizabeth so crudely, but he could not deny the truth of his argument. He clenched his jaw in determination and set about finding the fortitude necessary to carry him through to the end of his ordeal.

The last of the accused provided Seton with the opportunity to order a delay in proceedings the moment she was dragged forward and placed on the stool. She was not insensible as Agnes Newie had been, nor was she as vile and objectionable as Elspet Leyis. She did not struggle against the ropes at her wrists and ankles but glared up at her prosecutors through a thick fringe of matted, red-brown hair. The whites of her hostile, defiant eyes shone brightly against the dark filth that caked her from head to foot. Seton thought she must have rolled in mud and allowed it to dry but realised the error of his assumption the moment the stench hit his nostrils. She reeked of shit and pish so badly it caused him to gag and made his eyes water.

'In the name of God!' He cried out in disgust, cupping his hand over his mouth and nose in a vain attempt to spare himself from the stink and taste of stale urine and dried excrement. 'Why is this wretched woman in such a filthy and repellent state?' He demanded of the assembled company.

'I would not suffer an animal to be kept in such a poor and squalid condition!'

'She does it to herself, Minister Cowper.' Logie informed him with a shrug of his shoulders. 'We have drenched her with buckets of river water a dozen times but she smears herself with her own filth the moment she is able. My own wife had her washed and changed just last night but we found her already encrusted in dung when we roused her this morning.'

'We are to have our entertainment.' Kincaid hissed with amusement from Seton's side, his mouth hidden behind his hand. 'These mad bitches never disappoint.'

'I will not suffer this stench!' Seton snapped in irritation. 'Have the women take her out and scrub her. I will not continue until she is set before me in a clean and decent condition. Throw the shutters open so the room might air while we await her return.'

Kincaid lounged back in his seat, an expression of smug satisfaction on his face.

'See! I told you there was no need to fret. We are yet to begin and already the proceedings have been drawn out. We may well still be here come the next Sabbath day.'

Seton gasped when the minister's wife and the Old Laird's housekeeper led Violet Frazer back to her place on the stool. The sunlight streaming in through the open shutters turned her hair the fiery red of glowing embers now it was no longer crusted with filth. Her skin was pale and flawless and her slim figure was accentuated by the simple and worn dress dug out from some cupboard or attic in Marlee House. All of this paled into insignificance when set beside her eyes. They were as pale blue as the clearest of summer skies and fixed on Seton's with a directness and intensity that caused his jaw to drop. He did not think he had set his eyes upon a more beautiful woman since the first time he caught sight of his Elizabeth as she strolled by Edinburgh's Tolbooth on her brother's arm. It took every ounce of his will to turn his gaze away from her.

'Praise be!' Kincaid whispered in awe. 'The good Lord must be watching over me. I'll take my sweet time pricking this fair strumpet! I could make it last until Michaelmas and still not be done with her!'

Seton winced at the thought of him poking and prodding the girl and did not offer a response to his lewd comments. He instead gestured to the Young Laird as he had raised his hand to indicate his desire to speak.

'I offer thanks for being given leave to address this commission, good sirs.' He began, his voice clear and his delivery confident. 'Violet Frazer is the worst of the unholy witches who have so plagued us these past months. It would be an unforgivable dereliction of my duty to my tenants and the good people of this parish if I did not attest to this. Behold the coarse and loathsome creature who now stands before you! Let me ask you this before all else. What good and virtuous Christian woman would wallow in her squalor and soak herself in her own putrid excrement? Surely, no godly man who has seen this evidence of her foul nature would then go on to defend her against the charge of witchcraft. If either of you good gentlemen would doubt her guilt and be taken in by her beauty, the testimony you are about to hear will quickly disabuse you of any misguided notion of mercy or charity. Her presence in this parish stains us all with the sin of heresy and pollutes our nostrils with the stench of her shameful, unnatural and deviant actions. We must burn away the corruption she has wrought if we are to spare the souls of all who have been blighted by her blasphemy. We must purify with God's holy flame and scour clean all she has defiled. The testimony of our witnesses will convince you of the truth of it. Let Mabel Lamb speak first. All here would swear to her purity and righteous character.'

The girl who stepped forward at James Moncur's command was a lamb in nature as well as in name. She was small, plain of face and, though still a girl, was poised on the very edge of womanhood. She seemed to quail before Seton in her timidity and could scarcely bring herself to lift her head to meet his eye. She clasped her trembling hands before her as if in prayer and glanced constantly towards the Young Laird to seek his encouragement and his support. Seton spoke softly when he invited her to begin but even his most gentle tone was enough to startle her and cause her shoulders to shake.

'I am Mabel Lamb, daughter of David Lamb, a cowherd and drover of this parish.' She began hesitantly, her voice so quiet Seton had to strain his ears to catch her words. 'I know Violet Frazer to be a witch for only a witch would consort with the Devil. I was collecting wild strawberries for my mother when I came upon her by the side of the stream with a black dog at her side. I could see its great, pointed ears above the long grass.' The words began to tumble from her mouth as her confidence grew, though her delivery was toneless as if her speech had been committed to memory through repetition.

'I opened my mouth to call out to her but was brought to silence when she spoke to the beast. The blood seemed to freeze in my veins when the hound answered her, not with a bark or a growl, but in the voice of a man. I heard it as clearly as I heard you when you bade me to speak, good sir. His voice was so deep and hoarse it caused me to shiver though the day was warm. 'Do not fret, my bonnie lass.' He reassured her. 'You did right to send for me. No harm will come to you now I am at your side. Know that I will not hesitate to strike down anyone foolish or reckless enough to make the attempt!' She thanked him for coming so quickly and for giving her comfort. She then invited him to embrace her. My heart near seized in my chest when he suddenly rose up on his legs in the form of a rough and dishevelled man with wild and unkempt hair and eyes that were unnaturally dark!'

A few women gasped at this diabolical revelation but were brought to immediate silence when Seton gestured at them in irritation.

'I turned to flee as he changed shape.' Mabel Lamb continued, growing ever bolder as her testimony progressed. 'But my legs were frozen in terror. I stood transfixed as he wrapped her in his unholy embrace and rocked her back and forth as a man might rock his lover. I caught sight of his face just as he leaned in to kiss her neck. My horror was so great I called out in fright.' Mabel paused and met Seton's gaze directly for the first time. ''Twas none other than her own father brought back from the dead!'

Seton had to hammer his fist against the table to make himself heard above the uproar caused by the girl's abominable utterance. His eyes met those of Violet Frazer as the tumult subsided and he saw her give an almost imperceptible shake of her head in silent denial of the girl's extraordinary accusation.

'I will not tolerate these unseemly disturbances.' He barked, his annoyance clear from his furrowed brow. 'I will not hesitate to eject all who are incapable of holding their tongues. Let the girl complete her testimony without further interruption or you will suffer the consequences for it!'

'There could be no mistake about the man's identity.' Mabel Lamb asserted, her chin now held high from a heightened sense of self-assurance. 'I knew James Frazer well and considered him to be a kind, upstanding and respectable fellow. It broke my heart to see his corpse resurrected by dark and diabolical powers. His cheeks were dirty and sunken from long months in the grave. I feared I would die when he set his black eyes upon me and only then was I able to turn and run. I dared not stop until I was safe at my father's hearth.'

'Tis true!' A woman at the Young Laird's side called out, her plainness causing Seton to assume she was the girl's mother. 'She burst through the door in such a state of terror and breathlessness we could make no sense of the words spilling out of her mouth. We feared she had fallen into madness until my husband forced a wee drop of whisky between her lips to calm her and soothe her spirits.'

'Out!' Seton ordered her. 'I did not give you leave to speak. See this woman to the door, Mister Kincaid! She has no place here if she is unable or unwilling to follow my instructions.'

Seton's outburst had the desired effect and the gathered worthies and peasants were left shocked and subdued by his harsh discipline. They remained silent and gazed at their feet while the pricker escorted Mistress Lamb from the hall.

'May I address you, sir.' The Young Laird enquired, his tone rendered unusually deferential by the sudden banishment of the mother Lamb. Seton gave a curt nod to bid him to continue. 'If Violet Frazer would deny the truth of this brave girl's testament, then command her to lift her hair and allow us to examine her neck where Beelzebub laid his lips upon her. Her guilt will be confirmed if he has left his mark upon her to claim her soul for himself.'

The accused lifted her hair aside without protest when she was instructed to do so. The angry red mark was a little behind her ear and stood out in livid contrast to her pale and otherwise unblemished skin. She held Seton's gaze and seemed to arch her neck towards him as though she was inviting him to press his own lips against her and bury his face in her fiery locks. Her lips twitched upwards in the beginnings of a smile as if she sensed Seton's sudden desire for her. Her subtle, kittenish flirtation caused his cheeks to redden and he forced himself to turn from her and call for the next witness to step forward.

The farmer's wife had none of Mabel Lamb's shyness or reserve. She stamped forward, her face pinched with bitterness and her eyes burning with raw hatred.

'This is Jill Gowrie.' James Moncur announced, once again taking it upon himself to marshal the witnesses against Violet Frazer. 'She is wife to Bob Gowrie, a tenant of this estate. I do not doubt you will find her testimony to be as damning as Mabel Lamb's.'

'I will be the judge of that.' Seton snapped back in annoyance at the arrogance of his presumption. 'Say your piece, Mistress Gowrie! I can see you are champing at the bit in your haste to so unburden yourself.'

Jill Gowrie required no second invitation to give voice to her wrath and felt no need to look to the Young Laird or to anyone else for encouragement. She might have been taken for the homely sort, on account of her simple dress and round and rosy cheeks, if it was not for the fierce and seething expression on her face. Her frown darkened with rage as she glared at Seton in open hostility and she glanced away only to fire dirty and malevolent looks in the direction of the accused.

'That foul and wanton bitch has done great injury to my family by way of charms and curses and other dark sorcery!' She snarled, the force of her words causing flecks of white spittle to fly into the air as she spoke. 'Twas last autumn when I caught sight of her hurrying away from our gate after being disturbed at my work by the unnatural tinkling of a bell. I knew it heralded some act of witchcraft for the sound of it caused shivers to run down my spine. I made to go after her but stopped when I spied a cross of buckthorn planted in the manure pile. From that day on, all four of our cows refused to give more than a few drops of milk no matter how hard we coaxed them or how roughly we pulled at their teats. My husband has tended to cattle for all of his days and is well acquainted with their peculiarities and perversities and with the ailments they suffer. He tried every remedy known to him but all of his efforts were in vain. Desperation and the threat of ruin forced him to abandon his pride and seek advice from our neighbours. Nothing they suggested had any good effect, though we fed them with all manner of things, washed them in the river, applied poultices to their udders and put them to pasture with calves in the hope of bringing on their milk. My family was left with barely enough milk to drink and there was no surplus to sell or to churn to butter in order to earn coin.' The thought of this suffering caused tears to pour from her eyes and she paused to brush them angrily from her cheeks.

'Twas then, just as my children began to grow gaunt and hollow of cheek, that my worst suspicions were confirmed. I chanced upon the vile, dark-hearted bitch in the lane and saw her struggling into the village under the weight of two full pails of milk. She had so much she cared not if it sloshed and spilled as she walked along. How can her two cows produce a greater quantity of milk than all four of ours? It goes against all laws of nature and God! Only witchcraft can explain such a thing! Only sorcery could enable her to draw off the milk from our beasts and take it for herself. Tis the Devil's work! Everyone agrees it can be nothing else. She has bewitched my beasts with her spells and her charms and leaves my children to starve! She must burn for her sins, good sir! She must burn if our suffering is to be brought to an end.'

Jill Gowrie's shoulders slumped as though the effort of giving her testimony had drained her of all energy. Her eyes lost their hardness and hostility and she gazed at Seton in a silent and desperate plea for justice. This softness was short-lived and evaporated the instant Violet Frazer spoke.

'Liar!' She said, her voice clear and steady with no hint of anger or hysteria.

13

Seton was surprised when Kincaid announced the adjournment. The witness testimony had absorbed him so completely the morning seemed to have passed by in an instant. His appetite was fully restored and he took full advantage of the Young Laird's continuing largesse. There was mutton to go with the bread and cheese and good claret to moisten their throats rather than the usual bitter and cloudy ale.

'A man could become accustomed to this.' He declared as he rubbed at his stomach.

'I could grow accustomed to strumping that little trollop.' Kincaid retorted with a heartfelt sigh. 'I'll wager she is as firm and juicy as the plumpest of peaches. I am so eager to prick her, I almost wish you would dismiss all the witnesses so we could proceed straight to the tests.' He then groaned in frustration. 'It would be a pity to burn her before she is plucked. Perhaps we might steal into the barn and have use of her once she is condemned.'

'Christ, Will!' Seton hissed at him, twisting his head around to make sure they were not overheard. 'Must you talk such filth? I am a married man and would not countenance such an outrage!'

'Damn your eyes, John Seton!' The pricker drawled unabashed. 'You can lay no more claim to sanctimony than I. I have seen how you gaze at her and did not miss the coy look she favoured you with. She has no need of charms or spells to so enchant you.'

'Enough of this!' Seton insisted. 'The Young Laird grows impatient. He will seek to dispense with this last witness without delay so we might complete the swimming test before the day is out. I will need my wits about me if I am to succeed in frustrating his ambition.'

'I hope you will grant me this last indulgence.' James Moncur requested when Seton declared the proceedings open. 'This final witness will lend weight to the testimony already submitted to this commission. Marion Hay is of good and humble family and is known to all to be a devoted Christian, an obedient wife and a kind and attentive mother to all seven of her surviving children. Her long and close acquaintance with the family of the accused brings a new and more intimate perspective to the case against her. Such independent corroboration will, I am sure, aid you in the reaching of your judgement.'

Marion Hay might have been described as buxom in her youth but the years had not been kind to her. She was well past her child-bearing years and her grey and sagging skin spoke of a life full of hardship and care. A lumpy growth of some kind dangled from her left eyelid and seemed to weigh it down so it hung lower than its partner on the other side. The wart jumped around obscenely whenever she blinked her eyes and Seton could not help but gape at it in horrid fascination as she laid her accusations out. Her nerves afflicted her so fiercely she often took to blinking furiously and so set the protuberance to dancing.

'I knew Violet's mother well.' She began, her voice made high-pitched from anxiety. 'She was a fine and godly woman and it is a pity she was cursed to bear only a single child strong enough to survive its infancy. The greater pity was the foul and sinful nature of that child. I have never known a girl to be as wilful and disobedient as Violet Frazer. I once chastised her for swimming naked in the river. She did not blush or ask forgiveness for this affront to decency but laughed and leapt back into the water. She floated there as bare as when she was a baby born and taunted me horribly. What eight-year-old would dare to so abuse a respectable and upright Christian woman? She ran wild from the moment she could walk and would pay no heed to her poor mother. Her father beat her black and blue, as was his Christian duty, but she was immune to whatever discipline he dispensed. She caused them so much anguish it wore at their spirits and sent them both to early graves.'

'I have no interest in tales of errant children.' Seton interrupted her. 'If every disobedient child grew up to be a witch, our country would have been overwhelmed by sorcery many years ago. Do you have any testimony to offer likely to be of relevance to this commission?'

'I do, good sir!' She retorted, her head wobbling from side to side in indignation. 'I called upon her not long after her poor father had passed. I entered the house when she bid me to do so and was confronted by a rat standing on its hind legs by the hearth. It did not scamper away at the sight of me, as any natural creature would, but returned my gaze without flinching and rubbed its paws together as if warming them at the flames. It glared at me, good sir, as if I was the unwelcome interloper and not this foul rodent. I have set my eyes upon this diabolical creature several times since then. Just two months past, I watched from the hedge as Violet conversed with it and then, to my great horror, she bared her breast and invited it to suckle her. The sight of it lapping at her teat sickened me to my stomach and I made away as quickly as I was able.'

'Mistress Hay speaks true!' James Moncur announced with an emphatic nod of his head. 'Every time I step into the barn the accursed rat is close to her and scuttles off at my approach. It is known that a witch's familiar must suckle at her teats if it is to have sustenance. It will wither and die if denied its feast.'

Violet Frazer had remained impassive since renouncing Jill Gowrie's testimony and had limited herself to a faint smile of arrogance and wry amusement. The Young Laird's intervention prompted her to shake her head and give a snort of derision.

'I would counsel you against such scorn.' Seton admonished her. 'The weight of evidence against you is quite damning and I have seen little likely to persuade me of your innocence.'

'Tis nothing more than hearsay and tittle-tattle.' She shot back, undaunted by Seton's rebuke. 'How much weight will you give to their false and flimsy testimony when there is no confession to corroborate a single word of it?'

'Tis a fair question.' Seton conceded, turning his head towards the men around the Young Laird. 'The lack of a confession cannot be considered to be of no significance. What methods were employed to induce her to admit her guilt?'

'We pressed her hard in our questioning.' William Kerr replied, his head bowed as if he feared suffering another scolding at Seton's hand. He had cowered like a beaten dog since being rebuked for kicking Elspet Leyis on the riverbank and had lacked the courage to look Seton in the eye since then. 'But she resisted all of our efforts most stubbornly. We subjected her to the same coercion that proved sufficient to persuade the other two accused to admit the truth. We denied her food, water and sleep for four full days but she did not rant and babble in delirium like the others did. She remained resolute in her stubborn defiance and refused to give voice to her heresy. It was then I knew beyond all doubt she was a witch in possession of some diabolical power. No natural woman would have the strength to endure the punishment of such dire deprivation. I do not doubt that even the hardiest and boldest of men would have broken in the face of such extreme hardship.'

'The Young Laird then instructed us to test her with fire.' William Kerr continued, now sufficiently emboldened to cast furtive, sideways glances in Seton's direction. 'Not a single word passed her lips when we seared the flesh of her arms, belly and thighs with iron rods heated until they glowed red like fire. She hissed when her skin blistered and sizzled but refused to divulge the foulness and sinfulness of her true nature in exchange for bringing her torment to an end. We then applied a boot fashioned from two slabs of timber and a bolt of iron. We tightened it until her foot was bruised black but she did nothing other than whimper and moan and wilfully ignore every legitimate question put to her. The minister then ordered us to remove the contraption lest we leave her crippled without having secured an admission of her sins.'

'The Young Laird then sent the pastor away and had us remove the heavy byre door from its hinges and lay the witch beneath it. He told us we should see if she could bear its weight as happily as she bore the burden of her crimes.' Kerr looked to James Moncur for confirmation and received a curt nod in response. 'It took six men to lift the door but the filthy sorceress did not make a sound when its great weight pressed down upon her. We piled stones and boulders upon the door from noon until the sun began to set. We stopped only when we heard the bitch wheezing and whispering to herself. The Young Laird dropped to the ground in his fine blue coat to better catch the words of her admission, but he had soiled the cloth for no good reason. Her mutterings were no confession.'

'What words did she speak?' Seton demanded, his curiosity piqued by the tale of the girl's fortitude and courage in the face of such pain and torment.

'She mocked us, sir.' Kerr replied, a slow shake of his head communicating the great depth of his disapproval. 'She prayed as the life was being slowly crushed from her and, in so doing, gave grave offence to God. She prayed, but not for her soul or for forgiveness from on high. She instead called on God to forgive the men who now murdered her and beseeched Him to absolve them for their weakness and ignorance. It was blasphemy, sir. When the Young Laird cried out in rage and frustration, she fell to fits of laughter and subjected him to ridicule with no thought for his rank or standing. Sore aggrieved at having dirtied his good coat for no good reason, he ordered all six of us to stand upon the door to choke off her merriment. Twas then that the minister returned. He commanded us to release her if we did not want to hang for murdering her when we had no authority to try and execute her for her crimes. The Young Laird was furious and cursed the pastor before going off to write to you in Glasgow to beg for your assistance in bringing this outrage to a satisfactory, swift and lawful conclusion.'

'How did she ridicule the Young Laird?' Seton asked, the question driven partly by curiosity and partly by mischief.

'I would not like to say, sir.' Kerr replied, almost squirming in discomfort. 'I would not like to offer offence to him by repeating her false and insolent lies before this company.'

'Then you will write them out for me. I must have a full and complete account if I am to reach a sound judgment in this case. Will! Give him quill and parchment so he might record what words were spoken.'

'I cannot, good sir.' Kerr replied, his cheeks flushing with embarrassment. 'I never learned my letters. The quill and parchment would be of no use to me.'

'Then speak the words, good blacksmith.' Seton commanded him. 'I would know what was said.'

'She meant to insult and provoke him. She called him a lazy, spoilt and greedy boy who had ever been an embarrassment to his good father. She called him a thief, a liar and a faithless, black-hearted master and said his birth was the worst misfortune ever to befall this parish. She accused him of coveting the land she inherited from her father and of being so lacking in Christian morals there were no depths he would not stoop to in order to enrich himself. She did not curse or swear but her insolence was no less offensive for the lack of profanity. No man would have blamed the

Young Laird if he had taken his whip to her and stripped the flesh from her back. There was no shred of truth to her vile and false accusations. Anyone here would swear the same.'

Seton had to bite his lip to keep himself from smiling in amusement. James Moncur's face had turned a dark shade of red as the blacksmith spoke and he now glared at the hapless fool as if he wished to murder him.

'The lack of a confession is undeniably troublesome.' He began, cutting short his enjoyment of Moncur's discomfort. 'Particularly as she was subjected to such great pressure to elicit an admission of her sins. I must therefore adjourn this hearing to give further consideration to the witness testimony before returning tomorrow to provide the accused with the opportunity to respond to the accusations made against her.'

'Is that really necessary?' The Young Laird demanded, the words exploding from his lips in fury. 'The great weight of testimony against her cannot be denied and no reasonable man would accept anything uttered by that foul bitch to contain any trace of veracity. Tis patently pointless! Let us dispense with this futile distraction and put her to test at dawn. Let us prick her, expose her immorality for all to see and have done with it!'

Seton matched Moncur's glare with his own and returned his stare for several moments. When he finally spoke, his voice was steady and filled with authority.

'Sir, you know full well I have no authority to deviate from the legal process laid down by the Privy Council and mandated by King James himself. I am obliged to put all testimony to close examination before I am able to turn to the more scientific methodologies. Even if I did possess some degree of latitude, any educated man would know I am unable to exercise it when the given testimony is too tenuous to be fully relied upon. All of the witnesses are women and, as such, no lawful commission can accept their word unchallenged. Members of their sex are, by nature, weak and unreliable witnesses with a tendency to exaggerate and embellish and be driven by petty spite and the lure of material rewards. The law would rightly have me interrogate them and I will do so on the morrow.'

Moncur threw his arms up in exasperation but made no further protest. Seton then gestured towards the housekeeper and beckoned her forward.

'I will instruct the accused to refrain from rolling in her own filth when she is returned to her stall. If she does not obey, I must impose on you to ensure she is presented here at dawn tomorrow fully scrubbed and in clean attire. I will not suffer her filth and stench through a close examination.'

'Aye, sir.' Margaret replied, nodding her head so enthusiastically all of her chins wobbled in agreement. 'I have boiled her old dress clean and it is drying on the back green for that very purpose. I will rise with the lark and have her before you in presentable condition at dawn.'

Kincaid slapped Seton on the shoulder when he brought the proceedings to a close and the villagers began to shuffle from the hall.

'You did well to put that bastard in his place.' He exclaimed with no small satisfaction. 'Now let us test the full extent of your powers. Even I am not convinced you have the ability to fill a full day with your cross-examination of this fiery wench. I will wager five shillings on it and will pay it willingly if we reach this hour tomorrow without having cast her on the water.'

14

Seton awakened before the first light of dawn and found himself in better spirits than he had expected. The weight of his deception and the fear of being discovered still preyed upon him but they were not at the forefront of his mind. He yearned for the smoke and filth of Edinburgh and indulged himself in daydreams of returning there to confound both the sinister Flesher and the vile Carmichaels before setting about reclaiming his sweet Elizabeth and pulling her into his embrace. His impatience to be away was tempered by curiosity and he found he was intrigued to see how Violet Frazer would perform when he questioned her. The odds were stacked against the girl but he detected a strength in her and thought she might well stand her ground and mount a more vigorous defence than her accusers had reason to expect.

He ventured out into the chill morning air to clear his head and strolled down towards the river. A thick mist clung to the fields and hills like a soft, grey blanket. The sun had just begun to show itself on the far horizon, its muted brilliance not yet strong enough to burn the haze away and reveal the clear blue skies above it. Birdsong heralded the new dawn and all manner of the tiny creatures hopped across the dewy grass, their hungry beaks pecking furiously in search of unwary worms. He counted the rabbits as he walked, his slow and steady progress not disturbing their languid gnawing and the twitching of their noses. The peace and tranquillity of the scene served to soothe his soul and he sighed in resignation when the sound of voices and tramping feet intruded on his solitary and silent meditations.

The villagers shrank away from him when he emerged from the mist with sufficient suddenness to bring their conversations to an abrupt end. Those closest to him offered terse and reluctant greetings while the others cast furtive glances in his direction before quickening their pace and making for Marlee House without having to engage with him. He took no satisfaction from the fear generated by his supposed position and imposing appearance. The novelty of the effect he had on these people had dwindled away to nothing and he thought only of the task before him.

Will Kincaid was already lounging in his chair behind the prosecutor's table and greeted him with a wink.

'Five shillings!' He reminded him with a grin. 'I'll count them into your sweaty palm if the girl is still dry when she crawls into her cell this eventide.'

Seton was unable to give the pricker any response to his gleeful challenge for the Young Laird had taken it upon himself to call the proceedings to order. The three accused were led into the hall with their wrists bound before them. Agnes Nevie was guided to her place on the low bench against the back wall. Her eyes were glazed and she gave no sign of being aware of her surroundings as she was pushed down into her seat. Elspet Leyis followed closely behind, her head bowed and her shoulders slumped forward as if she lacked the strength or the will to hold herself upright. Violet Frazer was the last to enter the chamber. The contrast between her and the other two forlorn and feeble creatures could not have been more striking. She strode towards the stool with her back straight, her chin held high and with an expression of calm determination on her face. She met Seton's gaze and held it, her eyes flashing with defiance. Her beauty and spirit seemed to entrance him for a moment and he had to force himself to turn away to keep himself from staring for longer than was seemly.

'Miss Frazer.' He began, keeping his eyes fixed firmly on the documents on the table before him. 'You stand accused of the most grievous and evil of misdeeds. It is incumbent on me to impress upon you the seriousness of the crime of witchcraft. If found guilty, you would be summarily condemned to death. Though you resisted all attempts to induce you to confess your sins, you will doubtless concede that there is a significant weight of testimony against you. I am bound to hear your own testimony and to grant you the opportunity to refute all and any of the accusations made against you. However, I must counsel you against disrespecting the authority of this commission and would urge you to resist the temptation to give vent to spite or recrimination. If you are incapable of conducting yourself with courtesy and civility, you will leave me with no choice but to have you forcibly silenced. Such a course of action would deprive you of your right to be heard and, as such, would be regrettable. My only interest is in the facts.'

'Then I must inform you, good sir, that these false accusations are not at all concerned with witchcraft, spirits or fairy folk.' She declared, her voice clear and steady. Her tone was calm and measured and only the set of her jaw and the tight clenching of her teeth betrayed the cold fury within her. 'Tis all to do with lust, greed and spite.'

'Ha!' The Young Laird called out in derision. 'No sooner does she open her lips than the lies come spilling out from between them. Was Mable Lamb, a young, innocent and blameless child, acting out of lust, greed or spite? Or was she terrorised by the abomination down by the stream? Her mother was quite eloquent when she described the state of hysteria it brought her to!'

Seton opened his mouth to upbraid Moncur for his outburst but closed it again when Violet Frazer gave answer to his challenge.

'I do not doubt she was hysterical. She is a slow and simple child much given to nervous excitement. I do believe she was genuinely mistaken in what she claims to have seen and I hold her blameless for her error. My contempt is reserved for those who would take advantage of her skittish and excitable nature to further their own dishonourable interests. Did you not see how she looked ever at James Moncur for his approval as she spoke? Did you not see the pretty dress she wore? Her father earns barely enough coin to keep his children from starvation, let alone enough to clothe them in fine cloth from Perth. How could she come to cast her grey and ragged attire aside without silver from a gentleman's purse to so replace it?' Her face momentarily twisted in bitterness as she spat out the word 'gentleman', the force of its expulsion sending spittle flying into the air.

'It is not your place to make accusations against your betters!' Seton scolded her in an attempt to restore the dignity of the proceedings and to silence the hubbub of chatter caused by the implication of impropriety made against the heir to Marlee House. 'I will have you gagged if you are unable or unwilling to hold your temper.'

His eyes fell upon James Moncur as he spoke and he was surprised to detect no small measure of guilt in his expression. The Young Laird's sly and shifty demeanour pricked his curiosity and this, along with his personal dislike of the man and his own sense of mischief, drove him to pursue the line of inquiry further.

'In any case, what possible motive could the Young Laird have to offer silver to this child?' He demanded, conscious of Moncur glaring at him and hissing between his teeth in fury. The girl's smile of satisfaction told him she had laid a trap before sweetly enticing him to blunder headlong into it.

'Tis his greed that drives him and the object of his avarice is the land I now occupy. The Old Laird gifted those acres to my father out of love and gratitude for the services done to him when he led his men out in defence of the Old Queen and her throne. He would have bled his last after the battle at Langside if my father had not staunched his wounds with his own hands and dragged him away from the Earl of Moray's soldiers. Title to the land was gifted to my family in perpetuity but the Young Laird seeks to renege on this blood debt so he can enhance his dwindling inheritance. He offered me a pittance for those acres and, when I steadfastly refused him, turned to threats and now to false accusations. He would see me dead and burnt to steal my birthright!'

'I will not stand for this!' Moncur bellowed, his cheeks rendered puce from rage or shame. 'The bitch lies to escape the flames! These foul and baseless allegations do not negate the girl's testimony. The child saw her consort with Satan and she can offer no proof to refute it! Tis enough to condemn her without further corroboration.'

'It is undeniably the most serious of all the allegations, Miss Frazer.' Seton agreed. 'Do you deny cavorting by the stream and can you offer any proof in opposition to Mabel Lamb's account?'

'I do not deny being at the stream on that summer's afternoon.' She replied, a slight curl of her lip the only sign of her frustration. 'I was in the company of my uncle and not in that of a black hound, the Devil or my dear father's corpse newly dragged from its grave in the kirkyard.'

'Ha!' The Young Laird roared in jubilation. 'She has the cheek to lie shamelessly but lacks the wit to offer falsehoods that cannot be easily contradicted. Her family have lived in this parish for generations and all here know she has no uncle. Her father had only three sisters, two of whom died in infancy and a third who was a spinster until the plague carried her off. Her mother's only brother drowned in the Ericht not two years past! She damns herself with this wild and outrageous fabrication! You must bring this travesty to a close and subject her to the tests!'

'I call him uncle but he is my father's cousin.' Violet insisted, her plea directed at Seton rather than at James Moncur. 'He raises sheep for Lord Ogilvy of Airlic up by Alyth. You will find no kinder or more godly man than he. The Old Laird would likely vouch for him as he too served in the defence of the Old Queen and is known to him. Go! Send for him! He will attest to the truth of my account!'

'I would be more inclined to give weight to your arguments if you could offer some explanation for the more lurid claims contained within Mabel Lamb's testimony.' Seton replied. 'The transformation from dog to man, for instance, or the fact of the Devil taking on your father's likeness. I cannot see how you would explain these away?'

'There was no dog with us, good sir.' Violet began, screwing her eyes up as if she was straining to recall every detail of the day in question. 'My uncle was tired after his journey and lay down in the tall grass with his knees pulled up in front of him. I think it likely it was his knees and black trews poor Mabel saw poking up above the grass and mistakenly took them to be the ears of a dog. Tis no wonder she was frightened when he jumped back to his feet. It was clearly no diabolical transformation, just a trick of the light made worse by a young girl's imagination. The presence of my father's corpse can be more easily explained. My uncle and father shared a certain family resemblance. They were of the same build and colouring, though my uncle is of slighter frame and carries less flesh around his face. I can see why she might have taken him for my father when she saw him at a distance. This dull and superstitious girl has concocted a fantastical tale from her misreading of a scene of complete innocence and has been encouraged to embellish it by others content to see me burn in order to relieve me of my land. Call my uncle here and you will have the truth of it.'

'I may well do so, Miss Frazer.' Seton replied, taking care to conceal how impressed he had been by her reasoned and logical account. 'But what of the other testimony against you? I fear you will not find it so easy to rebut. What would you say to Mistress Gowrie? She is no dull-witted girl and wears no new and pretty dress or silver rings upon her fingers. She has accused you of bewitching her cattle and of stealing their milk for yourself. Will you also accuse her of conspiring to seize your land from you?'

'Twas not her who desired something of me, good sir. Twas her fat and lazy husband who spied upon me and plagued me with all manner of improper and objectionable propositions. She directs her spite at me rather than accept the unwelcome fact of her husband's inconstancy. She would see me burn to spare herself from the shame of knowing that her lewd and bawdy spouse would rather plough my fresh field uninvited than tend to her bare and arid pasture.'

Seton covered his mouth with his hand to hide his amusement at her turn of phrase. A ripple of muted laughter swept around the hall and Violet Frazer had wit enough to see the opportunity to sway those present in her favour and to move quickly enough to press her advantage home.

'My dear father was hardly in his grave when that fat pig began to pester and spy on me. I could scarcely leave the house without catching sight of him skulking in the trees or peering at me from behind the hedgerow. He would gaze at me openly and without apology whilst drooling and salivating like a hungry dog. He would often rattle at my door when he was full of ale and unsteady on his feet. Once, when I was foolish enough to unfasten my shutters, I saw him there, his trews around his ankles and his swollen manhood gripped tightly in his hand. When I scolded him and commanded him to go, he cried and begged me to come out and touch it. He promised me silver if I would only do it once. He grew angry when I refused him and threatened to strip me bare and ride me like the bitch I was. I did not sleep a wink that night but sat with my back against the door and my father's sword across my knees. Ask the minister if you do not believe me! I was so afeart I sought him out the following morning and begged for his protection. He was so disgusted he took the lecherous pig aside and chided him for his wanton and shameless behaviour.'

'Tis true.' Minister Logie confirmed with a grave expression on his face. 'He was mortified when I confronted him and gave an oath to restrain his sinful urges in the future.'

'Tis she who is the liar!' Jill Gowrie exploded, her cheeks scarlet and her brow knitted in murderous fury. 'She set her eyes upon another woman's husband and bewitched him. Robert is a good and honest man and would never have acted so disgracefully if not for the dirty whore's enchantment. When he refused her foul advances, she took revenge and made her charms to drain our cows of all of their milk. How can her two cows produce more milk than all four of ours without some diabolical intervention? Ask her to explain it! Let her deny her witchcraft now!'

'Tis easily explained within the laws of God and nature.' Violet replied, maintaining her restraint in the face of Mistress Gowrie's rage. 'Bob Gowrie is too fat and idle and too concerned with the contents of his trews to walk your beasts all the way to the common pasture. He sits on his arse and leaves them to graze in a paddock where the clover and grass have been chewed down to the earth. Go and see for yourself, Minister Cowper!' She pleaded, fixing her striking blue eyes on Seton. 'His poor cattle are so thin and underfed it is a wonder they have the strength to squeeze out a single drop of milk between them. You will find my own beasts in far better condition. They are fat and healthy and their udders are filled to bursting. Go and milk them yourself and you will see how quickly they fill my pails to overflowing. It is the result of hard work and good husbandry. No charms or sprites are magically stealing milk away.'

Seton was persuaded by her calm and logical reasoning and nodded his approval. He swept his eyes around the chamber and saw the same emotion reflected in the faces of the majority of the villagers. The Young Laird and Jill Gowrie glowered at him in resentment while poor Bob Gowrie was shame-faced and was sweating so profusely great rivers of it ran down his hot cheeks.

'Ask her about the rat!' Kincaid hissed at him from behind his hand. 'Ask her about how it sucks at her titty.'

'What of your familiar, Miss Frazer?' Seton asked in response to Kincaid's somewhat seedy prompting. 'A good woman has testified to seeing it in your company and the Young Laird himself has observed it in your vicinity on more than one occasion. What explanation would you offer for this?'

Violet Frazer knew she had given a good account of herself and had succeeded in swaying the opinion of those present in her favour. This knowledge caused her to grow in confidence and she smiled sweetly as she answered Seton's question.

'If only witches have rats in their homes and barns, then you will have to burn every last man, woman and child in the country. Even the Laird's barn is overrun with them. It is why has keeps his hounds there but even their jaws are not quick enough to kill them all. It would be more surprising if the Young Laird was able to enter the barn without disturbing at least one of the filthy and loathsome creatures.'

'Natural rats do not suckle at a witch's teat!' The Young Laird interrupted her. 'Do not be diverted by her lies! You have seen the Devil's mark on her! In God's name, I do beseech you, sir, let the pricker do his work and demonstrate the truth of these accusations without any further delay!'

'I have given no creature leave to suckle on my teats.' She declared, the directness of her gaze causing Seton's cheeks to redden. 'And Marion Hay has witnessed no such thing. She has not darkened my door since we laid my father in the ground and so could not have seen what she claims to have seen. Why would she visit out of courtesy if she knew me to be cursed and likely a witch? Would she not have been afraid for her mortal soul? Did she not know it is both a sin and a crime to consort with someone you know to be a witch? It makes no sense and the reason it makes no sense is because it is a lie. Look at her feet if you wish to discern her motive! I would wager that those fine black boots were bought with a gentleman's silver!'

'I will not suffer these baseless smears and insults a moment longer.' James Moncur barked, his face screwed up in anger. 'Prick the bitch and be done with it.'

'All in good time, good sir, all in good time.' Seton replied, taking great enjoyment from the frustration his words and even tone were causing the Young Laird. 'I have much to consider in determining how best to proceed. I will adjourn until the morrow and devote the afternoon and evening to weighing the testimony of the accusers against that of the accused.'

15

Seton swept from the hall the moment the adjournment was called. He ignored the hostile glares cast in his direction and paused only to ask Margaret to bring a plate of lunch to his chamber. She brought a tray up to him only a few minutes later and placed it on the small table at the far wall. He laughed when his eyes fell upon the meagre fare laid out for him. The crust of bread and the dry, hard cheese were accompanied by only a small cup of ale.

'I must have greatly displeased the Young Laird.' He declared with a shake of his head. 'I assume he has instructed you to deny us meat and claret?'

Margaret shuffled uncomfortably and wrung her hands out of nervousness. Seton shrugged his shoulders and patted her arm in a bid to put her at her ease.

'Violet Frazer is an impressive young woman, is she not? She gave a very good account of herself this day.'

'I have always liked her, good sir.' Margaret replied, casting a glance over her shoulder as if she feared her master might be lurking somewhere close enough to overhear her. ''Tis a sin for her to be mired in this foul business. The Old Laird would have put a stop to it if only he had the strength to do so.'

'Did she speak the truth about the Old Laird and her father?' Seton enquired. 'Did Laird Marlee really ride out in support of Queen Mary after she was forced to abdicate her throne?'

'Aye, that he did' Margaret responded before sighing and shaking her head. 'He was young and too headstrong to heed his father's advice. He answered the Earl of Argyll's call and went to defend Queen Mary from her enemies. We were told he fought bravely at the battle at Langside in spite of being sorely outnumbered. He stood his ground long enough to enable the Old Queen to make away but was cut down and left for dead. He would have died there if Violet's father had not borne him away on his shoulders. It was his great misfortune to be on the losing side. The Moncur family was near ruined when more than half their lands were confiscated as a punishment for his disloyalty.'

'But he still granted land to Frazer in return for his service?'

''Twas a matter of honour for him. He always said he would have gifted him three times as much ground if only the estate had not already been so greatly reduced. James has always resented him for losing so much of the family's holdings and doubly so for giving away more to a man who was merely a servant.'

Seton sipped at his ale and pondered what the housekeeper had told him. He found it hard to imagine the wizened and withered old man riding out with his sword in his hand.

'Why would such a fine, upstanding woman take to rolling in her own filth?' Seton asked when his thoughts returned to Violet Frazer. 'The dirty and stinking creature first brought before me stands in sharp contrast to the canny and capable girl who spoke so well this morning. Did she suffer a temporary loss of her faculties? I can think of no other explanation for it.'

'You are a man, so it is little wonder you do not understand it.' Margaret replied with a rueful smile. 'She did it to repulse those men sent to guard her. What do you think Bob Gowrie, William Kerr and several of the others would have done with her when they had her bound and defenceless for long hours in the dark of the night? They gaze at her like starving dogs eyeing a bone. Would you trust them to refuse to give in to their lust? Violet did not and so did all she could to repel them.'

Seton nodded to acknowledge the sense of her rationale but was prevented from pursuing the subject further when Kincaid burst in through the door in a state of agitation.

'Christ!' He cursed when Margaret had left them. 'The bastard near roasted me. My face is wet but I cannot tell if it is from my own sweat or from the spittle he showered me with. I thought he might strike me when I refused to put her to the tests in defiance of your instructions.'

'Then it is well the Young Laird will have time enough to recover his temper.'

'How so?' The pricker asked as he helped himself to the crust of bread on Seton's tray.

'Violet Frazer has given us enough to occupy ourselves for two days or more. I will send you to Alyth to fetch this uncle or cousin of hers. He is to be told nothing of what has occurred here so as to avoid tainting his testimony. Tell him only that the commission has summoned him here as a witness in his niece's trial. The Old Laird will either confirm his identity or prove Violet Frazer to be a liar. If he is who she claims him to be, the uncle will prove which account of the incident by the stream is the true one and which is the lie. While you are gone, I will go and inspect both the Frazer and the Gowrie cattle to determine whether sorcery or poor husbandry has been at work. I will also have the accused placed under constant supervision. It is known that familiar spirits rely on their mistresses for sustenance. If Marion Hay saw what she claims to have seen, starvation will force the vile creature to come and suckle at Violet's breast and we will have witnesses when it latches onto her. I intend to take my turn at the watch as she will be unable to deny her heresy if I have witnessed it with my own eyes.'

The pricker seized the cup up from Seton's tray and held it aloft in salute before draining what little was left of its bitter contents.

'Twas my lucky day when I encountered you, John Seton.' He declared with evident satisfaction. 'I would not have had the wit to extend these trails for half as long as you have done, but I will play my part as best as I am able. I will travel slowly towards Alyth and may tarry in Blairgowrie awhile. I hear there is an inn just by the bridge over the Ericht where a gentleman might buy himself the favours of a gypsy harlot in exchange for a shilling or two.'

'Take care not to empty your pockets there.' Seton cautioned him. 'And do not tarry overlong. I would have this business done before the Sabbath so we might take ourselves away with our purses heavy with silver.'

Kincaid nodded in agreement as he gnawed at the dry and unappetising cheese.

'You will need to have your wits about you while I am gone, my friend. The Young Laird is heartily sour and filled with gall. I see him glaring at you with daggers in his eyes. I would advise you to bar your chamber door whenever you retire. It would not surprise me if he was to seek to do you harm when he is deep in his cups and his temper is unrestrained.'

The Young Laird did not disturb his sleep. It was the young witch who filled his dreams and caused him to toss and turn the night away. The blueness of her eyes and the coyness of her smile haunted him like a ghost throughout the hours of darkness. He tried to picture his Elizabeth in his mind but the vision evaporated the moment his head sagged against his pillow and he tipped from wakefulness into sleep. When he awakened in the tangle of his blankets, he could not help but wonder if she had enchanted him. He shook his head to dispel the thought and prepared himself for the day ahead.

The announcement of his intentions was met with neither surprise nor protest. The villagers seemed to have anticipated the direction his investigations would take and several of them nodded in approval as he listed the measures he had decided upon. James Moncur remained impassive when he declared that Will Kincaid was to be sent to Alyth to fetch the witness but shook his head in irritation and disgust at the mention of cattle inspections and close supervision of the accused. Seton sighed in relief when the proceedings were drawn to a close without objection or delay. He saw Will Kincaid off on his brother-in-law's horse before setting out towards the village on foot.

The fresh morning air reinvigorated him and he strode purposefully through the village. A few people offered him reluctant greetings as he passed but most averted their eyes as if they had not seen him and a few made sudden and unsubtle changes of direction in order to avoid him altogether. Only Minister Logie and his wife stopped to engage him in conversation. They complimented him on the wisdom of his decisions and the rigour of his investigation but did so in tones so hushed they almost whispered the words. The poor pastor risked doing an injury to his own neck by constantly casting his eyes around him as if he feared being seen in his company. Their relief at bidding him farewell was so palpable Seton did not know whether he should laugh or take offence.

He found Bob Gowrie's modest holding a half-mile to the west of Marlee village. The cottage could not quite be described as dilapidated but there was an undeniable air of neglect about it. The rough wooden door hung askew at a drunken angle and the moss growing upon the roof was thicker than the uneven and weathered thatch beneath it. Grass and weeds grew through the floor of a broken cart left to rot a few paces to the left of the hovel. An area of rough pasture lay beyond the house but he could see no cattle upon it. An attempt had been made to build a wall of stones around it but the effort seemed to have been abandoned before even a quarter of it had been completed. Jill Gowrie appeared in the doorway, her arms folded tightly across her chest as she glowered down at him. He advanced towards her undaunted by her hostility and called out to enquire about the whereabouts of her cows. The slamming of the door was her only answer, the force of it sufficient to send rotten splinters flying into the air. Seton chuckled at her petulance and pressed on with his investigation.

It did not take him long to locate the beasts. The lack of grass and clover on the pastureland had sent them into an isolated stand of trees in search of cud to chew. Seton was no farmer but even he knew that leaves were no substitute for grass or hay. The lower branches of all the trees had already been stripped bare, forcing the poor animals to strain their necks upwards in an effort to reach the higher limbs. The cows were flea-ridden, emaciated and lethargic, just as Violet Frazer had described them to be. Some disease had taken hold of them, causing large patches of their skin to become hairless, scabby and dry like ash. Seton thought the condition might be infectious and so decided against any closer inspection lest he, too, be similarly afflicted.

He called out as he passed the Gowrie's crooked door but neither Bob Gowrie nor his scowling, torn-faced wife came out to return his greeting. He followed the road west for another good mile before coming in sight of the Frazer place. He paused to remove his coat, for the sun was now strong enough to cause him to sweat even though much of the journey had been completed in the shade of the trees lining the track. The contrast between the two holdings could hardly have been starker. The Frazer farm was as neat and ordered as the Gowrie place was neglected and untidy. The cottage was in a good condition, its door and shutters hanging straight on their hinges and its thatch even and free of moss. A path of rough flagstones had been laid before the doorstep and a vegetable garden planted away to the right. The stone walls and wooden fencing to the rear of the property were upright and well-maintained and there was evidence of recent repairs.

Seton found the two cows in a field bordered by a wide and meandering stream. Even at a distance, he could see that they were fat and healthy as they chomped happily at the meadow's rich, green grass. He was distracted from his examination of their heavy and swollen udders when he caught sight of a young girl splashing through the water with a wooden bucket gripped in each of her hands. She sang as she came but halted and fell to sudden silence when her eyes fell upon him. Seton removed his father-in-law's wide-brimmed hat so he would appear less threatening and called her forward as pleasantly as he was able.

'Come, child. See to the beasts! I fear their udders will burst if you do not relieve them of their milk.'

The girl was perhaps a year away from womanhood and wore the surly expression common to children of that age. She eyed him with suspicion for a few moments longer before the urgency of her task persuaded her to advance. She came on cautiously, her frown deepening the closer she came to him.

'Do not let me divert you from your task.' Seton encouraged her with a smile. 'Violet Frazer bade me come here to see what good milkers she has.'

'I know who you are.' The girl snapped, her tone both hostile and wary. 'My father farms the land across the stream and sends me to milk Violet's cows so they will not sicken while she is away. If left too long, they would die a slow and painful death no good beast deserves.'

The girl then dropped to her haunches beside the nearest cow and began to milk it. Her fingers gripped its teats with an expertise born of long practice and sent a steady stream of milk squirting into her pail. Seton watched with fascination as she fell into a steady rhythm, her cheek pressed hard against the animal's flank.

'Are you not afraid you will come to harm tending to a witch's beasts?' He asked her out of curiosity.

'My father would not send me if he believed a word of it!' She snorted. 'We have known Violet all of our lives and know she is no witch. If she is guilty of anything, it is of being stubborn and wilful in refusing the Young Laird's offer for her father's land. A woman cannot manage alone and she should have taken the silver, though the price was low, and used it to attract a husband to look after her. My father warned her of the folly of showing defiance to our betters but she refused to pay him heed. Now she suffers for it.'

Seton did not press her further but watched in silence as she drained the cow of its milk. The beast lowed softly while she worked as though it thanked her for relieving its bloated udders.

'May I taste the milk?' Seton asked when the girl had almost filled the pale. 'I would like to test its quality.'

The girl rose stiffly to her feet and gestured towards the pail with cupped hands.

'By God, it is hot!' Seton laughed when he dipped his fingers into the liquid.

A ghost of a smile flickered on her lips for the briefest of moments before her more natural sullen expression returned once again. Seton then lifted his cupped hands to his lips and drank the milk contained within them.

'It is so thick and creamy.' He declared. 'It sits so heavily in my belly I doubt I will have need of bread and cheese for lunch.'

The girl gave no response for she had already picked her other bucket up and was marching resolutely towards the second of Violet Frazer's beasts.

16

Seton considered it to be a mercy when there was neither sight nor sound of the Young Laird when he returned to Marlee House in the middle of the afternoon. He had no desire to suffer his brooding malevolence without Will Kincaid at his side and so shut himself away in his chamber as soon as he was able. He intended to take his turn at watching Violet Frazer through the hours of darkness and so took to his bed so he would be rested when darkness fell. Sleep eluded him though he was tired and footsore after covering so many miles of country road in the summer heat. The house creaked and cracked even in the absence of other occupants and this lent an air of oppression to the place.

Rather than dozing to restore his strength, Seton found himself fretting and worrying about matters both here and back home in Edinburgh. His fear of being exposed was his greatest anxiety and he tried to comfort himself by reasoning that the greater part of their deception was now behind them. If he could bear a few more days of mental torment, he could leave Marlee House behind and return to Edinburgh with his pockets full and his prospects much improved. This hope prompted him to daydream about the coming reunion with his Elizabeth. He prayed to God to grant him the restoration of the relationship they had enjoyed before the prospect of easy riches had lured him away to Bordeaux and onto ruination. He rehearsed the words he would speak, the apologies he would offer and the promises he would make when he was alone with her again. He was certain he could charm her and talk her around if only he was given the opportunity to do so.

He also indulged himself in fantasies of throwing handfuls of silver at the feet of the dreaded Flesher and his overbearing father-in-law as they gaped at him in astonishment. The thought of such a triumph seemed a handsome reward for suffering only a few more days of worry and anguish. This happy reverie served to raise his spirits by the time the light shining through the cracks in the shutters faded and began to turn to darkness.

Margaret fussed around him like a mother hen when he descended to the kitchen. The Young Laird's absence freed her from his strictures and allowed her to be more generous with both the quantity and the quality of the food and drink she laid before him. Thick slices of succulent venison were washed down with several goblets of the Old Laird's favourite claret.

'Tis better that you have the enjoyment of it.' She chirped happily. 'Now the Laird no longer has the stomach for anything stronger than milk or water.'

Seton had to protest and wave her away when he was stuffed full and his trews grew uncomfortably tight at the waist. He even refused the offer of a last glass of claret lest it cause him to become so inebriated he would be rendered incapable of staying alert for the duration of his watch. It took a great effort to persuade her to stop her fussing and provide him with a lantern to light his way to the barn housing all three of the accused.

He was glad of his cloak when he stepped outside, for the heat of the day had been replaced by an almost wintry chill since the setting of the sun. He shivered a little as he crossed the yard but was grateful for the cool night air as it cleared a head made thick by too much food and drink. A dim light at the far end of the barn's dark interior guided him to the side of the young man watching over Violet Frazer as she slept on the straw. He had thought the lad to be asleep as he approached but he rose wearily to his feet at the sound of Seton's footsteps and yawned as he stretched to relieve the stiffness in his back. He grunted and shook his head when Seton asked if he had anything to report.

'Not so much as a mouse, sir.' The youth replied as he struggled to stifle another yawn. 'I would have welcomed some excitement to keep me alert but there was none to be had. If you had taken longer to relieve me, you would likely have found me fast asleep on my stool. Try pacing if your eyelids grow heavy, good sir. It helps for a while.'

He then vacated his stool, picked up his lantern and left Seton to his duty.

He settled himself on the stool, its surface still warm from its previous occupant's buttocks. The barn was not as silent as he had expected it to be. The heavy wooden beams and rough timber boards creaked and cracked constantly as they cooled and were gently buffeted by the light wind. Unseen livestock shuffled in their stalls, smaller creatures skittered through the straw in search of some morsel to gnaw upon and birds perched high above would periodically flap their wings and squawk in alarm at some invisible predator. Violet Frazer slept on through all of this, her breathing deep and regular in spite of the discomfort of having her hands and feet bound tight. These ropes were secured to another tethering her to a beam above her head. He watched her for a while and could not help but admire her beauty. The dim and flickering light did not diminish the redness of her hair or the fullness of her lips and the worn and shapeless dress did nothing to disguise her ample figure. He dreamed of her when his head grew heavy and he lost the struggle to stop his eyes from closing.

He came back to wakefulness with a start and then jerked backwards in fright when he found her face only inches away from his own.

'Would you see me burn, good sir?' She whispered, her lips so close to him he felt her breath upon his cheek. 'You must know that all testimony against me is false. I am guilty only of refusing to submit to one man's lust and to the greed of another.'

Seton's heart hammered in his chest but he could not bring himself to tear his eyes away from hers.

'The evidence against you lacks substance.' He stammered, still trying to gather his wits. 'That much I will admit. But, as with the other women, the truth of it will likely have to be proved by the tests. If witch you be, the waters and the bodkin will condemn you to the flames. If the waters accept you and the bodkin makes you bleed, no man will be able to deny your innocence.'

'You would place your faith in the pricker then?' She demanded with a bitter laugh. 'I took you to be a wiser man than that.'

'Will is a good man and is highly skilled in his craft.' Seton protested. 'His spike exposed and condemned near a hundred fiends in Glasgow. Did you not see it for yourself when Agnes Nevie and Elspet Leyis were tested? No good and honest woman could feel no pain and shed no blood when pierced by such a long and vicious spike. I saw it at close quarters and knew it to be a diabolical and unnatural thing.'

Violet Frazer threw her head back and laughed loud enough to set the roosting birds above their heads to flapping on their perches.

'You really did not see it?' She demanded, shaking her head in disbelief and genuine amusement. 'I can scarce believe you were fool enough to be taken in by such low cunning.'

'I am no fool!' He snapped back, his cheeks flushing with anger at her mockery. 'I watched with my own eyes as their flesh was pierced without effect. My skin crawled to be in such close proximity to Satan's works.'

'Would you blame Satan for making you gullible enough to be taken in by a simple conjurer's trick?' She demanded, her teeth flashing in the lantern's light. 'No flesh was broken! The pricker brandished his spike and tapped it against the table to show its strength. He then poked and prodded those poor women to make them squeal and so convince you of the sharpness of his tool. Then, as he approached the Devil's mark, he placed the true bodkin back into his pocket and misdirected the lot of you by circling around to the far side of the table. He then drew a spike from his other pocket and jabbed at the women to no effect. Twas not a true bodkin he employed. Twas a fake with a hollow handle to allow the needle to retract harmlessly when he pressed it against their flesh. By such foul trickery, he has sent innocent women to their pyres and will condemn us to share their fate if you lack the courage to stop him. You know in your heart he is rotten to his very core. You may convince yourself he is here for silver coin but your conscience knows he is not. He revels in the humiliation and suffering of women and you unwittingly aid him in his perversion.'

'I do not believe it.' Seton protested, though he could not stop himself from recalling how odd the pricker's theatrical performance had seemed to him when he first witnessed it.

'Then check his coat pockets when he returns here with my uncle.' She demanded. 'I guarantee you will find a bodkin in each of his pockets. One true and one false!'

Violet then stretched her hand out towards him, her fingers surprisingly slim and delicate for someone accustomed to farm work. He knew something was amiss but could not immediately discern the source of his unease. His eyes widened when he realised her wrists were no longer bound, the tight knots somehow unpicked and the ropes cast aside. A small blue spark jumped between them just as her fingertips brushed against the back of his hand. He recoiled in fright, almost tripping over the stool in his haste to escape her grasp.

'Do not dare to bewitch me!' He growled at her, his heart thundering in his chest. 'I will not be drawn into your thrall. You will burn if you turn your sorcery upon me!'

Violet did not fly at him as he feared but instead laughed, shook her head and wagged her finger at him like a mother scolding her son.

'I may well burn, John Seton, but I will likely live long enough to see you hang. One touch was enough for me to know you are neither minister nor witchfinder. The severest of punishments are reserved for imposters such as you and your foul and black-toothed accomplice.'

'How dare you accuse me so?' Seton raged, though his heart had near seized in his chest on hearing his name from her lips.

'I dare because I see you for what you are. If you and your false commission should condemn any one of us to death, then know I will not hesitate to publicly denounce you and expose you for your sins. You have reached a fork in the road and must now choose which path to follow. If your choice is the righteous and honourable one, I swear that you will be well rewarded for it. If you give in to the weakness at the heart of you, I know you will suffer for it. Flames consume but they also burn away the old so that the new may flourish. Think of that while you sleep your watch away!'

The barn was in darkness when Seton jerked back into consciousness amongst the straw and dirt of its floor. He was disoriented and had to force himself to take deep breaths to control the feeling of panic swelling in his chest. The early morning light shone dimly through the cracks between the rough planking of the barn walls. He was able to make out vague shapes in the shadowed gloom as his eyes adjusted to the murk. The wooden stool lay on its side to his left and the lantern stood on the earth to his right, the flame of its candle having guttered out long hours past. Violet Frazer lay asleep in her stall, her face angelic, her breathing deep and steady and her hands bound tightly in front of her. He rubbed at his face in an attempt to clear his head and rouse himself to wakefulness. He racked his brain in an effort to determine whether the disconcerting encounter with the accused had been real or merely a dream fuelled by claret and a stomach overfilled with venison. He decided to put it down to a troubled sleep but could not quite shake off the feeling of unease that soured his stomach and made his shoulders tight with tension.

The sound of distant voices brought him to his feet and he set about righting the stool and brushing the straw and dust from his clothes. He turned when the barn door creaked open and lifted his hand in greeting to the blacksmith.

'Good morning, William.' He called out. 'I trust you slept well.'

'Tolerably well, good sir. 'The blacksmith replied as he doffed his dirty woollen cap. 'Did you have company in the night or was your watch undisturbed?'

'It was an unremarkable night, free of any diabolical visitations, thank God.' Seton replied, forcing himself to seem cheerful. 'I pray your own watch will be similarly uneventful.'

Margaret greeted him the moment he entered the hall and ushered him towards the table where she had laid out a bowl of porridge and a small jug of thick cream.

'Well?' She demanded when he had seated himself. 'How many demons came to her while you watched over her? None, I would wager.'

'Then you would be right, Margaret. Nothing came to trouble either of us.'

Seton had no real appetite but decided to try the porridge and cream in the hope of settling his churning stomach. He froze as he reached for the jug. The small red mark on the back of his hand was in the very spot where Violet Frazer had touched him with her fingertips. He scrubbed at it with the palm of his hand but could not rub it away.

17

The porridge did nothing to ease Seton's guts but sat there as hard and heavy as a stone. A rising panic sent him rushing for the sanctuary of his chamber and, once safe within its confines, he jammed a chair against the door to bar the way should anyone come with the intention of seizing hold of him. The day passed by with agonising slowness, each hour a torment of fear, paranoia and indecision. His head spun wildly from one extreme to the other, his ability to order his thoughts disrupted by his mental torment. Had he dreamed the encounter with the witch or had she employed some fiendish power to read his mind and so discern his true identity? He succeeded in convincing himself it was a dream and berated himself for his stupidity and superstition. It stood to reason that the girl was not capable of releasing herself from ropes pulled tight by the hands of men strengthened by years of hard manual labour. He laughed at his own foolishness and breathed more easily until his eyes were once more drawn back to the small blemish on the back of his left hand. Was it a mere flea bite or clear and physical proof of vile sorcery?

This internal battle raged throughout the afternoon, each of the opposing arguments gaining temporary ascendancy before being forced into retreat when a rival premise seemed to strengthen and erode its competitor's potency. He packed and unpacked his bags three times or more, once carrying them as far as the door before dropping them to the floor. The desire to be away from Marlee House and far from the risk of discovery was tempered by thoughts of the silver still owed to him and by some sense of loyalty to his companion. The lure of open countryside was intensified by the oppressive and claustrophobic atmosphere of the dark, creaking and foreboding house.

He leapt up in fright when knuckles were rapped gently against his door just as the skies had begun to darken. Visions of men lying silently in wait for him on the landing sent him to the shutters with the intention of throwing them open and jumping down to make his escape. He could have wept with relief when the housekeeper called out to him.

'I have brought a tray for you, good minister. You cannot work away at your parchments with nothing to sustain you. I have beef with onions, turnip, fresh-baked bread and more of the Old Laird's claret!'

'I give thanks to you, Margaret.' Seton declared when he had removed the chair and pulled the door open. 'I was so absorbed in my work all thoughts of food and drink were pushed from my mind. What a feast you have prepared for me!'

'The Young Laird is still away, so I am free of his restrictions.' Her eyes then widened in shock and concern. 'In God's name, sir, but you are as pale as death! Do you sicken?'

'I am just tired and hungry, Margaret.' He reassured her, forcing a thin smile onto his lips in a bid to allay her concerns. 'I did not sleep at all last night and have been so engrossed in my work I neglected to take some rest this afternoon.'

She fussed and fretted around him for a few moments longer and then left him to his meal. The aroma of roasted beef and onions set him to salivating and he fell upon the feast with great enthusiasm. He cleared his plate and consumed half the jug of claret within moments of Margaret leaving him. The effect of the beef and wine was immediate after a long day spent in a state of great agitation. Seton's eyelids grew heavy and he struggled to stop them from closing. He stumbled towards the bed and fell into a deep sleep the moment his head hit the pillow.

He was ripped from his restful and dreamless unconsciousness by rough fingers grasping at his shoulder. He hit out in confusion and terror, his fist connecting hard with flesh and bone in the dim light of a lantern.

'Christ, John!' Will Kincaid hissed at him, rubbing his right bicep with his left hand. 'Stop your screeching! You will have the whole house up with your insanity!'

Seton took a deep breath to steady himself and patted at his chest to still his racing heart.

'Christ, Will! You frightened me half to death! Why would you creep up on a man asleep in his bed?'

'Creep up on you? You were snoring so hard a whole army could have marched up those stairs and you would have heard nothing of it. Come! You must rouse yourself. We have much to discuss in the few hours left to us before dawn.'

Seton yawned and stretched his shoulders in a bid to relieve their stiffness.

'I feared you would tarry in Blairgowrie for much longer. Surely, you did not run through your silver so quickly?'

Kincaid shook his head and rolled his eyes as he examined the contents of the claret jug.

'I spent three shillings on ale and whores but extracted little pleasure from either.' He confided in a whisper. 'I had a full tankard in one hand and a little dark-haired beauty in the other when a fat and loud-mouthed merchant strode into the tavern with such arrogance it was as if he owned the place. He was a braggart and so full of his own importance it set my teeth on edge. You will have met his kind before. The inns of Edinburgh are always filled to the brim with such swaggering blowhards. They make a pretence of conversing with one person but are intent on making all present their audience whether they will it or not. His voice was so loud and piercing I did not miss a single word as he boasted of the success of a lucrative trip to Glasgow. I was sorely irked by his bragging and was about to tell him to pipe down when he shared news of such dire consequence it caused my heart to stop in my chest.' The pricker then paused to drink from the jug as if to console himself.

'What news?' Seton demanded, his stomach once more churning in dread.

'It seems that my master, John Cowper, has been brought close to ruin by his enemies within the clergy. All efforts to suppress news of the Great Witch of Balwearie's false testimony have come to naught. The hard-faced harridan who has made public the witch's confession has ignored all threats and attempts to silence her. Widow Walker has been dragged before the Presbytery three times or more and ordered to desist from blaming the minister for the executions of those innocents who were falsely condemned. She defies all threats of flogging and the scold's bridle and goes from street to street denouncing my master to all who will listen. The common Glasgow folk are incensed and are only kept from rioting by the presence of militia. Word of this has reached Edinburgh and has caused the Privy Council to withdraw all commission granted for the prosecution of witches.' Kincaid reached out and grasped Seton's wrist in his hand. 'We must complete our work, collect our silver and be away before word of this reaches this backwater!'

'Then let us steal away before the dawn!' Seton pleaded, the prospect of escape lifting a great weight from his shoulders. 'I will not be unhappy to be done with this. I fear we have already ridden our luck too far. We could be at Perth before first light if we depart without delay.'

'Would you run when there is still silver upon the table?' The pricker demanded, his grip tightening on Seton's wrist. 'Think of all you have endured this past week. Would you walk away from our expenses and the fees we would be due for overseeing the executions? It would take you more than three years to earn the same amount of coin in your father-in-law's putrid warehouse. Three years surrounded by stinking sheepskins instead of one last day here amongst these peasants?'

Seton's shoulders slumped forward in defeat. He could not refute the sense of Kincaid's argument but was downcast at having his imminent liberation snatched away from him just as it was tantalisingly within his reach. Kincaid sensed the change in him and moved quickly to press home his advantage.

'Then you must dispense with your examination of the accusations against the Frazer bitch as quickly as you are able. If I have her pricked and condemned before noon, I can press the villagers into service and have wood and peat stacked high around the stakes before darkness falls. We will collect what is owed to us the moment they have screamed their last and will take to horse with their pyres to light our way!'

'Will her uncle corroborate her account?' Seton demanded, his mind already turning to the task ahead of him.

'Aye!' The pricker replied with a scowl of disapproval. 'He will march in here at first light set on defending her. His account matches hers in every detail and I have no doubt it will be persuasive.'

'Then none of the accusations will stand. The Gowrie's cows were half-starved just as she claimed they were. The lack of milk is clearly due to laziness and neglect and not to witchcraft, spells or sorcery. Jill Gowrie has made her accusations out of bitterness, her spite driven by a jealous rage caused by her husband lusting after a younger and more comely wench. Neither is there any truth to the claims made by Marion Hay. No rat, whether natural or familiar, has approached her or attempted to suckle at her breast though she has been watched constantly since the moment of your departure. Mistress Hay seems to have been induced to utter these falsehoods in exchange for the Young Laird's silver pennies.'

'Good!' Kincaid nodded with satisfaction as he spoke. 'Then you can dismiss the testimony with all speed and move onto the tests. For my part, I will duck her with all the haste I can muster. The pricking will then reveal the truth and we can bring this business to an end.'

'Then let us drink to it! My nerves are sore in need of it.'

'I will leave you to drain the jug.' Kincaid replied before yawning hard enough to cause his jaw to crack. 'I am weary after so long in the saddle. We rode so hard my arse is bruised and tender. You must let me crawl into your bed and sleep awhile. I must have some little rest if I am to have my wits about me when dawn breaks upon us on our last day in this miserable place.'

Seton sipped at the claret and listened as the pricker's breathing grew deeper and slower as he fell into sleep. He waited until he began to snore and snuffle gently before edging silently towards the chair Kincaid had vacated only moments before. He had draped his coat across its back when he first entered the chamber. Seton kneeled down and cast a furtive glance in the pricker's direction to make sure he was truly unconscious. It took him a few moments of fumbling before his hand closed on the bodkin's smooth wooden handle in the coat's right-hand pocket. He tested the spike against his fingertip and was rewarded with a sharp prick and a single drop of blood. He replaced the tool just where he had found it and pulled at the folds of cloth to reveal the pocket on the opposite side. A sense of relief washed over him when long moments of blind groping revealed nothing more sinister than a crusted handkerchief, a length of string and a small pocket knife. He sent a silent prayer of thanks to God as he pushed those items back into the pocket. The interaction with Violet Frazer had been a figment of his fevered and claret-soaked imagination after all. He would have danced a jig from the joy of it if he had not still been on his knees.

A sharp pain caused him to wince as he withdrew his hand. Blood welled up from a ragged scratch across the base of his thumb and he sucked at it to stem the bleeding. He felt at the inside of the pocket with his fingers, wiggling them tentatively as he forced them into a tight fold in the cloth in search of whatever had caused his injury. He cursed when his fingertips encountered something smooth and hard. He grasped the object and pulled it from its hiding place. The second bodkin was almost identical to the first. The handle was smoother and less worn and the spike half an inch shorter, but the differences between them were so slight only a close and detailed inspection would have revealed them. Seton pressed his fingertip against the tip of the needle and found it was so blunt it was almost rounded. He pressed harder and felt his heart sink when the spike slid smoothly until it was fully concealed within the hollow handle.

'Bastard dog!' He hissed in temper at being so cruelly deceived.

The discovery caused his mind to reel and he knew he would enjoy no rest during the few hours left before dawn. He might blame and castigate Kincaid and his contemptible deception for condemning two, if not three, women to death, but he, too, had played his part and was equally responsible. It made no difference that he was guilty of stupidity rather than vile trickery. The pricker's appetite for humiliation and suffering would have gone unsatisfied if not for his connivance. This unwelcome realisation weighed heavily on his conscience and caused him to hold his head in his hands in despair.

On the bed behind him, the bastard dog slept on in his exhaustion, his slumber undisturbed.

18

Seton shook Kincaid awake at the first sounds of activity on the floor below. Hushed voices and boots shuffling on wooden boards heralded the arrival of villagers intent on witnessing the trial's conclusion. A few came in the hope of seeing sanity and justice restored, but most came for the excitement and spectacle of seeing a witch condemned and three consumed by the flames.

'The house will be packed to the rafters today.' Kincaid announced happily as he rubbed his hands over his clothes in a vain attempt to smooth the creases away and to brush off the dust and dirt of the road. 'People will travel from miles away for a burning and further still for the chance to gawp at a fair wench when she is stripped bare and shaved. I will confess to dreaming of it as I slept. The thought of Violet Frazer naked and spread-eagled before me is enough to quicken my heart. I near soiled my undergarments as I dreamed of it.' He winked at Seton as he shared this unsavoury confidence and smiled widely enough to reveal that his teeth were as corrupted with rot as his soul must surely be. 'Do your part quickly, John Seton! I will not be rushed when I prick her. I mean to linger for as long as I am able and so make the most of it. Lord knows when I will next be called upon to perform the tests and I doubt if I will ever again have such tender flesh to probe with my fingers.'

Seton felt such contempt for the pricker in that moment he was certain the wretch would be able to read it in his face. His fears proved to be mercifully groundless as Kincaid was oblivious to any change in the atmosphere between them and continued to blather on happily in his repulsive excitement.

'You must instruct the Young Laird to have his men stand ready.' Kincaid ordered him, wagging his finger like a stern minister delivering a rebuke from his pulpit. 'Her uncle is likely to protest when I strip her and will need to be restrained and removed from the hall. I have the sense he is no stranger to violence and have no desire to be the object of his fury.'

'Let us pack our bags and divide our silver now.' Seton suggested, deliberately ignoring the pricker's request. A beating was the least he deserved. 'I want away from here the moment we are done.'

'You speak sense.' He agreed as he attempted to untangle his greasy and matted hair. 'I will fetch my own bags and bring them here and you can look on as I count out our spoils.'

Seton watched closely while the rogue counted the silver as all trust in him had vanished with the discovery of the false bodkin. He had known in his heart that neither Agnes Nevie nor Elspet Leyis were witches but had allowed himself to be convinced of their guilt by this black-toothed fraudster. He was as furious with himself for being taken in as he was with Kincaid for deceiving him so completely.

'There!' Kincaid announced when he had finished with his counting. 'I have divided it all into two equal piles. I will let you choose which one to take if you doubt either my honesty or my accuracy.'

'I will take the one on the left after you have added the five shillings you promised me if I could fill a full day with my examination of Violet Frazer. You said you would pay it willingly.'

Kincaid did not dispute the point but added the five shillings to Seton's share without complaint or any sign of ill-humour.

'I will let you have another five if you are done with Violet Frazer before the sun reaches its highest point. It will be well worth the cost if it buys me an hour to linger over her delights.'

The hall was packed tight, just as Kincaid had predicted it would be. The crush of bodies and the heavy stench of bad breath and unwashed oxters was oppressive enough to bring Seton to a halt in the doorway. The sight of two hundred eyes gazing back at him was quite disconcerting and he had to draw a sharp breath to steel himself before advancing. The curious peasants shrank back from him as he came, some stepping on the feet of those behind in their haste to avoid obstructing the dread witchfinder and his pricker. One poor man cried out as his toes were crushed but pushed his hand hard against his mouth to muffle his squeals of pain out of fear of suffering Seton's displeasure.

Kincaid poked him in the ribs and jerked his head towards a tall man standing behind Violet Frazer on her stool. Seton did not need the pricker to confirm his identity. Alexander Frazer had placed his hand on his niece's shoulder in a silent declaration of his intention to protect her. Seton locked eyes with the grizzled shepherd and knew immediately why Kincaid was in fear of him. It was like gazing into the eyes of a deadly predator. His face was weathered and lean, his cheekbones jutting like blades against wind-lashed flesh and his eyes as cold and hard as shards of ice. Seton's stomach tightened, some instinct telling him he was in the presence of a creature capable of cold-blooded murder if the situation demanded it. The older man held himself with an uncommon stillness, but Seton suspected he was capable of exploding into violence in an instant. The Flesher had the same aura of calm detachment and held out the same dark promise of extreme cruelty and sudden, ferocious brutality.

The girl's gaze was free of malice and hostility but was somehow more discomfiting than that of her glowering uncle. Her pale blue eyes were wide and her expression earnest, but the faint smile upon her lips hinted at some shared secret. The threat of exposure was also there, though Seton could not tell if this was real or only a figment of his imagination.

'Let us bring these proceedings to order!' He declared with a confidence and authority he did not feel. 'I will begin by dealing with the accusations against Violet Frazer and will dispense with them with all speed.'

It took Kincaid long moments to realise the promised haste was not forthcoming. Seton did not cut to the chase as agreed but delivered a long monologue detailing each and every step of his investigation into the claims made in the testimony of Jill Gowrie and Marion Hay. The pricker confined himself to the occasional concerned glance while Seton was describing the poor state of repair of the Gowrie's cottage and informing the assembly of the presence of a broken and rotten cart on the land in front of it. He was even able to restrain himself while his companion reported on the condition of each of the Gowrie's cattle in turn and engaged in speculation as to what ailments each of them might be suffering from. He was no longer able to conceal his agitation when Seton dawdled overlong on his account of the walk between the Gowrie holding and the Frazer place. He began to fidget in his chair and tapped at Seton's ankle with the toe of his right boot to hurry him along in his recollection of the rich and creamy milk produced by the Frazer cows. Those gentle taps increased in force until he was kicking at Seton's ankle as he recounted the complete absence of rats in Violet Frazer's stall during the long hours of his night-time watch in the Old Laird's barn.

'The testimony of Jill Gowrie and Marion Hay must be dismissed on the basis of the minister's findings.' Kincaid announced when he could contain his impatience no longer. 'Let us call Alexander Frazer forward so we might hear his account of the meeting between him and Violet Frazer and ascertain the truth of the accusations made before this commission by young Mabel Lamb.'

'We must first establish whether he is who both he and his niece claim him to be.' Seton interjected in an attempt to thwart the pricker's efforts to hurry the proceedings along. 'I will hear not a word from him until his identity has been confirmed. We were told that he was known to the Old Laird in his youth. Let him now be taken upstairs so Laird Marlee might vouch for him from his sickbed.'

'Tis already done.' James Moncur gloated with a contemptuous smile. 'I took him to my father at first light. He recognised him almost immediately and spoke his name without being prompted. So, there is no need for you to dither and vacillate any further. Call the man forward and put him to question!'

Alexander Frazer stepped up to the prosecution table when he was commanded to do so and gave his oath to speak the truth and nothing but the truth before God. The Young Laird cursed audibly in disapproval when Seton invited the witness to share details of his background so the good citizens of Marlee could gain some insight into his character. The shepherd was no more eager than James Moncur to see the proceedings drawn out and frustrated Seton's ambitions by moving to directly address the matter at hand.

'I have known this girl since she was a babe in arms and can tell you there is not a shred of truth in any of the accusations made against her!' He growled, his words clear in spite of having been spoken through teeth gritted in barely suppressed fury. 'She is stubborn, like her father, and is wilful, like her mother, but that does not make a witch of her.'

'While your spirited defence of your niece is commendable, good sir, you must confine yourself to providing answers to my questions.' Seton scolded him. 'The purpose of this commission is to establish the truth and I will not be obstructed in my duty. If you lack the restraint to do as I command, I will have you removed forthwith. Is that clearly understood?'

The shepherd gave a curt nod in response, though Seton did notice that his fists were now clenched tightly at his sides.

'Then tell us of the day in question, Mister Frazer. Tell us how you came to be by the stream when Mabel Lamb happened upon you and was so terrorised she almost lost her wits.'

'I was away when my cousin, Violet's father, passed on. Lord Ogilvy tasked me with driving his sheep south so he might earn a better price for his mutton in the markets of Carlisle and Newcastle.

The burghers there took us for ignorant Scots and thought to cheat us by offering less than the beasts were worth. Tis often those of the highest rank who stoop to the lowest of tricks.' Frazer turned to glare at the Young Laird as he spoke and his lips twisted into a sneer. 'No kin of mine will be so easily extorted.'

Seton gestured at him to get on with his account.

'I was unwilling to bow down before those swindlers and so set course for Durham in search of an honest market for our flocks. Twas there I received word of my cousin's death. I turned my feet north the moment Lord Ogilvy's business was concluded and came directly here to Marlee to pay my respects and to see to Violet's welfare. I was exhausted and footsore when I found her by the stream and so lay down in the grass while she brought me water to drink.'

The shepherd then chuckled, his expression transforming into one of kindness and gentle amusement.

'How Violet laughed when she caught sight of the little girl spying on us from the trees. She squealed when I rose to my feet and ran off as fast as her little legs would carry her. I thought nothing more of it until Mister Kincaid came knocking at my door. Twas entirely innocent. I swear it before God and this commission.' The shepherd's smile then faded from his lips and his face darkened once again. 'I will also swear to defend my niece against anyone who dares to threaten her with false accusations of sorcery or attempts to steal her land away. Any man intent on doing her injury will find me in their path with my sword in my hand and malice in my heart. I have seven brothers, four sons and more than thirty cousins a day's ride away from here. Be sure they will come in haste and fury if you give them reason to so do!'

His words hung heavily in the air. All present knew they were fully meant and none doubted the threat was real and not empty, as most men's were.

'Tis a crime, Mister Frazer.' Seton informed him in an attempt to reassert his authority. 'To make such threats before a commission imbued with all of the authority of the Privy Council. I will allow it to pass on this occasion due to tempers being frayed. I would not be so understanding if the offence was to be repeated. We will adjourn awhile to allow you to recover yourself and to give these poor people the opportunity to take themselves outside to enjoy a breath of air.'

Kincaid followed Seton upstairs to his chamber and turned on him the moment he closed the door behind them.

'What in the name of God was that?' He demanded furiously. 'You could have dealt with all testimony in an hour or less but have wasted the whole morning to no good effect! How am I meant to duck and prick her and still have time enough to condemn and burn her before darkness falls?'

Seton was denied the opportunity to respond when the chamber door squealed open on its hinges and the Young Laird stepped into the room.

'I came to ask the self-same question.' He snapped in irritation. 'But Mister Kincaid seems to have saved me the trouble of articulating it for myself. What say you, Minister Cowper? Tell me how I have come to be insulted and threatened in my own home without you so much as raising a finger to prevent it! Explain why it is reasonable for you to drain my coffers only to allow proceedings to drag on interminably. Come! Let us delay no longer! Let us move to the pricking and be done with it. We have all seen the Devil's mark upon her neck. Do not vex me by insisting on the integrity of the legitimate procedure. Let Mister Kincaid be about his work so we might expose her foul nature for all to see!'

'Very well.' Seton conceded to the great surprise of both Kincaid and Moncur. 'I will give Mister Kincaid leave to proceed the moment you pay us all outstanding fees and expenses. I am tired of your complaints and will proceed more happily in the administration of justice when I am free of your material restraints. I mean to be away from here the moment the trials are concluded.'

Kincaid's face lit up in delight and he favoured Seton with a wink of approval, his faith in his companion restored by his deft manipulation of their paymaster.

'Let's prick the bitch!' He crowed with a wide grin on his face.

'Indeed.' Seton replied, his own smile containing none of the warmth of the pricker's.

19

'I hereby dismiss the testimony of all three of Violet Frazer's accusers in its entirety.' Seton announced solemnly when the proceedings were reconvened. 'My own investigations found no merit in the claims made by Marion Hay and Jill Gowrie and my questioning of Alexander Frazer served to corroborate Violet Frazer's account and so disprove Mabel Lamb's version of the meeting between uncle and niece beside the stream. In the absence of a confession, we will proceed directly to the pricking test. Mister Kincaid! Please be about your business.'

Kincaid hesitated, his glance switching from Alexander Frazer to Seton and then back again.

'Surely it would be best if you were to have him removed, good sir.' The pricker insisted. 'I must strip and shave her and I fear he will be unable to control himself and allow me to proceed in my duties unhindered.'

'You are right to be afeart, my black-toothed friend.' The shepherd muttered, his voice little more than a whisper. 'I will strip the flesh from your bones if you dare to lay a single finger upon her. You have my word on it.'

'Minister?' Kincaid pleaded, his eyes wide in panic. 'How can I be expected to proceed when he threatens me with violence? You must eject him, by force if it proves necessary!'

'Gentlemen.' Seton appealed to them both, his tone reasonable and intended to soothe. 'I see no need for any unpleasantness. The Devil's mark, if that is what it is, is plainly visible on the neck of the accused. The Young Laird was good enough to point it out to us earlier in the trial. We need not waste time in searching her further. Proceed, Mister Kincaid! Prick the mark so we might all bear witness to her guilt or to her innocence.'

Kincaid gazed back at him in confusion, a range of competing emotions reflected in his face. There was anger, exasperation and a trace of genuine hurt at being denied the pleasure of salivating over the delights of Violet Frazer's most intimate places. A great number of the villagers shared his disappointment and muttered indignantly when they realised they were not about to enjoy the salacious spectacle they had hoped for.

'Minister!' The pricker insisted, his frustration and petulance scarcely concealed. 'There may be other more prominent marks hidden in her private parts. We both know that is where they are most commonly concealed. I should conduct a careful and thorough inspection so we might locate and test the largest of them.'

'The one on her neck is more than large enough for the purposes of the test, Mister Kincaid. I doubt you will find a more promising blemish elsewhere. You should proceed without delay.'

'Very well!' The pricker snapped, his fury causing Seton such amusement he had to bite at the inside of his cheek to keep himself from smiling.

The pricker entered into the pricking ritual with far less vigour and showmanship than he had displayed when putting Elspet Leyis and Agnes Nevie to the test. He followed his well-worn procedure faithfully but was lethargic and peevish in its execution. His face was sour from being denied the opportunity to defile a maiden fair enough to cause his blood to pump and he cast murderous glances in Seton's direction as he worked. He held his bodkin aloft for all to see before stabbing it hard into the tabletop to demonstrate the strength of the short but vicious spike. The villagers gasped, as they were meant to do, but Kincaid's face registered no trace of satisfaction from the effect he had on the gawping peasants. He jabbed Violet Frazer in the ribs just below her breast, his eyes wary and fixed on Alexander Frazer lest he should react and explode into violence. The shepherd did not so much as blink when Violet squealed and hissed a curse at her tormentor.

'See!' Kincaid called out to the assembly. 'Uncorrupted flesh has no defence against the purity of the steel. When pierced, it will bleed and cause those so injured to call out in pain.'

A flick of his wrist sent the bodkin point into the back of Violet's hand. She jerked away from him in fright, a trickle of blood flowing from the puncture wound. Kincaid then ducked down and stabbed at her calf. She pulled away instinctively and so caused the pricker to miss his mark and scratch her foot instead. The ugly gash was not deep but blood flowed from it all along its length and dripped onto the wooden boards.

'See the effect of good steel on natural, unadulterated flesh!' Kincaid roared. 'Do we not bleed when our flesh is torn? Yes! We do bleed, just as the good Lord intended it. Only Satan's touch can make flesh impervious to such injury! Only flesh made foul by his black and twisted lips can resist the steel. Only witches are so marked when they swear their souls to him! Violet Frazer bears just such a mark upon her neck! Let us test it now and so reveal the darkness and corruption of her soul!'

Seton kept his eyes fixed upon Kincaid's hands as he spoke. The pricker slipped the bodkin deftly into his right pocket as he raved about flesh and steel. A look of confusion and panic crossed his face when he pushed his left hand into his pocket and fumbled around in the folds of cloth as if in search of some elusive object. Seton revelled in the spectacle of the deceiver falling prey to his deception. He suppressed a smile of satisfaction as he patted his own pocket and felt the weight and shape of the false bodkin against his fingers. Kincaid suddenly stood bolt upright and all colour drained from his face as he grasped the horror of what was unfolding. He turned slowly towards Seton with his teeth gritted hard and his face twisted in savage fury.

'Please proceed, Mister Kincaid.' Seton ordered him in as amiable and pleasant a tone as he could muster. 'Do not keep us in suspense! Let us see the darkness and corruption of her soul for ourselves.'

The pricker held his ground and glared back at him for so long he feared he might fly at him intent on doing him harm. He took some comfort from the presence of the shepherd, though he had no real reason to believe the fellow would come rushing to his aid. He knew he was safe when Kincaid's shoulders slumped forward in defeat and he reached into his right pocket to extract the true bodkin.

'Gentle now!' Alexander Frazer warned him when he turned towards his niece. 'Just a wee scratch. There's a good laddie!'

Kincaid was almost tender in his treatment of the girl. He brushed the hair from her neck with his fingers to reveal the blemish on her skin. He did not grasp the bodkin in his fist as he normally did but held it delicately between thumb and forefinger as he wielded it. Violet Fraser winced when he pressed the spike against her skin but did not cry out. The villagers all leaned forward when he pulled his implement away and strained their eyes in an effort to see what truth the steel had revealed. All there seemed to hold their breath until a single drop of blood ran down her neck like a crimson tear. Then all was uproar.

Seton ignored the growing cacophony though he was aware of voices calling out in relief and celebration and others raised in outrage and disappointment. Violet Frazer returned his gaze and gave him a nod of acknowledgement. He now knew their exchange in the barn was not the result of too much venison and claret. He waited for the tumult to subside before hammering his fist against the table to bring the proceedings back to order.

'In the name of God and King James and by the authority of the Privy Council!' He boomed as he rose to his feet. 'I declare Miss Violet Frazer to be innocent of all accusations made against her. I find her innocent of the charges of witchcraft, of consorting with the Devil and of giving sustenance to a familiar spirit. She is exonerated and is free to go without fear of persecution or impediment!'

'I must object in the strongest of terms!' The Young Laird protested, his face aghast and flushed red with anger. 'You did not adhere to the proper and lawful procedure. You prevented Mister Kincaid from carrying out a thorough examination. The witch must have a mark elsewhere on her person. Pray good minister, give him leave to search for it. She is a witch! I am certain of it.'

Alexander Frazer took a single pace forward but even that small action was sufficient to cause James Moncur to flinch back from him in fear of being assaulted.

'Did you no' hear the minister?' The shepherd barked. 'He just declared her innocent and so put her and all she holds beyond your reach. You will answer to me and mine if you are foolish enough to attempt to pursue her further.'

'The matter is closed.' Seton declared with finality. 'No proof of guilt was provided through testimony, confession or tests. The procedure is quite clear and a declaration of innocence was the only course left open to me. You are welcome to lay an appeal before the Privy Council if you so wish, but I would strongly counsel you against it, good sir. Tis likely they will prove less lenient than I when confronted with such flimsy testimony and so much clear evidence of bribery. You would do well to heed my advice and accept the loss of this case and of the land you so covet with some small measure of grace. It would be foolhardy to do otherwise.'

'I doubt you will persuade him, sir.' Kincaid interjected in a tone of bitterness. 'You should accept his judgment so we might make our preparations for the other two. If you set the villagers to collecting wood and peat without delay, the pyres will be high enough to light before darkness falls. Then you will at least have the consolation of having rid yourself of two of the witches who have so infected your estates. Give the order now, I beg of you, I will leave this place all the happier if I have seen the flames consume them and reduce their flesh and bones to smoking ash.'

The pricker's tongue flicked between his teeth as he awaited the Young Laird's response. Seton felt real hatred for him in that moment for the hunger in his eyes revealed the twisted perversity of his nature. Denied the pleasure of humiliating Violet Frazer, he now sought to satisfy his deviant appetites by feasting on the fear and torment of two women as they burned.

'If the two of you are so eager for more pricking, then I will not deny you the pleasure of it.' Seton seethed in temper, his heart hammering in his chest at the thought of what he was about to do. 'Bring the widow Leyis and the widow Nevie forward! I would have you prick them again to confirm their guilt before we commit them to the flames.'

'You should take care, Minister Cowper.' Kincaid warned him, each word loaded with menace. 'It would not do to exceed the authority of your commission before these good people. I would not like to see you so exposed.'

'I see no risk of exposure here, Mister Kincaid.' Seton shot back. 'I have full confidence in the authority granted to me by the Privy Council. Did you yourself not inform these people that it vested the full authority of both King James and the Privy Council in my person? I am sure you did when first we came. I intend to use those powers so justice might be done and be seen to be done by the good people now crammed into this chamber. Now, bring the widows forward and be about your work!'

With the outcome already certain, Kincaid did not linger over the tests as he had when he first administered them. He ushered Minister Logie's wife forward and instructed her to lift Agnes Nevie's skirts and pull her undergarments down. Seton looked away rather than witness her indignity anew but took comfort from the knowledge that such an outrage was of little consequence when her life was hanging in the balance. The widow was as oblivious to her surroundings as she had ever been but she gasped when Kincaid pricked her groin.

'Does she bleed?' Seton demanded of Mistress Logie.

'Aye, good sir.' She replied, nodding with relief and satisfaction. 'The needle has pierced her flesh and blood runs freely from the wound. Tis not the Devil's mark after all, praise God!'

The procedure was then repeated on Elspet Leyis. She had recovered somewhat after her ordeal but offered little resistance and shut her eyes tight in shame when Mistress Logie bared her privates so Kincaid could complete his test. She winced when he jabbed her with his spike and tears rolled down her cheeks when Mistress Logie held up a finger stained with blood in repudiation of the earlier test. The widow then reached out and clasped the pricker by his shoulder.

'My thanks to you, Mister Kincaid.' She said, some of her old strength and wilfulness evident in her voice. 'It has been a while since I had so much benefit from so small a prick!'

The pricker blushed as red as a bride on her wedding night and knocked her hand away in disgust. Elspet's laughter echoed back from the rafters until it was lost in the din of the villagers' hilarity. Kincaid shot a sullen glance in Seton's direction before pushing his way through the throng on his way to the stairs. Seton allowed himself a smile of amusement at the rogue's discomfort. He thought it fitting for him to suffer some small humiliation given his willingness to subject so many poor women to public shame and degradation. He would have dwelled on this happy thought for much longer if it had not been for his reluctance to leave Will Kincaid alone upstairs with his bags and his silver. He banged his fist against the table and called for silence. He did not wait for the chatter to die away entirely before delivering his hurried pronouncement.

'In the name of God and good King James and by the authority of the Privy Council, I declare Elspet Leyis, Agnes Nevie and Violet Frazer to be innocent of all charges against them. I find them innocent of the charges of witchcraft, of sorcery, of the casting of spells and the making charms, of consorting with the Devil and of giving sustenance to familiar spirits. All three are hereby exonerated and are free to go without fear of further persecution or of unjust impediment!' He then paused and looked around the packed chamber. 'This commission is now concluded! Please clear the room!'

He did not wait for any response but made immediately for the stairs, ignoring the pleas of both Minister Logie and the Young Laird as they clutched at his sleeve and begged for a moment of his attention.

20

The pricker froze when Seton burst in through the chamber door and caught him in the act of tipping the contents of his bag onto the unmade bed.

'You would steal from me, you ill-bred villain?' Seton hissed at him. 'Are you so low and dishonourable you would add that sin to all others you have done to me?'

'Treacherous, snivelling dog!' Kincaid seethed as he rose to his feet, his teeth bared in anger. 'You have the check to point the finger at me after all I have done for you. I should have expected no less from such a weak and pathetic fraudster. I held you in contempt when I first encountered you in that low, Grassmarket tavern. It sickened me to be in the company of a wretch so wrapped up in self-pity he whined and sobbed like a broken and miserable bitch and bemoaned the consequences of a mess entirely of his own making. I curse myself for my own weakness in not leaving you to your fate! How often did I have to carry you when you grew faint-hearted and lost all courage?

How much silver would have been lost to us if I had been half as feeble and spineless as you? And how have you repaid me for saving you from your own stupidity and recklessness? With trickery and betrayal! You deserve to rot in your father-in-law's stinking warehouse with your wife kept far from you. She would likely thank me for sparing her from the life of disappointment you would surely condemn her to!'

'To hell with you!' Seton growled, his fists clenched at his sides. 'I curse the day fate brought me into your company! I hold myself to blame for not sensing the rottenness and corruption of your soul. I knew you to be repulsive at my first sight of you but my senses were clouded by the promise of easy silver and the prospect of discharging my debts. I allowed myself to be blinded but now I see you clearly for the foul and hideous creature you are. Your fury has nothing to do with the few shillings we might have lost or won. You rage at me because I have deprived you of the sick and perverted pleasure of seeing those poor and innocent women scream and struggle as the flames consumed them. I will be forever shamed by my failure to strike you down for your deviance when you drooled and slobbered over the nakedness of those first two women. My only consolation is in knowing I denied you the depraved delight of so defiling the third. Tis only my cowardice and fear of the noose that keeps me from exposing your crimes and seeing you condemned to hang from the gibbet as you surely deserve!'

'Tis you who will hang, you gutless pig.' Kincaid sneered, the bodkin suddenly in his hand. 'I will ride directly to Edinburgh and see to it that the Privy Council learns of all you did here. They will have no shortage of witnesses willing to testify against you. The word of the Young Laird alone will be enough to put a rope around your miserable and worthless neck. I have no doubt he will take to his horse the moment he is summoned, such is his hatred for you. My only regret is that I will be far away and will be denied the joy of seeing you spasm and jerk as the life is choked from you.'

'Imbecile!' Seton cried out in disbelief. 'You will be strung up at my side if you are stupid enough to expose me. Do you think they will not prevail upon me to reveal the identity of my accomplice? Do you imagine I would resist their torture out of loyalty to the worthless and repulsive rogue who betrayed me?'

'Tis you who is the imbecile! Only a thick-headed fool would share his name with a stranger before embarking on such a risky and fraudulent enterprise. I know you, John Seton. I know your history, I know the names of your wife and your in-laws, I know the address of your residence in Edinburgh and I know the details of all your dealings in Bordeaux and Leith! I know more than enough to condemn you, while you know nothing of me.'

'By Christ, you are even more deluded than I thought.' Seton spluttered in incredulity. 'I know your name and your history with John Cowper in

Glasgow. I doubt it would take long to track you down.'

'They might well be able to locate Will Kincaid.' The pricker retorted with a sly and self-satisfied grin. 'Though the trail would lead them to a kirkyard in Johnstone and the gravestone I took the name from. I doubt they will be able to hang him as he has been in the ground for so long they are unlikely to find enough sinew left to hold his bones together.'

'Ha!' Seton shouted out in triumph. 'You are not half as cunning as you suppose yourself to be. When your lips were made loose by tavern ale, you spoke of your father and your lord and master down by Stirling. Did you forget the tale you told me by the fireside in the Black Swan? You sold your master's mutton and kept the proceeds for yourself. It would take no more than a day or two to find both father and master and so discover your true identity.'

'Then it is well I lied to you. You will find no trace of me in Stirlingshire nor of any master mourning the loss of mutton or coin. You might look down on me as one of lower rank but you have not brains enough to come close to outwitting me. I will have my revenge on you and take myself away with impunity.'

'Bastard dog!' Seton spat, his heart now thundering in his chest. 'You would betray me out of spite?'

'Tis no more than you deserve, John Seton. Now, let me pass if you do not want to feel the point of my spike!'

Kincaid advanced with menace but froze in his tracks, his eyes wide in fright and fixed on the doorway at Seton's back. John turned his head slowly and let out a sigh of frustration when he saw James Moncur glowering back at him, his brows furrowed and his expression grave. Seton and Kincaid exchanged a glance, both of them wondering how much the Young Laird had heard of their exchange.

'Did you think to steal away weighed down by my silver when you failed to condemn a single one of these bitches?' Moncur demanded of them. 'Tis reasonable for me to demand the return of half of what I have paid given the poor quality of your work. Come! Let me have it so we might avoid any unnecessary unpleasantness!'

Kincaid seemed paralysed with fear and indecision and gaped helplessly at their host. Seton searched the young noble's face but could find nothing to indicate whether their deceit had been exposed or if his antagonism was fired only by the bitterness of a man denied the outcome he desired. He chose to do what he did best and risked all on his ability to employ bluff and bluster to good effect.

'I would counsel you against making such threats and demands of officers commissioned by the Privy Council, good sir.' He stated calmly, pulling himself to his full height to lend authority to his words. 'Such base extortion is a crime and, as such, is beneath your dignity. You must accept my judgement with good grace, no matter how much it may vex you.'

'It does vex me, minister! It vexes me greatly!' The Young Laird retorted, punctuating his words by jabbing his forefinger hard into Seton's shoulder. 'I am so vexed I will ride for Edinburgh the moment my silver is returned to me. I mean to seek out the honourable Lords of the Privy Council and bid them to overturn the travesty of justice you have just inflicted upon me and the good people of this parish. I doubt they will be much impressed by your rank incompetence and your unwillingness to rid us of those foul and diabolical hags. You will be censured, I will make sure of it.'

Seton felt almost light-headed with relief, though his heart still raced from coming so close to having his crimes exposed. It was beyond him how James Moncur had not heard more of his argument with Kincaid as he made his way upstairs. He did not dwell on it but sent a silent prayer of thanks to God above.

'Such a course would be most unwise, good sir.' He drawled when he had composed himself and his confidence was fully restored. 'I would advise you against holding these trials up to the scrutiny of any higher authority. They would likely uncover many unpalatable truths and be moved to take punitive action against your good self and those close to you.'

'Do not think to threaten me, sir. They will find nothing to reproach me with, though I cannot say the same for you and your low-born companion.'

'Very well!' Seton replied, nodding as he held Moncur's gaze. 'Then I, too, will take to horse and ride for Edinburgh to lay all of my concerns before them. I had thought to let them pass but would abandon all thoughts of leniency if my hand was to be forced.'

'What damned concerns?' The Young Laird barked, a hint of nervousness now entering his tone.

'Let me see.' Seton trilled, his voice light and calm as he held up each of his fingers in turn as he counted off the offences. 'You subjected all three of the accused to torture without first seeking the authority to do so. The Privy Council frowns upon such lawless barbarity, especially if it does not lead to a finding of guilt. I need only present the accused to the Council as proof of your cruelty. Their melted flesh, deformed feet and torn nails will surely condemn you.'

'Then I will admit to being overzealous in doing the Lord's work and seek their pardon. They will have little concern for the suffering of such peasant stock.'

Seton shook his head though he knew Moncur's assumption was likely correct.

'You submitted a false confession in evidence when Agnes Nevie was incapable of making such an admission and was ignorant of the terms you yourself instructed Minister Logie to write down. You attempted the same trick with Elspet Leyis and would have done the same with Violet Frazer if she had lacked the strength to defy you.'

'You think they will take the word of these women over my own? You clutch at straws, Cowper. I will take my chances.'

'Then there is the evidence of bribery.' Seton continued, the sight of a vein pulsing furiously at the corner of Moncur's left eye giving him the encouragement to press on. 'Was there a single witness who did not benefit from your largesse? A new dress for Mabel Lamb, fine boots for Marion Hay and a widow's land and her hovel for the blacksmith's family. All others who testified were driven by spite, their transparent lies so feeble they crumbled under the most gentle and tentative of questioning. How would they fare when faced by the honourable Lords of the Privy Council? Would you stake your reputation on their ability to withstand such close examination? I doubt if any one of them could last a full minute before breaking down and confessing to lying at your behest!'

'They will do as I bid them.' Moncur insisted, though his tone was less forceful and his stance more stooped and less confident than before. 'They would not dare to betray me! Their livelihoods depend on it!'

'And how would you fare if they were to examine your motives? What judgement would they make of your character when told of your attempts to steal the inheritance of a young and fatherless girl? What would they think of a man low enough to condemn her to death in order to seize lands granted in perpetuity by his own father? They would think you a villain and Alexander Frazer would confirm it. They might dismiss the word of a slip of a girl but he was most upright and impressive, would you not say? Lord

Ogilvy of Airlie seemed to hold him in sufficient esteem to trust him with the sale of his livestock and the handling of the proceeds. The Privy Councillors would undoubtedly listen to him if such a noble lord was to vouch for his character. I think they would find him persuasive.'

James Moncur did not respond and his eyes blinked rapidly as if he was calculating the odds of success or failure.

'Then there would the prosecution of your own tenants, servants and neighbours.' Seton shrugged his shoulders nonchalantly as if such a thing was of little consequence. 'They might hang but are more likely to be flogged, branded or banished from this parish. I doubt you would be much concerned by such trifling matters but you should think of what it would cost you in lost income.'

'And what charges would be made against them to merit such punishment?'

'Lying before an appointed commissioner is a serious offence and all but one of your witnesses can be shown to have given false testimony. Then there is the capital offence of knowingly consorting with a witch. Your own tenant, Douglas Crichton, admitted to seeking the assistance of Elspet Leyis when he lost his father's good hunting knife. She said she would invoke the fairy folk to search the verges of the road between here and Perth and he promised her silver in return for her services. I have seen others strung up for much less. Then you must consider how many of Marlee's inhabitants parted with coin for the charms manufactured by Agnes Nevie at her fireside and how many farmers and parents called on her when their beasts or their children were sick and in need of her healing powers. Given all she has suffered at their hands, I am certain she and her friends would not hesitate in naming every last one of them! To benefit from such sorcery is deemed to be as bad as the practice of witchcraft itself. If you were to succeed in persuading the Privy Council to reverse my judgement, you would also condemn at least half the village to dire punishment. Go! Ride for Edinburgh if you must! It is not I who will suffer the consequences!'

'Damn you to hell!' The Young Laird bellowed, his shoulders hunched forward in defeat. 'Get out before I lay my hands on you! Go! Take yourselves from my sight before I change my mind and do something we all will regret!'

Kincaid required no second invitation. He lifted his bag from the floor, squeezed past the Young Laird in the doorway and scuttled away as fast as his legs would carry him. Seton would have followed suit if his belongings had not been scattered across the crumpled blankets. He suppressed the urge to hurry and took the time to pack carefully even though he could feel the Young Laird's eyes boring into the back of his head. He turned when he was done and opened his mouth to offer some words of farewell to the scowling Moncur.

'No!' The Young Laird spat. 'I will hear no word from you. Keep your mouth tight shut if you would not have me cast you down those stairs and break your worthless neck. Go now, before I forget myself!'

21

It took every ounce of Seton's courage to step past the glowering and furious James Moncur without flinching away from him. He resisted the urge to dart down the stairs as Kincaid had, though he kept his muscles tensed in anticipation of a sudden assault from behind until he reached the very last step. He found only a few stragglers still in the hall, their voices low as they gossiped, speculated and opined on what they had just witnessed. Only Minister Logie and his wife were willing to meet his eye and did not back away in fear as he advanced towards the door. The minister offered his hand and gave a nod of approval.

'The Old Laird will be happy.' He announced as he squeezed at Seton's fingers. 'He thought this whole travesty to be an abomination and was certain you would bring it to a just and fitting conclusion. You had me worried there for a while though.' He admitted with a rueful smile. 'With the widows condemned and Violet about to be pricked, I feared all three were sure to be burned.'

'May God bless you, good sir.' Mistress Logie gushed, her eyes glassy and moist. 'A terrible injustice has been averted thanks to your wisdom and goodness. You must visit with Laird Marlee before you depart. I know he would want to offer you his personal thanks, though he is now much weakened and scarcely has the strength to speak.'

'I will not trouble the Laird in his sickbed but will leave him to his rest.' Seton replied, his tone gentle as he was moved by their gratitude. 'In any case, I should not tarry here. While the father may approve of my judgement, the son is far from happy. I think it would be better if I did not encounter him again. His hold on his temper may not be as firm as I would like. I am also keen to catch up with Mister Kincaid. He travelled here on one of my horses and I am eager to remind him of it and to ensure he does not ride off without me.'

'Oh!' Mistress Logie gasped in shock. 'Then I fear you are too late, Minister Cowper. I was outside with Violet Frazer a few moments ago and your Mister Kincaid thundered past on his horse from the direction of the stables. We thought him to be in a terrible hurry for he galloped away wildly.'

Seton cursed inwardly. The villain was likely away on his brother-in-law's steed and he would be forced to part with a large amount of his silver to procure a suitable replacement. Such a sum would condemn him to at least two and perhaps as many as three years of toil in the Carmichael warehouse.

'Then I should be after him without delay.' He declared through lips pursed in irritation. 'Did you see the road he took, Mistress Logie? I assume he was headed towards Perth?'

'No, minister.' She replied. 'He followed the track towards Crieff. I could see him as he raced through the trees.'

Seton wasted no time in bidding the Logies farewell and strode purposefully towards the front door. He groaned in frustration when the housekeeper called out to him just as he pulled it open. Margaret was giddy with relief from seeing the three women exonerated and chattered away in her excitement. She was oblivious to Seton's agitation as she showered him with thanks and praise and tried to persuade him to go and pay his respects to Laird Marlee and so allow him to express his gratitude. His sense of decency caused him to put his frustration aside and treat the woman with courtesy given the many kindnesses she had done him. When his patience was drawn too thin, he reached for his purse and dug out three shillings in the hope of filling her with such thankfulness she would release him to go off in pursuit of his former companion. The gesture did not have the desired effect but served to heighten her emotions and seemed to make her less willing to let him be on his way. He finally won his freedom when, in desperation, he took her into his tight embrace and whispered words of thanks directly into her ear. This unseemly show of affection caused her to smile with pleasure but filled her with such embarrassment her cheeks burned red and she lost the power of speech. Seton turned from her while she was so disarmed and hurried towards the barn to retrieve his horse.

He had only advanced a dozen paces when another female voice called out after him. He cursed again but with less vehemence than before. The prospect of being waylaid by Violet Frazer was somehow less objectional and irksome than being delayed by Margaret and the minister and his wife. He found himself captivated by her smile and mesmerised by her gaze the moment he turned to her. Her beauty was even more striking now she was no longer burdened by the threat of death.

'I come to offer my thanks to you, good minister.' She said when she came up to him. 'I owe my life to you and will be ever grateful for your courage. A weaker man would have seen me tied to a stake and burned to death as darkness fell.'

'Then show your gratitude by telling me how you knew!' He demanded. 'Do not flutter your eyelashes and feign innocence! Tell me how you knew of the pricker's trickery and of my deceit! Come now! There is no one close by to hear us and you know I am no witchfinder and have no interest in your persecution.'

Violet paused and tilted her head to one side as if she was weighing him up. Her smile slowly widened until it became a grin of amusement.

'I have the touch, or at least that is what my mother called it. She said it was a God-given talent. I need only brush your skin with my fingertips to know what is in your heart. Tis not sorcery or witchcraft but is pure and benign.'

'Others might not so agree.' Seton warned her. 'You would do well to keep it to yourself.'

'I have told no other and know your discretion can be relied upon, good sir. Ride for home knowing that your life has changed for the better as a consequence of your righteous courage. Enjoy your newfound fortune and resist all temptation to fritter it away on trivialities or rash and foolish enterprises. Do some good with it!'

'I appreciate your kindness but must confess that my future is quite bleak. If I am lucky, my life will be one of servitude. If the good Lord does not favour me, the pricker will carry out his threats and I will end my life at the end of the hangman's rope before the summer is out. My good wife will be made a widow and will likely curse my name and the shame it brings upon her.'

Violet reached out and gently gripped his shoulder with her slender and delicate fingers. There was no spark but Seton felt a warmth spreading out from where she touched him.

'Do not despair, John Seton.' She whispered, her eyes wide and fixed on his. 'Do not despair as I did when I was certain I would burn. The good Lord intervened on my behalf and sent you here to be my saviour. You will be rewarded for your courage and your kindness, I swear it. You, too, will be spared the flames and you will rise from the ashes and be renewed.'

Seton suddenly felt quite dizzy and had to shake his head in order to restore his equilibrium.

'What of you?' He asked, still a little dazed. 'Can you be sure the Young Laird will give you peace when he was so set on taking your land for himself?'

'I am certain I will be quite safe.' She laughed, pointing towards the place where her uncle leaned against a wall and watched over her. 'I doubt if anyone would be so foolish as to trifle with me after my uncle threatened them with the fury of his whole family.'

Seton nodded his agreement. No sane man would risk such wrath and even a madman would think twice about it. He took his leave of her and set off in search of his horse. He was somehow emboldened by his exchange with her and was now confident he would catch up with the pricker and succeed in persuading him to abandon all thoughts of betraying him.

The little comfort he took from her words did not last the afternoon. The skies began to darken the moment he swung into his saddle and angry black clouds filled the heavens from one horizon to the other before he was even out of sight of Marlee House. The first few fat and heavy drops of rain barely penetrated the canopy of leaves above his head, but this opening salvo soon turned into such a deluge it soaked him to the skin and filled his boots with water. His determination to cover the ground lost to the pricker forced him onwards through rain so thick he could barely see the track five paces ahead of him and winds so strong he had to cling onto his reins to keep himself from being ripped from his horse's back. He was willing to push on through his discomfort but had to reluctantly admit defeat when the track was reduced to a mud so thick his horse began to falter and struggled to place one hoof before another without slipping and sliding in the mire.

He sought shelter in a humble cottage on the far side of Crieff. A single shilling bought him a steaming bowl of thin gruel and a filthy, ragged blanket to huddle under in his misery. The grim-faced and uncommunicative farmer's meagre hospitality did not stretch much further than this and he merely grunted and gestured towards a bare patch of earth on the far side of the room. Logs were piled high in the hearth but were so wet and green they gave off more smoke than light and heat. Any faint hope of drying his clothes was dashed by the water dripping constantly from the thin and ancient thatch above his head. At least three generations of slack-jawed, inbred peasants lay sprawled upon or between the few sticks of rough and rickety furniture in the family's possession. They gazed at him in mute and open hostility and gave no response when he attempted to engage with them. Exhaustion might have brought him the gift of sleep if it had not been for that sea of wide, unblinking eyes staring back at him through the smoky gloom. He wondered if greed might drive them to slit his throat in the night and take his horse and the contents of his bag for themselves. He did not dare to do so much as doze once this thought was lodged firmly in his mind.

The day dawned dark and dank and only the sullen, resentful and dirt-smeared faces of his hosts forced him up and back out into the unrelenting drizzle. He groaned as he pulled himself up and into the saddle, his back painful and protesting after a night of suffering on cold, hard earth in sodden clothes. He gritted his teeth and urged his horse onwards, his spirits low and his head heavy with thoughts of the trials ahead of him. He prayed as he went, pleading with God to ensure that the pricker was meeting with at least the same torments and adversity as he. He tortured himself with imaginings of Will Kincaid somehow riding ahead of the weather, his clothes dry as he pulled further and further away. He let his shoulders slump forward as hopelessness threatened to overwhelm him and drive him to the depths of despair. The elements seemed intent on matching his mood and buffeted him with harsh gusts of wind and sent sheets of rain to chill him to the bone.

It is often the small and inconsequential things that cause men to lose heart and surrender to despondency. The loss of his father-in-law's fine hat should have troubled him little but it threw Seton into a fit of melancholy so deep he was unable to shake it off. He cursed bitterly and was brought close to tears when a sudden flurry ripped it from his head and sent it soaring over fields and rough open pasture. Its wide brim acted like a sail and the wind got underneath it and carried it away at such a speed and at such a height he soon lost sight of it altogether. He knew that the depth of his sorrow was disproportionate given the relative insignificance of what he had lost, but he mourned it all the same. He was so dismayed he began to consider the wisdom of abandoning his pursuit in favour of a more drastic course. The prospect of riding south and over the border might have been an attractive one if it had not entailed leaving his Elizabeth behind in order to save his neck.

22

Seton was so absorbed in his own misery he was scarcely aware of his horse plodding on and up the long slope leading to the hamlet of Auchterarder. He did not have the strength or the will to lift his eyes from the muddy, waterlogged track directly in front of him and barely noticed the few hardy locals who had braved the foul weather and nodded to him or raised their hands in greeting as he passed. He was already beyond the small, ramshackle kirk when some instinct prompted him to rein his horse in and come to a halt. He turned his head slowly and felt his stomach clench in disbelief. He blinked furiously to clear the water from his eyes and to ensure they were not deceiving him.

He scarcely dared to breathe as he dismounted and approached the horse tied to the rotten wooden rail at the front of the kirk. The beast was caked in mud almost to its neck but the patch of white stretching from its forehead to its nostrils was clearly visible despite being spattered with muck. Seton could not quite bring himself to accept what he was seeing. He reached out with trembling fingers and traced the pattern carved into the leather stirrup. There was no mistaking it. Thomas Carmichael had conceived the design himself when he commissioned James Myles, the royal saddler, to craft the saddle for him. He had been forced to endure long hours of his brother-in-law boasting about how fine it would be and crowing about how much silver it had cost him to have it made. Both he and Elizabeth had been compelled to attend its unveiling and to gasp in wonder while offering lavish compliments through false smiles and gritted teeth.

'Praise be!' Seton whispered to himself, almost reeling from a sense of elation. 'My prayers are answered!' The relief of having caught up with Will Kincaid so quickly and so unexpectedly was added to that of having spared himself from the discomfort of having to explain the loss of the beast to his pious and disapproving brother-in-law.

His euphoria faded as he turned his thoughts to what arguments might be employed to bring the pricker to reason. An appeal to his decency was unlikely to succeed but his silence might well be bought with some of the silver earned in Marlee. He thought he might be willing to part with as much as half of his hoard in order to avoid further bitterness and recrimination. Seton jumped back in fright when a voice called out to him from the door of the kirk.

'Good morning, my son.' The white-haired minister greeted him, his shabby robes already spotted with rain. 'Though this foul weather could hardly be described in such terms.' He paused to revel in his own wit before allowing his smile to fade and his expression to grow more serious. 'May I be so bold as to ask if the owner of this horse is known to you?'

'Aye!' Seton replied, offering the minister his hand in a bid to hide his nervousness.' I know him well having spent these last weeks with him in service to Laird Moncur up at Marlee. He left for home ahead of me and I wondered why he tarried here when he was so anxious to return to his old mother in Glasgow.'

The old man clasped his hands together and became so shifty and uncomfortable Seton feared Kincaid had told him some story that differed from his own account.

'Then I am afraid I must be the bearer of the worst of tidings, though it breaks my heart to do so.' His brows furrowed in concern and his voice grew mournful as he spoke. 'Your friend met with calamity as he forced this poor beast along this hill while the heavens poured down upon him. It was foolish of him to make the attempt when the road was flooded by such a torrent it was almost impassable. He would have been spared his fate if only he had sought shelter and waited for the worst to pass. His poor horse lost its footing in the mud and threw your friend to the ground so hard his neck was snapped from the force of it. He will not have suffered for long, my son. You should draw some little comfort from that knowledge.'

'He is dead?' Seton stuttered, his head swimming from the shock of the minister's pronouncement. 'I cannot believe it!'

'Come!' The minister commanded him as he waved him towards the door of the kirk. 'I can see that the news has hit you like a thunderbolt and has left you greatly upset. Come inside so you might gather yourself.'

Seton's heart soared at the sight of the pricker's pale and lifeless corpse laid out on a table at the rear of the kirk. He had to bite at his lip to keep himself from smiling. His fortunes had been transformed in an instant, just as Violet Frazer had predicted. The shadow of the noose had been lifted from him and new hope blossomed within his breast. With silver enough to repay his debt to the Flesher, he thought he might well win his Elizabeth back. He resolved to make the attempt though he knew he would still have to suffer humiliation and toil at the hands of her father and brother.

'He does look peaceful now.' The minister commented, misreading Seton's faint smile as some sign of pity or fondness for the foul, black-hearted creature. 'He is with the angels now, you must think of that.'

Seton nodded and murmured his agreement though he did not think Kincaid looked peaceful at all. The departure of his foul and corrupted soul had done nothing to hide his ugliness. The elders had evidently treated him with a gentleness and a dignity he did not deserve. They had combed his hair, wiped much of the mud and dirt from his face and clothes, set his neck so it was almost straight again and folded his cloak around him to hide his injuries. All of their efforts had done little to conceal the extent of his disfigurement. Three of his brown and decaying teeth had been smashed and broken with the rest now coated in congealed blood. The left side of his forehead was badly bruised and part of his skull had been caved in, leaving his face even more twisted and grotesque than it had been in life. Seton was surprised to find he felt no pity for his former companion, his threats and spite having served to rob him of all compassion.

'He lives on in the Kingdom of Heaven, my son.' The minister reassured him in a hushed and respectful tone. 'You must take comfort from that.'

Seton was certain Will Kincaid now dwelled in a much less pleasant place but lowered his eyes and nodded. He stayed silent for a few moments longer so the minister would think he was praying and paying his respects to his dear, departed comrade.

'Will you bury him here in the kirkyard, good pastor?' Seton enquired, keeping his eyes lowered as though he mourned. 'His mother is too old and frail to risk the journey here when the weather is so foul. Perhaps she will be well enough to accompany me here when it is less inclement. I know she will want to say a prayer at his grave.'

'I would do it happily.' The minister replied, his expression suddenly devoid of all sympathy and filled with something far less Christian. 'But there would be a gravedigger to pay, a coffin to purchase and all manner of other sundries to be thought of.'

'How much?' Seton retorted without bothering to soften his tone. He had encountered enough grasping and greedy men to know when one was intent on relieving him of some of his money.

The minister rubbed at his chin, more concerned with silver coin than with the saving of souls.

'Five shillings?' He suggested tentatively, his intonation telling Seton that the price was being inflated to win some modicum of profit.

He raised his eyebrow to show the minister his disdain but reached for his purse all the same. In truth, he would have beggared himself to see Kincaid safely in the ground and would have happily paid the minister twice what he had demanded. He counted out five shillings into the minister's hand and then, on impulse, added another two.

'For the elders.' He told the minister. 'By way of thanks for their care towards my associate. Please give it to them along with my good wishes.'

'You will not stay for the burial?' The cleric asked, almost succeeding in masking his joy at having the shillings safely in his grasp. 'The ground will be soft after so much rain. The gravedigger's work should be done before the day is out.'

'If only I was able, good pastor.' Seton replied, shaking his head to demonstrate the depth of his regret. 'But I must be away if I am to carry these sad tidings to his old mother before returning to my own family. I have been gone for so long they are already likely to think me lost to them.'

Seton bid the old man farewell and started for the door intent on being on his way. He had pulled it open and was about to step out into the filthy street when the minister called after him.

'Wait, good sir! You must take the poor fellow's belongings to his mother. The having of them might bring her some small comfort in her grief.'

Seton's jaw fell open when the minister reached between the pews and lifted Kincaid's bag from where it had been secreted. He took it from the pastor's hands and the weight of it caused his heart to quicken. It took all of his strength to steady himself and resist the urge to take his leave with unseemly haste.

He rode on until he was well clear of the village and beyond the sight of prying eyes before leaping down from his saddle. He tore at the bag's buckles with fingers made clumsy by his excitement and tipped Will Kincaid's worldly possessions onto the sodden verge careless of any damage he might cause them. He was quick to cast aside an old knife, a torn and dirty scarf, a woollen cap and three blackened candle stubs. He lingered over two silver candlesticks and four spoons, all of which he had seen before when they sat upon Laird Marlee's dining table. He set them aside on account of their value with the intention of adding them to the contents of his own bag. He then turned his attention to the twisted bundle of unwashed clothes and set about unravelling them. His nose wrinkled in distaste as he scrambled to untangle the tightly bunched items and his fingers brushed against a handkerchief crusted in something unspeakably disgusting. He gagged when the odour of stale sweat and dried pish rose up from the pricker's soiled undergarments. His eyes watered when the stench hit his nostrils but he did not allow it to divert him from his task.

He plucked the purse up from its foul hiding place and weighed it in his hand. The girl had been right when she said his fortunes would be restored. With the pricker's fat purse now added to his own, he could afford to settle his debt to the Flesher and pay most of what was owed to his father-in-law. He might still have to labour in his stinking warehouse to cover the entire amount, but it would likely take only a year, or two at the most, to fully discharge whatever small sum was left outstanding. A solitary sheep was his only witness when he cried out in his delight and clenched his fists above his head in triumph. The spectacle caused the bedraggled creature to pause for only a moment before it returned its attention to gnawing at the grass.

He left the pricker's clothing to be scattered by the wind and remounted his horse with both bags tied securely to his saddle. He rode on with his back straight and his chin held high and could not help but smile at the first signs of the skies beginning to clear. The rain grew lighter as he went and had stopped altogether by the time he crossed the swollen waters of the Black Ford. He amused himself with the thought of what gift he might buy for Elizabeth in Stirling in the hope of winning her favour anew.

23

The last hour before dawn was Thomas O'Malley's favourite time of the day. With the last of the animals slaughtered, he could rest after his night's labours and turn his mind to matters of business in the few moments of darkness and quiet left before the sun rose and the city burst back into life. He kept no ledgers or written accounts. Every penny loaned, every shilling unpaid and every pound of interest accrued was stored away in his memory. It was his habit to start each new day with a reckoning of what was owed, what was overdue and what recovery measures were necessary in the hours ahead.

He grunted and arched his back until it cracked, earning himself some momentary relief from the stiffness caused by so many hours of wielding both axe and cleaver. He rubbed his hands clean of blood and offal with a filthy cloth and shook at his leather apron until the worst of the clotted gore had fallen to the ground. He gulped great mouthfuls of ale from the jug his wife had brought him, but it did nothing to improve his sour mood.

The loss of two of his apprentices to the plague had left him badly short-handed and he was now exhausted and even more irritable than was usual. He had paid no heed when they first sickened. He cared not if they sweated with fever or if their shit soaked their trews and ran down their legs as they worked. The stench did not come close to overpowering the abattoir's reek of blood, fear and open guts. It was the outbreak of sores and pus-filled boils around their mouths and noses he could not ignore. Word of their sickness would have spread like wildfire if they were seen in his slaughterhouse and his customers would have turned to other butchers to avoid catching the disease. He had sent them away with the promise of a return to work as soon as they were recovered but he knew it was a promise he would not be called upon to keep. Neither of them was likely to last the month now they were denied their living. They would not have the means to buy the bread and cheese required to sustain them through the fevers and to replace what would be lost when their bowels turned to rot.

O'Malley turned to examine himself in the mirror of polished silver nailed to the back wall of the shop. He had taken it from a gentleman in Leith whose liking for dice exceeded both his luck and his skill. He had emptied the poor bastard's grand house of all of his possessions and still he borrowed more and threw it away in the taverns down by the docks. When he had nothing left to sell or to pawn, O'Malley had opened his guts with his favourite knife. He smiled at the memory of how the fine and affable gentleman had screamed empty threats and hollow curses at him when his puddings slid and slithered out to steam on the cold floor. The mirror was the only item of his he had not sold or melted down for the silver. He could not bring himself to part with it when the mere sight of it gave him such pleasure.

The reflection gazing back at him from the polished surface was not a handsome one. The brows were too heavy, the neck too thick and the skin too scarred from years of bare-knuckle fighting and too pock-marked from a childhood of squalor and disease. The left eye appeared to be smaller than the right as it was set further back in his skull. This was the result of being blind-sided by a vicious roundhouse when his father was drunk and in one of his foul tempers. The blow had knocked him out cold and left him in a stupor for two full weeks after the assault. At twelve, he had been too slight of frame and too fearful to defend himself and so was forced to seethe in impotent fury and skulk around like a ghost to avoid incurring his father's displeasure. It had taken more than two years for his courage and his muscles to build. He had lain in wait for the old bastard in a dark alley and had set about him with both feet and fists when he staggered by on his way home from the tavern. He battered his head so badly he was left bleeding from his eyes and his ears and lay sobbing in the gutter while Thomas pissed on him and told him he would finish him if he ever came into his sight again. The old man never darkened his mother's door again nor troubled her or her offspring with his fists. Thomas had caught sight of him in the street on two or three occasions since then, but he had possessed wisdom enough to change direction or to duck into a close to keep out of his son's sight.

O'Malley ran his finger around his eye socket and traced the rough edges where the bone had knitted back together. There had been a time when the bone would flex when he pressed on it but those days were long past. He did not turn when the Tolley boy crept in through the door but continued to stare at his reflection as if he had not noticed him. The little runt sidled into the shadows in the corner of the room and watched the Flesher with wide and wary eyes. His parents had died almost two years before. His mother was one of those unfortunates carried off by the winter coughing sickness. She died a long and agonising death, her lungs slowly filling with her own blood until she drowned in it. The husband lasted a little longer but took to drinking to ease his sorrow. His heart seized in his chest after a long day of supping spirits. His companions only realised he was dead when they offered him a drink and he did not immediately accept it.

O'Malley had taken the boy in when he caught him gnawing raw flesh and gristle from the bones thrown onto the midden at the back of the shop. He let him sleep on the slaughterhouse floor and fed him on scraps of skin, fat and offal. He had hoped he might prove to be of some use as he grew but he was a sore disappointment. He was weak and feeble and shivered in fear whenever he was in the Flesher's presence. He did try to put on a brave face but O'Malley saw through the façade. It was not a hard thing to do when the wretch's knees trembled so hard they knocked together loud enough for him to hear it. He despised the lad more for his sickening eagerness to please than for his lack of guts. He was so desperate for some morsel of faint praise he would rush to do whatever he was bid as if his very life depended on it. O'Malley thought he would likely run to lick his arse clean after a heavy night on the ale and the oysters if only he ordered him to do so. The thought brought a smile to his lips. It might well provide him and his wife with some amusement after a pint or two.

'You better have some news for me, boy.' He growled when he had kept the little fool waiting in suspense for long enough. 'Be warned! I am in no mood for disappointment after a hard night at slaughter. Tell me what you saw at the Carmichael house! Leave nothing out!'

'The old man left at first light and went off towards the Grassmarket as he always does.' The boy began, his eyes wide and blinking.

'Aye.' The Flesher replied as he rubbed at his chin in contemplation. 'I heard there were five cartloads of sheepskins lined up at the western gate just before dawn. He will have gone down to oversee the delivery when it arrived at his warehouse. What else?'

'Their carriage was brought to the door just as the baker's boy was making his rounds. The son and the daughter climbed into it while their groom strapped their trunks to the back.'

'Trunks?' The Flesher asked, the question directed at himself rather than at the Tolley boy. 'Someone means to be away from the city for some time. You followed them, I presume?'

'I ran behind the carriage all the way to Musselburgh.' The boy boasted before pausing in anticipation of some recognition of his feat. He continued with his account when his words were met with only silence and a stony and expressionless glare. 'They stopped at a fine house on the seafront and went inside. The groom unstrapped the baggage and took it in after them. Carmichael's son came out a while later and the carriage turned back for Edinburgh.'

'A fine house on the seafront? Why has Carmichael hidden her away and who has taken her in?' The Flesher racked his brain for answers to these questions and was oblivious to the expression of quiet satisfaction on the boy's face. Several moments passed before he became aware of the tension in the boy's shoulders and his eagerness to speak. 'What?' He demanded in irritation at being kept waiting.

'Mistress Elizabeth is sorely distressed by the sudden and unexplained disappearance of her husband.' The boy gushed in a rush of excitement as he recited words spoken by someone of greater rank and education. 'Her father has sent her to lodge with her maiden aunt so she may take in the clean sea air to aid in her recovery.'

O'Malley looked the boy up and down and raised his eyebrows in surprise.

'And how did you come to know such things?' He asked, failing to entirely mask his admiration.

'The aunt came out to wave the carriage off and fell into conversation with her lady neighbour. I crouched down in the bushes and heard every word of it.'

The Flesher narrowed his eyes and seemed to regard the Tolley boy in a new light.

'Perhaps you are not the pitiful creature I thought you to be.'

The boy grinned in delight and his cheeks reddened at receiving such thin and grudging praise. O'Malley dared not let him bask in it overlong for fear of it going to his head.

'What of our Mister Seton? Did you catch sight of him striding about as if he was the only cockerel in the farmyard?'

'No. I did not see him though I stayed on the corner until the night watchmen chased me off.'

'Stay at it! He'll come crawling back before long to suck at the teat of old man Carmichael's wealth.' O'Malley spat on the floor in disgust. 'He'll be sorry for being late with his payment, you see if he's not. I'll take a finger or two and maybe an eye to reward the arrogant bastard for so disrespecting me. That'll teach him to look down his nose at me!'

'Why only a finger or an eye?' Young Tolley asked, emboldened by his recent good work.

'Why not slice off his cock or his balls to punish him for running away? He would surely regret their loss more than that of the others.'

'A man might mourn such a loss but he could conceal his injury if the wound did not rot.' The Flesher replied, quietly impressed by the boy's question. 'The beauty of a missing eye or finger is that it cannot be so easily hidden. The transgressor is punished but also becomes a walking reminder of the cost of default or late payment. It makes our debtors think twice and so keeps the silver flowing into my purse.'

The conversation was brought to a halt by the arrival of the Flesher's ugly and broad-shouldered wife and his two ugly and broad-shouldered daughters. The boy seemed to shrink back into the shadows as they passed him, his fear of them greater than his dread of the Flesher. O'Malley did not greet them but gave a slight nod of acknowledgement before they set about hauling a great weight of pork, beef and mutton out of the slaughterhouse and into the shop in preparation for the day's trading. The Flesher turned back to his ale and watched silently as they worked. His girls might have no head for business but they were as strong and as fearless as most men. The sight of them toiling without a word of complaint filled him with pride and a feeling of contentment. He smiled at the thought of how well they would take care of him in his dotage. The smile suddenly faded from his lips and he sniffed at the air like a dog catching the scent of a bitch in heat on the breeze.

'What is this?' He asked himself. 'Tis either silver or excuses coming my way! If it is silver, I will happily take it. If it is excuses, I will need to take an eye or a finger if I am to keep my temper.' He then turned to the boy. 'Bring my best knife, there's a good lad! It would not do to let him away while I go to fetch it.'

The boy ran for the slaughterhouse as if the Devil himself was on his heels and was back with the knife in his hands before the Flesher had pushed himself up from his chair. O'Malley took the blade and ran his fingers over the steel, taking a moment to marvel at the craftsmanship of the intricate engraving and the metal's subtle blue colour. There was no doubting its quality. It had been three years since he seized it from the unfortunate French exile and he had never needed to sharpen its blade in all of that time. The Comte de Marsaud had near wept at its loss but had never made good on his promise to return with enough coin to buy it back.

O'Malley stepped out into the grey light of dawn and gazed down the length of the Grassmarket. The road was beginning to fill with men, women and children hurrying to their work and with carts and packhorses carrying goods to market. He sniffed the air again before nodding to himself in satisfaction. The Tolley boy stood off to his side but could see nothing of any significance no matter how hard he squinted his eyes. Long moments passed before O'Malley let out a sigh of triumph.

'Here you are, my bonnie lad. Here you are at last.' He whispered to himself. 'Let us see what the morning brings. Whether it's silver or excuses, I will have what I am due.'

Seton had taken a bed in a tavern just inside the city walls when he arrived in Edinburgh the night before. He could have reached the butcher's shop by riding on for only a few moments longer but chose to stop rather than conclude his business with the Flesher after darkness had fallen. He hoped that daylight and witnesses would dissuade the Flesher from rash action and so keep his innards intact and out of his foul pies. He groaned and felt his stomach clench painfully when he caught sight of O'Malley's thick head and broad shoulders in the distance. He shook his head and cursed in disbelief. The bastard had to be in possession of some supernatural instinct to be expecting his arrival this morning. He had given no name at the tavern, had kept to his room to avoid detection and was certain he had not been observed. He shivered though it was not cold and wondered how terrified he would have been if he had not been carrying all the silver he owed.

He began to sweat as he approached under the Flesher's unyielding, unflinching gaze. He raised his hand in greeting but the beast made no gesture in response, his eyes slitted and shaded beneath his protruding and tightly furrowed brow. He tensed and stretched his shoulders as Seton reined his horse in, the movement perhaps intended to relieve some stiffness there or to serve as a reminder of what damage those strong shoulders and thick arms could inflict on a man's skull and neck if the situation should require it.

'Good morrow, good sir.' Seton called out, his voice less steady and more high-pitched than he would have liked. 'Tis good I have encountered you here.'

'Tis well you have come now, young sir!' The Flesher growled, his voice hoarse and gruff like two handfuls of gravel being rubbed together. 'I was beginning to fret about your well-being given the sudden nature of your unannounced departure. I was on the verge of sending men in search of you when there had been neither sight nor sound of you around the city these past few days. A less trusting soul might well have suspected you of running from your responsibilities.'

Seton shuddered at the sound of some poor creature squealing in pain and fear somewhere in the dark depths of the slaughterhouse. The Flesher read his thoughts and his mouth twitched in what might have been some grotesque form of smile.

'It would be you screeching on the block if I had been forced to fetch you back, young sir.' He hissed, his tone heavy with malice though he had not raised his voice. 'You have my silver?'

'Aye!' Seton replied, already reaching into his saddlebag to retrieve it. 'I have what is owed to you along with a little extra by way of thanks now that our business is concluded.'

He extracted the pricker's purse from his bag and leaned down with his arm stretched out towards the unsmiling butcher. The Flesher seemed almost disappointed by Seton's response and hesitated before reaching out to accept the purse. He seemed to weigh the bag of silver in his hand before giving a curt nod to indicate he was satisfied with it.

'How did you come by so much silver in so short a space of time?' He demanded when he found himself unable to fully suppress his curiosity. He prided himself on his ability to keep his nose out of other people's business but was so astonished by the way events had unfolded he could not help himself. 'I know you made not a single shilling from the claret you had transported here from Bordeaux. I was told it was so sour they cracked the casks and let it drain into the dock.'

Seton tapped his finger against the side of his nose.

'I have fingers in many pies, good sir. I will say no more than that.'

'All of your fingers would have been baked in a single pie if you had not come to me this day.' The Flesher snapped in irritation at being denied an answer. 'I was certain it would be necessary for us to become much more intimately acquainted.'

Seton felt his balls shrivel in their sack at the thought of such a horrific prospect.

'I'll see you again, young sir.' O'Malley said as he turned back towards the slaughterhouse. 'I'll see you very soon.'

'Not I.' Seton retorted, his face aghast. 'My borrowing days are now behind me. I will never darken your door again.'

'They all say that, so they do.' The Flesher chuckled without turning his head. 'They all make such rash promises, but back they come just the same. Old or young, high born or low, clever or dull-witted, they all come crawling back in the end.'

Seton watched until the Flesher and his boy disappeared into the butcher shop's dark interior.

24

Seton took a moment to settle himself and to wipe fat droplets of sweat from his forehead and upper lip. He had expected to be elated when the Flesher was finally repaid but his guts were still twisted in a tight knot and his fingers continued to tremble though he gripped his reins hard enough to turn his knuckles white. He cursed himself for ever being reckless and foolish enough to put himself in the debt of such a foul and vicious monster. Desperation might have driven him to the butcher's door but only his own insanity could explain his decision to cross his threshold. He swore a silent vow to never again involve himself in any business with such base and bestial creatures.

He urged his horse on and away to put the slaughterhouse and its dreadful and loathsome proprietor behind him. It was still too early for him to catch the Carmichaels at their breakfast so he set course for the castle and the peddlers who sold hot food from their stalls in its shadow. The place was teeming with all forms of life even at such an early hour of the morning. Rough-faced labourers stood in line with craftsmen, servants and lawyers and even fine gentlemen in their expensive cloaks awaited their turn to be served with plain food to sustain them until lunch. Seton's stomach was still too sour for fried mutton or pork so he exchanged a shilling for a bowl of steaming porridge, a crust of bread and a small cup of ale. He led his horse and that of his brother-in-law across the square to the grass verge and lowered himself down to break his fast. He watched the throng bustle about as he ate and turned his thoughts to the encounter ahead. His mood improved as the oats filled his belly and he imagined how the Misters Carmichael would react when he thumped his purse of silver onto the table between them. The elder Carmichael would likely splutter and suffer a fit while the smugness would be wiped from his son's face. The prospect caused Seton to guffaw in delight and he did nothing to restrain his amusement when those rushing by cast anxious glances in his direction. What did he care if they thought him to be mad? He was about to confound those who regarded him as a lower form of life and buy his way out of a lifetime of hard labour.

The only cloud on the horizon was the question of how Elizabeth would respond to his overtures. His smile faded as he considered how best to achieve the outcome he so keenly desired. Her father and brother would undoubtedly seek to impose their wills upon her and steer her away from any reconciliation. Their determination would likely be strengthened by his unexpected success in escaping the bonds of servitude they had intended to use to control and contain him. He had no doubt the odious pair had worked night and day during his absence to turn her against him. His daydreams of pulling her into his embrace seemed improbable now that his return was only moments away. His imaginings of her delight when he presented her with the fine cloth he had bought for her in Stirling were rendered pathetic and idiotic by the reality of the situation. The blue cloth would make a fine dress and its colour would set off the colour of her eyes most beautifully, but it could hardly be expected to make up for months of having poison dripped into her ears.

His shoulders began to sag under the weight of cold reality and his earlier optimism and confidence melted away like the last snows of spring. He cursed himself as an empty-headed fool when he realised that the Carmichaels would not be so overawed by his silver they would meekly lie down to him. He had allowed himself to indulge in delusion and fantasy. His new-found riches would be a trifle to them when laid beside the great wealth they had accumulated over long years of toil. They would likely refuse to accept a single coin from his hand and would accuse him of having come by it through dishonest and nefarious means. The pompous and sickeningly sanctimonious pair would also be reluctant to offer forgiveness for the theft of their clothes and their horses. They would denounce him as a thief, a fraudster and a habitual liar and would only baulk at reporting him to the magistrates to spare the family the shame of being associated with a convicted criminal.

Seton lost what little was left of his appetite and tossed the untouched crust of bread into the gutter with a petulant flick of his wrist. He watched as a ragged and filthy boy appeared from nowhere and seized the bread up. The little urchin was so encrusted in dirt the whites of his eyes and his teeth shone out from his dark face. He smiled in triumph and tore at his prize with great glee. Seton knew he was sinking into a state of abject self-pity but could not help but envy the waif's happiness and freedom from care.

Seton grew so disheartened in those moments he could not summon the strength to push himself back to his feet. He watched on morosely as the people of Edinburgh rushed in all directions as they went about their business. He might have spent half the day there if his horse had not chosen that moment to empty its bladder. The great stream of pish ran into the gutter and flowed downwards, soaking the boots and the shoes of the other good citizens taking refreshment on the grass verge. Men and women shouted out in shock and anger when the green and foaming cascade reached their feet.

'Dirty bastard! I'm at my breakfast here!' A ruddy-faced carter roared in fury and disgust.

More curses, threats and insults followed as the river of dark urine ran further down the gutter. Seton felt his face redden and his embarrassment forced him up and back into his saddle. He muttered an apology as he went and counted himself lucky that no stones were cast after him.

The roads were thick with carts, horses and pedestrians but it took only a few minutes for him to come in sight of the fine houses lining both sides of the Cowgate. Seton was so downcast and wrapped up in his own misery he did not register someone calling out after him as he went. When he eventually turned his head, he cursed at the sight of William Erskine, the Carmichael's lawyer, gesticulating towards him and imploring him to stop.

'Miserable bastard!' Seton muttered under his breath as he gently dug his heels into his horse's sides to urge him into a trot.

He had not forgotten Erskine's haughty condescension or his part in writing up the papers intended to damn him to years of toil in the Carmichael warehouse. The old lawyer had never bothered to hide his contempt for him and he had no desire to converse with him now. He allowed himself a smirk of petty satisfaction when the fat old shit began to gasp and wheeze and to spatter his trews with mud as he struggled to match the horse's pace. He would have kept this up all the way to Carmichael's door if he had not noticed something strange in the lawyer's tone and the manner in which he was addressing him. Erskine had never called him anything but 'Seton' and always spat the word out heavy with scorn and disapproval. The old fool was now red-faced and struggling for breath but was still crying out after him.

'Pray stop, Mister Seton! Please rein in your steed, good sir. I must speak with you!'

He was not motivated by pity or courtesy when he pulled on his reins and brought his horse to a halt, but was driven by curiosity as to why the odious and contemptible man was treating him with such an uncommon degree of respect.

'Thanks be to God I found you before you reached the house!' He wheezed, his face soaked with sweat and coloured an alarmingly dark shade of red. He clutched at Seton's bridle as if he lacked the strength to hold himself upright. 'I have had all of my clerks out scouring the city for some sign of you. I prayed that either they or I would be able to intercept you.'

'And why would you do such a thing, Erskine?' Seton barked without making any effort to disguise his dislike for the man. 'If your master means to keep me from my wife, he will need to block my path with better men than you and your ink-stained scribblers.'

'I sought only to spare you the horror of the calamity that has befallen us! I thought it would be better for you to hear the dreadful news from the lips of one who is known to you rather than to learn of it from a stranger or to see it for yourself.'

Seton was suddenly dizzy from fear and his stomach tightened into a knot of dread.

'Not Elizabeth?' He cried out in alarm. 'Has some misfortune befallen her?'

'Not her, sir.' The lawyer replied, his tone now gentle and filled with concern. 'She is, praise God, safe with her aunt in Musselburgh. Tis your father-in-law, Mister Carmichael, and his son, Mister Thomas! I would soften the blow if only I knew the words necessary to achieve such a thing. It breaks my heart to be the bearer of such terrible news but I can offer you only the hard truth of it.' Erskine paused as his eyes filled with tears. 'Both of them perished when the house burned to the ground in the night. They were both abed when the inferno took hold and had no hope of escaping the flames. I pray that they were overcome by the smoke and so were spared the unspeakable agony of being burned alive!'

Seton turned his head towards the far end of the Cowgate but was at too great a distance to make out anything of his father-in-law's house. A haze of thick smoke hung over the buildings but it was impossible to tell how much of it came from the inferno and how much from the city's thousands of hearths and cook fires.

'Tis such a horror and a tragedy!' The lawyer wailed miserably. 'I am still in shock and can scarcely believe they suffered such a terrible fate!'

Seton felt the blood drain from his face as Erskine's words began to sink in.

'How did it happen?' He asked, his voice little more than a whisper.

'It would seem that the housekeeper was refilling the oil in the lamp in the dining room, just as Mister Carmichael had instructed her to do each night before taking to her bed. She does not know if the wick was still aglow or if the glass was still hot from burning all through the evening. Whatever the cause, the oil ignited even as she poured it and the blaze took hold too quickly for her to control it. She tried to beat the flames out with her bare hands but was powerless to stop them from spreading. By the time she was driven out by the flames and the smoke, she was burned most horribly and the stairwell was too far ablaze for her to reach her master. The doctor believes she will live but she is so terribly disfigured I doubt she will ever work again. No civilised man would have the stomach for food if it was served by a woman whose flesh has been melted from her face and her hands. It would make you weep to see her, good sir. She is such a pitiful creature now. Once you have dealt with the funeral arrangements, you must see to it that some settlement is made so she is not beggared. It is the least you should do.'

'It is the least I should do?' Seton demanded, his face creased in confusion. 'You think I should make provision for William Carmichael's housekeeper?'

'Aye, sir.' Erskine replied as he reached out to grasp Seton's wrist. 'The responsibility will now fall to you. Mister Carmichael has no surviving male heirs and Mister Thomas died without ever marrying. As a result, all of his considerable assets, properties and business interests will pass to his daughter, Elizabeth, and so to you as her husband. The only consolation from this whole tragic episode is knowing that William's daughter will be the wife of one of the richest and most influential men in all of Edinburgh!'

Seton gulped and found himself struck dumb as he struggled to take in the sudden transformation of his circumstances. The weight of silver in his bag had seemed to be of great importance when he awakened in his bed in the tavern only a few hours before. The lawyer's tidings had made it a matter of little consequence when set against the great wealth he was about to inherit.

'I know you will mourn the loss of both William and Thomas, but you must not allow yourself to sink into sorrow and despair overlong. You must enjoy your newfound fortune and build on your father-in-law's legacy. You must also resist all temptation to fritter it away on trivialities and rash and foolish enterprises. You may do some good with it!'

Seton gaped at the old man in shock. The sound of Violet Frazer's words coming from Erskine's mouth sent a shiver down his spine and caused him to be momentarily stupefied. He blinked at the lawyer in astonishment and wondered what supernatural power had led him to give voice to the very same words Violet had spoken to him as he took his leave from Marlee House. Erskine mistook his bewilderment for shock and grief and patted at his shoulder to comfort him.

'Come, sir.' He implored him. 'I can see you are badly shaken. Let us take a seat in yonder tavern and order some whisky to restore us. There is urgent business we must attend to, but it can wait until you have steadied yourself.'

Epilogue

James Moncur was never a man much given to patience. The four months since Cowper and Kincaid had made their hasty departure from Marlee had done nothing to sweeten his nature. He paced the floor of the antechamber as he struggled to contain his growing frustration and irritation. It had taken more than three months to secure an audience with one of the honourable Lords of the Privy Council and now, on the day of his appointment with David Lindsay of Edzell, he had been kept waiting for half the morning and all of the afternoon. All manner of officials, petitioners and other worthies had been waved in through the doors and into Edzell's presence while the sneering and officious clerk ignored him and made a pretence of being unaware of his existence. All of his letters to Privy Council members had been ignored and he had been forced to impose on the kindness of one of his associates from his time in St Andrews. Francis Stewart was Lord Edzell's nephew and had immediately agreed to intercede on Moncur's behalf. Inducing the fellow to actually turn his promise into action had proven to be more troublesome than securing his support in the first place.

The Young Laird had been reduced to following Francis Stewart around the country as he moved from one family estate to another in order to indulge his various appetites. They had raced horses in Atholl, taken to hawking and boar hunting in Cupar and spent long nights at cards and dice in Dundee. Moncur could hardly bring himself to think of how much he had spent in the brothels and whorehouses of Perthshire and Fife. He did take great joy in his friend's company but lacked the means to match his extravagant and excessive spending. He feigned illness to spare himself the shame of pleading poverty when the wagers grew too rich for his blood but found himself mocked for his feebleness and frailty instead. He suffered his friend's ridicule and jeering with all the good grace he could muster but cursed them silently and prayed for the day when he could take himself away from their company. Francis would promise faithfully to put quill to parchment whenever Moncur raised the matter with him but would forget his vow with the consumption of the first jug of claret of the day. The Young Laird was down to his last five shillings when he finally cornered his companion whilst he was still fully sober and succeeded in coaxing him into dashing off a note to his uncle.

He had begun to despair when three weeks passed without any word from the capital. The sight of Violet Frazer and Elspet Leyis strolling around the village without a care in the world was enough to darken his mood and drive him to drink for days at a time. He could not help but notice the other villagers offering them warm greetings and vowed to remember their disloyalty when he became Laird and had more power with which to punish them. He could not even go to the kirk without being provoked because Minister Logie and his vile wife had taken it upon themselves to take the decrepit widow Nevie into their home. They claimed to be driven by Christian charity but their action was clearly intended as both an insult and an unspoken reproof. They propped her up in the second row each Sunday so he would be forced to walk past the drooling, insensible old bitch on his way to his place in the front pew. The indignity was almost too much for a gentleman to be expected to bear. He bemoaned the unsatisfactory conclusion to the trials and knew it had done great damage to his standing in the village. There was no one brave or foolish enough to say as much to his face but many were content to whisper it among themselves and quickly fell to embarrassed and guilty silence whenever he came into their presence.

The improvement in his father's health did little to ease his unhappiness though it was good to see him grow well enough to leave his bed to take his meals in his own dining room. Margaret fussed around him from dawn until dusk and did all she could to entice him to take solid food. Her efforts bore fruit and the old man grew less gaunt with each passing week and was soon able to hobble around the yard with the aid of a stick. His sight was all but lost to him but he still took great pleasure from sitting outside with the sun on his face. It was a pity the Old Laird's infirmity did not prevent him from giving voice to his great disapproval of his son's reprehensible conduct.

'I hold myself wholly accountable.' He would often declare when chewing on bread with the few teeth still left to him. 'Your poor mother's death left me too soft-hearted to chastise you harshly enough when your behaviour was wanting. A bit more of the rod would have done you no harm and would likely have made a better man of you.'

James could only endure his father's criticism in silence and comfort himself with thoughts of the injuries he would inflict on Cowper and Kincaid when he caught up with them. The solace he took from these dark fantasies diminished with each day that passed without receiving any response to his desperate pleas for support. He began to lose hope of ever receiving any satisfaction through due legal process.

The belated arrival of Lord Edzell's letter hauled him back from the depths of despondency. He immediately set about honing the arguments he would make in order to elicit the judge's sympathy. He spent a full week closeted away in his chamber, first writing his speech, then improving and correcting it before committing it to memory. By the time he took to his horse and left for the capital, he was certain that reason would surely prevail.

His confidence had begun to wane the moment he set foot in Holyrood. Lord Edzell's clerk talked down to him as if he was some kind of peasant and pointedly refused to refer to him as the Young Laird of Marlee.

'Mister Moncur.' He insisted with a roll of his eyes. 'We do not recognise such provincial, informal titles here. I will inform his Lordship of your arrival, though you may have to wait for some time. He has a great many matters of import to attend to this morning.'

The morning had dragged on into the afternoon and then into the evening. Moncur halted in his furious pacing when the door was pulled open and a balding, red-faced man stamped out with his teeth clenched in anger. The haughty clerk followed him out and gestured absently towards the door into the street.

'The King shall hear of this!' The man barked, thumping his silver-topped cane against the floor to emphasise the extent of his displeasure. 'I have no doubt he will be unhappy when he hears how badly I have been mistreated. It is a monstrous outrage and will not be tolerated!'

'Do as you see fit.' The clerk replied coldly. 'Though I doubt he will grant you a hearing. His Lordship has already made him aware of the depths of your incompetence. I daresay he will have no great desire to sully his hands or his reputation with the mess you have made.'

The clerk then turned back towards the open door but froze in confusion when he found the Young Laird blocking his way. He blinked several times in a show of astonishment before recognition dawned on him.

'Mister Moncur!' He sighed as if his presence was unbearably tiresome. 'I did not think you would still be here.'

'I have been here since morning, good sir.' Moncur retorted with open hostility. 'And still I wait though a dozen others have been ushered through those doors while I was left standing here like some damned peasant!'

'Come then!' The clerk snapped with no little irritation. 'His Lordship has already called for his horse but may be good enough to spare you a few moments before he departs.'

Lord Edzell was engrossed in some document and did not look up when the Young Laird came to stand before his ornate, parchment-strewn desk. He read on for a few moments longer, his finger tracing the last few lines as he reached the bottom of the page. He sighed and went to rub at his eyes but stopped with his hands half-way to his face when he caught sight of the Young Laird.

'By Christ, you startled me there!' He grunted before laughing and shaking his head. 'I suppose you must be my nephew's acquaintance. The little scoundrel wrote to me on your behalf. How, may I ask, did you come to know him? I presumed it was from his brief time studying at St Andrews, though he was scarcely there long enough to unpack his bags. I hope that is the case. I would be less happy if you were one of those low-life ruffians who spend their time drinking and gambling with him. The feckless wretch has near beggared my sister with his profligate spending. I have never known a boy more intent on letting good silver slip between his fingers.'

'I did meet him at St Andrews, my Lord.' Moncur replied with a bow of his head. 'I confess to seeing less of him since he abandoned his studies.' He lied in the hope of gaining Edzell's favour.

'Good! Very good.' His Lordship replied. 'Pray tell me what I can do for you, Mister Moncur. Be as brief as you can. I am expected at court and it does not do to be late.'

The Young Laird needed no second bidding and launched into the speech he had so carefully prepared. He gave his account of the witch trials at Marlee and took care to emphasise just how poorly the proceedings had been conducted and how badly the parish had been let down by the inexplicably lenient judgements. Edzell listened impassively for the most part but sat bolt upright when the prosecutor was singled out for the bitterest and most vitriolic criticism.

'Cowper you say?' The Privy Councillor interrupted him. 'Not John Cowper, the minister at Glasgow Cathedral?'

'The very same.' Moncur replied. 'That villain relieved me of a great weight of silver and left me with nothing in return.'

'You are certain it was Minister Cowper? You are not mistaken?'

'Aye, sir. It was he along with the pricker William Kincaid.'

'Did you not confront him when he left this chamber not five minutes past? He must have walked right past you on his way to the street.'

'Cowper?' The Young Laird asked in confusion. 'The only man who passed me was of middle age with a bald patch on his crown and a silver-handled walking stick in his hand.'

'That was Minister Cowper!' Edzell retorted, pointing his finger in the direction of the cleric's departure. 'I summoned him here to berate him for his disgraceful handling of the witch trials in Glasgow. Near a hundred of them were burned on the basis of false confessions and the word of the so-called Great Witch of Balwearie. Tis the greatest scandal of our age. King James has ordered all trials to be halted due to the scale of the fraud.'

James Moncur turned pale as Lord Edzell spoke and leaned hard against the edge of the desk as all strength seemed to flow from his legs.

'I am afraid you have been duped out of your silver by some foul fraudster who took Cowper's name in an attempt to embezzle you. If there was no lawful commission for your trials, then I am afraid I can offer no remedy for the expenditure you incurred. Neither can I offer you a commission to retry the accused when neither the King nor the Privy Councillors will give authority for any such trials.'

Lord Edzell caught James Moncur just as he collapsed and was able to heave him into a chair before he fell to the floor. He called for his clerk to bring water to revive him and stayed by his side until he recovered his wits.

John Seton halted so abruptly his wife carried on walking for several paces before she realised her husband was no longer at her side. They had come to stroll at Holyrood and listen to the King's trumpeters as they practised before going on to Erskine's apartment to take dinner with him and his wife. Her enjoyment of the evening and Seton's company came to an end when she turned back and saw him gaping in horror.

'John!' She cried out in alarm. 'Are you quite well? Your cheeks have gone terribly pale! I hope you are not sickening. I heard talk of an outbreak of plague in the hovels around the Netherbow.'

Seton was so frozen in fear he was oblivious to his wife's distress. The sight of James Moncur being helped down the steps of a building only a dozen paces ahead had left him shocked and rooted to the spot. If the Young Laird turned his head to the right, he would capture him there in the street with Elizabeth at his side. Panic welled in his chest as he could neither flee and leave his wife at his mercy nor defend himself if Moncur was to confront them. All he had won in recent weeks would be irretrievably lost if he was exposed for his fraudulent activities. All of his efforts to restore his wife's faith in him would be undone the moment the first accusation was made. He gasped in fright when the man at Moncur's side began to guide him across the street towards them. Only a few paces stood between him and calamity when Elizabeth unwittingly came to his rescue.

'What ails you, husband?' She asked as she came close to him and put her hands to his cheeks. 'By God, you are as cold as ice though the night is unseasonably warm. What ails you, my love?'

James Moncur paid no heed to the couple as he passed them on legs still weak and unsteady. Even if he had glanced to his right, he would likely have seen too little of Seton's face to recognise him as his wife's hands masked most of his features. Seton did not dare to speak until the Young Laird had hobbled away out of earshot.

'I will happily send our apologies to Mister Erskine and his good wife if you are not well enough to sit through dinner.' Elizabeth reassured him, her eyes full of concern.

'It is no ailment causing me to sicken.' Seton replied, taking his wife's hands in his. 'I am just tired of the city and its noise and its filth. Let us take a carriage to Linlithgow this very night! Why wait to escape the smoke, the stench and the disease?'

'But the new house is not ready, John.' His wife protested, though her eyes sparkled with delight at the prospect of putting Edinburgh behind them. 'The carpenters and thatchers have only just completed their work. It will be dirty and dusty, will it not?'

'Who cares for a little dust, my sweet? Half of our furniture is already there and the servants moved into their quarters more than a week past.

We would have all we would need to be comfortable.'

'What of matters of business?' Elizabeth demanded, her face reflecting her concern. 'Did Erskine not say he had much to discuss with you? He only invited us to dinner so he might engage you in debate about warehouses and deliveries and other such things. Perhaps we should stay in the city until they have been dealt with.'

'To hell with old Erskine!' Seton retorted, his heart set on an immediate departure. 'He can ride out to Linlithgow with his charts and his papers if they are so urgent. I doubt he will refuse when I pay him so much for his trouble. Let us cast caution to the wind and begin our new life without unnecessary delay! Think of the joy of being able to fill your lungs with fresh country air! Think of the fields for our children to run in and the woodland where they can play in the trees. Just say the word and I will call for our carriage! We can be there in time to sleep the night in our own bed.'

'There was always some mischief in you, John Seton.' She scolded him, though there was laughter in her eyes. 'I find I am coming to like it.'

They wrapped themselves in a blanket as the carriage rumbled and shuddered its way through the darkness and spoke of the life they would have in Linlithgow. Elizabeth rubbed at her belly and stared deep into her husband's eyes.

'What shall we call him, if he is indeed a boy? I thought we might name him in honour of my dear father.'

Seton grimaced at the suggestion and pulled his wife closer to him so she would not see the expression of distaste on his face. He now had the means to indulge her every desire but was determined to refuse her in this one regard. Her grief for her father and brother was still very raw and he would happily do everything in his power to comfort her with the exception of naming his child in honour of William Carmichael. The mere thought of the man and the way he had mistreated him was enough to blacken his mood. He also had no desire to have a constant reminder of the vile William Kincaid in his everyday life. Others might take to calling the boy 'Will' and he could not tolerate such a prospect.

'I thought we might name him Andrew, if it is a boy. I once knew an Andrew who risked all to ride out in defence of his queen. I like the idea of naming him for such an honourable man. It was also my late brother's name. His loss at so young an age has long been a source of grief for my family. Giving new life to his name would bring them great joy. I know my mother would like it.'

'Tis a fine name indeed.' She agreed, her softhearted nature causing her to partially concede in the face of her husband's anguish but without completely surrendering her own claim. 'We do not need to decide now. What if the baby is a girl? What name would we give to her? Not Elizabeth. I have always hated it. It is either too formal or is shortened to something ugly such as Lizzie or Bess. What about Constance or Grace? They are both such virtuous names.'

'I would not burden her with so dull an epithet. What about something more vibrant and colourful? What about Violet?'

'Violet? Is it not too frivolous, my love? Whatever would people think?'

'They would think it to be a pretty name for the pretty daughter of a clever and beautiful mother. That is what they would think.'

Historical Note

The Great Scottish Witch Hunt of 1597 was one of the most shameful episodes in the history of Scotland. Between March and October of that year, at least four hundred people, most of them women, were tortured before being tried for crimes such as witchcraft, consulting with witches, folk healing, midwifery, demonic possession and engaging in unorthodox religious practices. The number of those condemned and executed is unknown but has been estimated to have been in the region of two hundred souls. A more accurate estimate is unavailable because most of the trials were conducted by local officials in possession of commissions granted by the Privy Council in Edinburgh. The central authorities do not seem to have kept any records of the trials and most of the documentation from those held at the local level was either lost or subsequently destroyed. It is therefore impossible to determine how many others suffered lesser punishments such as banishment, branding, excommunication, being declared fugitive and being subjected to public humiliation.

A great deal has been written about the causes of the 1597 witch panic but there is no single satisfactory explanation. Plague and famine undoubtedly played their part in prompting aristocrats and peasants alike to go in search of scapegoats to blame for their suffering. The atmosphere of suspicion and mistrust would have been heightened by the ongoing struggle between Catholicism and Protestantism following the Scottish Church's break with the papacy nearly forty years earlier. The ongoing political conflict between James VI of Scotland (later James I of England) and the Presbyterian Church can also be cited as a contributory factor. The support of King James himself for the prosecution of witches can be safely assumed to have increased enthusiasm for and lent legitimacy to the practices of witch-hunting and persecution.

James I's obsession with witchcraft and sorcery can be traced to 1590 when his ship almost sank in a storm as he brought his bride, Anne of Denmark, back to Scotland. Rather than attribute his near miss to the vagaries of tide and weather, he became convinced that the storm had been summoned by witchcraft. He was determined to punish those he held responsible for endangering his life and seventy suspects were duly identified and apprehended before being put on trial in North Berwick. Many of them confessed under torture and admitted to raising the storm by way of rituals and spells involving the devil and the casting of a cat and a dead man's genitalia into the sea. King James was so outraged by these confessions he decided to oversee the questioning and torture of the accused personally. The records show that he watched as one of the accused was shaved of all body hair and was subjected to a violent wrenching of her neck intended to cause her great pain. The trials ran on for more than two years.

James was not content with merely participating in the trials of those accused of plotting against him. He also set about whipping up a hysterical fear of witches and witchcraft amongst the general population by commissioning a pamphlet, Newes from Scotland, to spread word of the North Berwick trials to all four corners of the kingdom. He then devoted himself to the writing of a philosophical dissertation on the science of demons intended to convince sceptics of the dangers of witchcraft and to rouse his officials to persecute those accused of sorcery and necromancy with greater vigour and determination. The effect of this work, 'Daemonologie', was to provide the royal seal of approval for all manner of injustice and torture in pursuing those who were thought to have sinned against God. It is little wonder that its publication in 1597 was followed by an unprecedented outbreak of accusations of witchcraft.

King James found a willing audience for his obsession in 16th century Scottish society. A wide range of superstitions were commonly held with many people believing in demons, demonic possession, the evil eye, fairies, witches, spells, charms, curses, ghosts, familiars, incubi, succubi and a wide range of other spiritual entities. Not all accusations of witchcraft were made out of fear or genuinely held beliefs. It seems that the witch panic was used by some to further their own interests and ambitions and by others to settle old scores and, in a few documented cases, to lay claim to property. Royal commissions were granted for the investigation of witchcraft and sorcery in many parts of the country, most frequently in Perthshire, Glasgow, Stirlingshire, Fife and Aberdeenshire.

Perhaps the most disturbing elements of the witch trials were the cruelty and injustice that pervaded them. The accused were routinely denied food, water and sleep, causing them to suffer hallucinations. This may well explain some of the fantastical claims made under questioning. These included flying through the air, floating on the sea in sieves and transforming into the form of hares, cats and other creatures. Torture was used to extract confessions and often involved the searing of flesh with hot irons, the crushing of feet, the removal of finger and toenails and the use of the scold's bridle. The trials themselves were a travesty of justice with the accused refused representation and with guilty verdicts being reached on the basis of forced confessions, flimsy, uncorroborated evidence and the outcome of the 'scientific' swimming and pricking tests. The witch hunts were also horribly tainted by misogyny. In his 'Daemonologie', James I declared that women, due to their weakness and frailty, were twenty times as likely to be entrapped by the Devil as men. In fact, in the King James Bible, released several years later, all references to witches were exclusively female. The trials themselves reveal an obsession with the sexual elements of witchcraft. Many of the accused admitted to engaging in depraved sexual acts with the Devil and many of them suffered the indignity and humiliation of being stripped and shaved so their intimate parts could be examined in order to detect the Devil's mark on their flesh. It is hard to imagine the suffering and terror these women endured at the hands of a long-suffering and fearful population and an ambitious aristocracy spurred on by a vengeful and superstitious monarch.

In the midst of this cruelty, hysteria and persecution, it is heartening to find evidence of a few isolated dissenting voices. Some members of the Privy Council and the wider legal establishment were not comfortable with the widespread use of torture but were unwilling or unable to change the course of events due to the opposition of their superiors. Even sceptical members of the clergy were unwilling to raise their heads too far above the parapet for fear of retribution. The Presbytery in Glasgow gives us the best example of this cautious approach. Several clerics in Glasgow were horrified by the actions of the minister John Cowper. He had engaged the services of Margaret Aitken, a woman convicted of witchcraft in Fife. Aitken had been able to bargain for her life by claiming that she was able to identify other witches by a special mark in their eyes. Aitken's false testimony enabled John Cowper to condemn hundreds of innocent women to death. Several unnamed clergymen were so horrified by this they set out to expose Aitken as a fraud. Aitken was presented with women she had previously condemned and her deceit was laid bare when she declared them to be innocent. She admitted to lying when confronted with this evidence and her part in the witch trials came to an end. Cowper's activities were severely curtailed by this scandal but were not brought to an end. The persecution of innocent women might well have continued if not for the courage and determination of one Glasgow widow.

Marion Walker enjoyed none of the protection offered by wealth, profession or rank but was willing to stand up against the injustice of the Glasgow witch trials. She acquired a copy of Margaret Aitken's confession and fearlessly made its contents known to the people of Glasgow. She was not deterred by the threats of dire punishment made against her by ministers and magistrates but continued to hold Cowper responsible for the unnecessary deaths. The ensuing outrage and scandal resulted in King James withdrawing all existing commissions for the trying of witches and effectively brought the Great Scottish Witch Hunt of 1597 to an end.

Three more decades would pass before Scotland suffered another witch panic.

It is humbling to think of the great courage required to stand up to the monarchy, the aristocracy, the clergy, the legal establishment and the baying mob at a time when women were being routinely condemned and executed on the most spurious of grounds. Scotland has often been blessed by the emergence of heroes in the darkest days of its history. Marion Walker must surely be counted as one of their number.

The Blood King

A dark prophecy

A fractured kingdom

A sea of enemies

The blistering new historical fiction thriller from Michael Alexander McCarthy.

410 AD – The land of the Britons is thrown into chaos when the despairing Roman Emperor withdraws his legions in a desperate bid to prevent the collapse of his disintegrating empire.

Left to their fate by their former masters and deprived of the silver that had flowed into their treasuries from the continent, the vassal kings turn their eyes to the north in search of new wealth to plunder.

The warring northern tribes lack the strength and unity to resist and seem destined to fall prey to the greed of their southern neighbours.

Just when it seems that the gods will offer them no salvation, there comes one king to rule them all and soak the earth with blood from sea to sea and from the Dark Isles to Great Caesar's Wall.

Death's Head
Hitler's Wolfpack

A poisoned legacy

Lies that echo down through the years

A desperate struggle for survival

'Death's Head' is the epic tale of one man's fight to survive the meat-grinder of World War Two's Eastern Front.

David Strachan is torn from his comfortable corporate life in Singapore by news of his grandfather's death and is forced to return to rural Scotland to deal with his last will and testament.

The old man's legacy proves to be far from simple.

Strachan soon finds himself drawn into a web of intrigue and regret that stretches back to the battlefields of France, the ruins of Stalingrad, the suffocating atmosphere of the Fuhrerbunker in the dying days of World War Two, the Nazis' last, desperate stand at Fortress Breslau and the launch of Himmler's suicidal Operation Werewolf.

The Kingmaker Series

The epic story of Scotland's bloody struggle to win its independence and free itself from the grip of powerful, greedy and vicious English Kings.

'Return to your friends and tell them that we came here with no peaceful intent, but are ready for battle and determined to avenge our own wrongs and set our country free.'

William Wallace to the English commanders before the Battle of Stirling Bridge (1297)

KingMaker

Army of God

A tyrant king

An army of ragged peasants

A great battle at Stirling Bridge

Scotland, 1297.

The Plantagenet King, Edward 1st of England, has deposed and imprisoned the Scottish King, John Balliol. While the Scottish nobles bicker and squabble over the crumbs from the English King's table, Edward's army terrorizes and brutalizes the Scottish people and seeks to subjugate them at the point of their swords.

Scotland, like Wales before it, seems certain to fall under Edward's dominion and to be crushed within his iron fist.

To the fury of this great and terrible King, his forces cannot turn occupation into conquest and force the rebellious Scots to succumb to Plantagenet rule.

Failed by their leaders, the Scottish peasantry defy the mighty Edward and fight to send him homeward to think again.

KingMaker

Traitor

A bitter betrayal

An overwhelming defeat

A descent into hopelessness

The stubborn and rebellious Scots have resisted Edward 1st of England's attempts to add the Crown of Scotland to that of England.

With furious determination, Edward sets about bringing Scotland under his control. As one failed campaign follows another, he risks financial ruin, open rebellion amongst his own nobles, the condemnation of the Pope and the enmity of powerful European kings. His determination to be remembered as the 'Hammer of the Scots' condemns Scotland to ten long years of slaughter, burning, rape and pillage.

Through intrigue, cunning and cruelty, he slowly but surely extinguishes the flames of rebellion until only faint embers of patriotism burn in the hearts of the peasantry. How can commoners like the men of Scotstoun stand against proud Edward's might when their superiors are crushed or lose courage and bend the knee?

KingMaker

Bannockburn

An epic clash of kings!

Scotland, 1306.

After ten long years of bitter struggle, the conquest of Scotland is complete and King Edward of England can finally rest and survey a kingdom greater than that of any previous English monarch.

The stubborn Scots do not leave him to revel in his legacy for long.

The Plantagenet King throws age and infirmity aside in rage when he is told that Robert Bruce has broken faith and seized the Scottish Crown for himself.

His vow to avenge this insult ignites a new phase of unprecedented savagery in the struggle between the Kingdoms of Scotland and England and will lead to an epic clash between the might of the English nobility and the Scottish King's peasant army on the field of Bannockburn.

John Edward and his men of Scotstoun again find themselves at the centre of a clash between two powerful kings that will devastate their lives and force them into acts of heroism so great they will echo down through the ages.

KingMaker
Death of Kings

Scotland, 1314.

Though weakened by the crushing defeat of his great army at Bannockburn, estranged from the English nobility and financially crippled, King Edward of England stubbornly refuses to relinquish his claim to the Scottish throne and to recognise Robert Bruce as King of Scots.

Determined to force the hand of the enfeebled Plantagenet King, Robert Bruce unleashes his loyal commanders to raid and pillage deep into England and Ireland to further diminish English power and wealth.

Though wounded and beset from all sides, Edward of England will not be so easily defeated and raises one army after another in order to frustrate Robert Bruce and bring Scotland back under English rule.

John Edward and the men of Scotstoun are at the centre of this epic, dynastic struggle as it rages across battlefields on Scottish, Irish and English soil. They must set aside their dreams of peace once again and attempt to win liberty and nationhood through brutal, bloody struggle.

Printed in Great Britain
by Amazon